FEB   2021

THE CAPTIVE

THE
CAPTIVE

A NOVEL

FIONA KING
FOSTER

ecco

An Imprint of HarperCollins*Publishers*

THE CAPTIVE. Copyright © 2021 by Fiona King Foster. All rights reserved. Printed in the United States of America. No part of this book may be used or reproduced in any manner whatsoever without written permission except in the case of brief quotations embodied in critical articles and reviews. For information, address HarperCollins Publishers, 195 Broadway, New York, NY 10007.

HarperCollins books may be purchased for educational, business, or sales promotional use. For information, please email the Special Markets Department at SPsales@harpercollins.com.

Ecco® and HarperCollins® are trademarks of HarperCollins Publishers.

FIRST EDITION

Designed by Angela Boutin
Frontispiece © malija/stock.adobe.com

Library of Congress Cataloging-in-Publication Data

Names: Foster, Fiona King, 1977– author.
Title: The captive : a novel / Fiona King Foster.
Description: First edition. | New York, NY : Ecco, an imprint of HaperCollinsPublishers, [2021] | Summary: "A rural noir about a woman on a pulse-pounding expedition to deliver a fugitive—and forced to confront her own past on the journey"—Provided by publisher.
Identifiers: LCCN 2020041843 (print) | LCCN 2020041844 (ebook) | ISBN 9780062990976 (hardcover) | ISBN 9780062990990 (ebook)
Subjects: GSAFD: Noir fiction.
Classification: LCC PR9199.4.F6834 C37 2021 (print) | LCC PR9199.4.F6834 (ebook) | DDC 813/.6—dc23
LC record available at https://lccn.loc.gov/2020041843
LC ebook record available at https://lccn.loc.gov/2020041844

21 22 23 24 25 LSC 10 9 8 7 6 5 4 3 2 1

To Etan

THE CAPTIVE

PROLOGUE

THE AUCTION WAS INTERRUPTED IN THE MIDDLE OF DRY GOODS: BUCKWHEAT flour, pea flour, an exorbitant lot of coconut flour.

"Holly would kill for that," Milo said, twitching their bidding card.

"Don't," Brooke warned him. They still had to pay for sugar—fifty pounds of it, at least, for the fall preserves—and anyway, their daughter's passion for exotic ingredients was only her latest mutiny. "You already promised her a phone battery."

Milo shrugged amiably and lowered the card.

The kids were alone at the farm, a few hours' ride away. They had wanted to come, of course. Holly, especially, strained against their isolation, living hours outside town. But the four of them couldn't all ride. A hard-rot blight had turned half of their last cranberry crop to dry, cotton-filled beads, forcing Brooke to sell two horses for cash. They were down to just her old mare, Star, whom Brooke and Milo had ridden together from home that morning, leaving at dawn and planning to stay overnight.

Brooke couldn't remember the last time the two of them had been away from the farm together; it would have been when Milo's mother was still alive to watch the kids. But Holly was thirteen now, old enough to be left in charge, and Sal, at eight, was no longer the thumb-sucking baby sister she had been. They would be fine for one night.

Brooke and Milo's getaway, if a supply run to Buxton could be counted as such, had been enjoyable so far. People kept finding Milo in the auction crowd—friends, former students, people he'd known for years—gripping his arm and embracing him. Brooke knew the pleasure Milo took in his hometown, and she was happy for him, though she kept her own greetings brief; she had never stopped being a stranger here.

On the platform at the front of the parking lot, the auctioneer, a lanky, freckled grandmother, palmed her megaphone, sending a rough, amplified crackle through the air. Someone was climbing the platform, Brooke saw. She took in the symbol on the man's open windbreaker; it was rare for a marshal to travel this far, two hundred miles from the federal border and the city beyond.

The marshal leaned in and spoke to the auctioneer. There was another crackle from the speakers.

"Pause for a warrant," the auctioneer announced briefly. She handed her megaphone to the marshal and folded herself into a chair, sipping bottled water.

The energy in the crowd shifted, damped by a current of unease. Buxton had come through secession gentler than most—it was farming country, logging country, and the fight had been distant—still, they held no more esteem for federal authority than anyone did this side of the border.

For a minute, the marshal looked out over the crowd without speaking. Just to make them uncomfortable, Brooke thought. Even now—thirty years since the rural territories seceded, twenty-five since their hard-won sovereign government dissolved—the feds still acted like they had power. That smug tightness around the mouth.

Not just the man's windbreaker, but his T-shirt and ball cap both bore the crest of the federal government.

"Do they make undies, too?" someone called out, to a skim of laughter.

The marshal sighed and lifted a paper, reading his text into the megaphone slowly, as if to children.

"Addressed to residents of the unincorporated village known historically as Buxton: A fugitive is believed to be in your area. Local households are warned this man may try to obtain a vehicle or horse. He is dangerous and possibly armed. He is wanted on numerous charges, including trafficking, assault, destruction of federal property, and the murder of a federal narcotics officer."

Conversation around Brooke and Milo began to resume. The feds had no jurisdiction in the ceded territories, but they claimed the right to prosecute offenses against themselves. Everyone in the parking lot knew this marshal wasn't here out of concern for local households. Federal property had been damaged and a federal officer killed; that was all.

"There's a bounty," the marshal said, no longer reading from his paper. "We're offering five hundred dollars for information leading to capture, five thousand for safe delivery."

A few more jeers from the crowd—it was classic of the feds to throw money at a problem rather than solve it themselves. Still, Brooke couldn't help picturing what a sum like that could do for them. Five thousand dollars was more than the farm made in a good year.

The territories had always been poor by city standards. But then, if you went by city standards—if you believed the TV shows set here—people like Brooke and Milo were fighting it out in some kind of apocalyptic wasteland.

Copies of the warrant were lowered into the crowd. As Brooke took a sheet and passed the rest on, the marshal spoke the fugitive's name aloud for the first time. The syllables echoed across the parking lot, amplified and fractured by the megaphone; Brooke felt a momentary impulse to bat them away from her ears like pests. She glanced down to check the warrant paper in her hand, hoping she'd misheard, knowing she hadn't. The name was spelled out in clear black letters: *Stephen Cawley.*

The page was dominated by the fugitive's face: fair-haired, blue-eyed, a scar from his lip to his chin. *On charges of Murder,* the paper warned. *Felony Escape, Traffic of Controlled Substances, Incitement to Violence, Destruction of Federal Property. Last known address: Shaw Station.*

The noise of the auction receded. Brooke's hands tingled and her pulse beat forcefully in her temples. She noticed she wasn't breathing, drew in a jagged lungful of air.

A memory of pain. Darkness. Her own voice, screaming: *Run!*

Holly and Sal were at the farm, alone and unprotected. Brooke pictured them as they'd been that morning when she and Milo left for town: Sal's slack, sleepy hug, Holly arguing right up to the last about being left behind to watch her little sister.

Brooke and Star could be there in an hour, if they rode hard.

The thought of Star introduced a new fear: the horse's brand was old and faint but unmistakable, enough to expose them to anyone who came looking.

Brooke laid a hand on Milo's sleeve to get his attention, and he broke off the conversation he was having with someone on his other side.

"I have to go," Brooke said.

"What is it?" Milo asked, concerned.

"Two hundred on sugar," she said, already turning away. "Max."

She hurried through the crowd to the public stables. Star was drowsing in her stall. Brooke reached over the gate and grazed the mare's velvet-soft muzzle with her fingers. Star blinked and pushed Brooke's hand gently, steaming damp breath into the palm.

Brooke ran her hand down Star's neck to the shoulder, where the old brand showed through her half-grown winter coat: two thin vertical lines, bisected by a hook. It had been done flat-faced and superficially, just enough to prevent the hair follicles from regrowing, back when Star was a foal. Covering it would require more aggressive scarring.

"I have to do something, girl." Brooke pulled her hand away, hoping Star could not sense the anxiety in her touch. It had to be done, and fast. The harness shop in town was unscrupulous about off-auction horse trades.

Star was the only thing Brooke had taken with her fifteen years ago, the closest thing she had to a friend. She would tell Milo simply that the mare's years were starting to tell; Star was pushing eighteen, and it made sense to sell her while they could still get something.

It had never felt good to lie to Milo, but Brooke knew he wouldn't question her; he was accustomed to her reticence. And now wasn't the time for her to offer up any more complicated explanation. She had to go.

She would tell him she was sorry about their overnight, but she didn't want the girls left alone with a fugitive on the loose. That wasn't unreasonable—the Cawleys were notorious, even here.

Brooke removed her scarf and looped it around Star's neck, knotting the fabric behind the horse's ears. She poured oats into the improvised feed bag. As Star munched, Brooke backed the horse into the corner of the stall where the gate hinged. She unlatched the gate and roped it across the mare's chest, wedging her in so she couldn't move. Then she rummaged through a heap of implements leaning against the stable wall until she found what she was looking for: two long-handled claw cultivators with iron tines.

There was a fire burning in the small woodstove. She opened the door and propped one of the claws over the coals.

Brooke took the other claw over to the stall and touched it to Star's brand. Star brought her head up, watched Brooke's face, and then returned to her oats. Brooke withdrew the cold iron for a moment, then placed it on the brand again. She did this four times, until the horse took no more notice of the metal and kept eating.

Brooke moved swiftly to the stove. She had to be quick if she expected to get the proceeds into Milo's hands before the auction reached livestock. Anything under ten years old, she'd tell him, that could pull machinery and be trusted with the kids. He could meet her at home with the new horse, the sugar, and the rest of their supplies. Brooke didn't intend to wait. The weekly truck carrying tar sands workers up the mountain road left in the afternoon, and she planned to be on it. Its route traveled right past the farm, and the driver would make room if she paid.

The claw in the stove was hot. Near its iron collar, the wooden handle was charred and glowing, not yet burned through. Brooke lifted it and hurried back to Star.

"I'm sorry, girl," she whispered, as she threaded the hot tines between the planks of the stall to cover Star's brand. Star flinched and tried to heave herself away, but she was wedged in tight by the roped gate. Brooke pressed the searing metal, sizzling and smoking, into Star's shoulder for five seconds, and then it was over.

She was no one's, now.

1

BROOKE FELT HER WAY DOWNSTAIRS, SOCK FEET SLIDING OVER THE WORN STEPS. The days were short this time of year, the mornings dark. Holly and Sal hadn't even stirred when Brooke knocked for them to come down to breakfast. Asleep, or pretending to be. Brooke herself had been sleeping poorly since the auction. At night, she lay agitated for hours before she finally passed out, exhausted, only to be shocked awake by every creak of the walls, every knock of the branches outside.

At the bottom of the stairs, Brooke swept her gaze over the living room, lit faintly by the glow of a lamp from the kitchen. Shapes long faded with familiarity—desk, bookshelf, sofa, toy box—had become sharp again these past few days, liable to strangeness. Brooke jerked the rug straight with a toe as she passed. She pulled Sal's boot from where it poked out of a crease in the sofa and laid it with its mate on the floor.

In the kitchen, Milo was hunched at the table in his bathrobe, coffee mug hanging at a slant. He'd set out a bowl of chia pudding for her, a spoon.

Brooke glanced quickly at the door: still locked, its glass panes shining black.

"Thanks." She pulled out a chair across from Milo.

"Mm," he answered with a crooked smile. Hair sticking up on one side, cheek still creased with sleep.

Milo didn't ask why she'd started locking the door after all these years, its mechanism so seized up from disuse that she'd had to drench it in oil before it would slide, just as he didn't ask what had possessed her to sell their last horse so suddenly, mere days before the cranberry harvest. It was four days since the auction, where the money Brooke left Milo had not been enough for a new horse—he had come hobbling home from where a friend dropped him at the road, carrying a hundred pounds of supplies—and still, he didn't ask.

He knew something was wrong; of course he did. Brooke could feel it in the care he took with her, the small affectionate gestures, the way he laid out her breakfast. She knew when she was being managed. But Milo had long ago learned there were things Brooke kept to herself, and he seemed content to trust her.

From the first, Milo had been open-hearted and untroubled in a way Brooke couldn't imagine. There was something about him, a frequency, a hum, something electric. Whatever it was, all he had to do was touch her and the alarm in her blood went quiet.

She wished he would touch her now.

She opened her mouth for the hundredth time to say what she should have said at the auction, and long before that. Again, words fled. She picked up her spoon and ate the pudding. She would tell him. She would. Just not this morning.

"I'm going to check the bogs," Brooke said instead. "The girls could clean out the rinsing shed. Get it ready for the harvest."

"I don't mind doing that," Milo said. "They've got enough as it is."

Milo had always been quick to spare Holly and Sal from chores. They were just kids, he often reminded Brooke; they should have fun. Brooke didn't argue today. She rose from the table and stirred extra water into the pot of chia so it wouldn't dry out before the girls woke.

As Brooke moved past Milo to get her coat, he took her hand and held the palm against his lips.

Brooke stilled. The effect, no longer a surprise, was still a comfort, as if the dial had been turned down on radio static.

Down, but not quite off.

"I'll be back in a couple hours," she said, brushing Milo's cheek with her thumb. He let her go.

On the porch, Brooke locked the door behind her and peered south, into darkness, listening. The land was silent, save for small, sudden scraps of sound, quickly hidden—mice and other night creatures, hungry and running.

Coming down the steps, she felt a whisper-thin rime of ice under her boots. The cranberries needed a few more cold nights to fully ripen, but the frost had held off late this year, and now winter threatened to descend before they could be harvested.

It was being right up against the northern mountains the way they were. The season could flip like a blade. People in town thought Brooke and Milo were crazy, living alone and unprotected so far out. Milo had had one of the best jobs in Buxton, teaching in the community school; he'd had his mother and his friends; yet he'd given it all up to buy a failing cranberry farm when Brooke told him she wanted to move farther from town. She'd hoped they would be hidden here. Their nearest neighbors were halfway to Buxton, at the farthest edge of tillable soil, a full day's walk.

Maybe people in town were right. No one could see them here, but neither would anyone know if they were in trouble.

Brooke followed the path downhill to the cranberry bogs that grew in the silty runoff of a mountain creek. Crisscrossed by a maze of irrigation ditches, the bogs stretched a mile wide—pink in spring, green in summer, blood red in fall. In the winter, when the bogs flooded and froze, the girls could skate above the hibernating vines. This time of year, the bushes were tangled and impassable. One thing in Brooke's favor: anyone coming from the south would have slow going.

The sky had begun to pale. Brooke climbed the dike that surrounded the cranberry bogs and surveyed the red-blushed plants in the dawn light. The foothills were quiet. There came the first fluting call of a thrush.

Brooke told herself she'd done the best she could. She'd acted quickly to sell Star, the last thread tying her to the past. She'd kept her family hidden. There was nothing else she could do, short of uprooting Milo and the girls completely—and how would she explain that? Where could she take them? Horseless, with not enough cash to last a season, their only choice was to carry on. Harvest the berries and make enough money from the fall preserves to replace Star.

Brooke would stay vigilant. She wouldn't let her guard down again.

The day of the auction, cursing her complacency, Brooke had run flat out from the end of their driveway and come hammering up the porch stairs to find Holly lying on the kitchen floor, eyes wide and staring. For one terrible moment, Brooke had thought she was too late.

Then she noticed the book in Holly's hand, the faraway expression on her daughter's face.

"Mom!" Holly sat up as Brooke stumbled into the room, kneeling awkwardly to wrap her arms around her daughter.

Once Brooke's breath returned to her, she told Holly that she'd come back from town early because there was too much to do at home, that Dad could handle the shopping alone. Sal, appearing from the living room at the sound of Brooke's voice, was thrilled to have her mother home, and dragged Brooke straightaway into the hive of blankets she'd constructed around the sofa, detailing her fort's many elaborate features.

That night, after Brooke combed and braided Sal's hair and tucked her into bed, she went to Holly's room. Her elder daughter was propped up on a pillow, reading. The book was one she'd read before, probably several times.

"Read out loud for a bit?" Brooke asked, lying across Holly's feet. Holly rolled her eyes but complied.

"Half a daikon radish. One cup sugar snap peas. One cup edamame beans. Two cups Napa cabbage. One ripe avocado. One small red onion. One carrot. A one-inch piece of fresh ginger."

Brooke closed her eyes, listening. Holly's voice trailed off.

"Why'd you stop?"

"I thought you fell asleep."

"No. Keep reading."

"For the dressing: Two tablespoons sesame oil. Three table-spoons rice vinegar. A squeeze of agave syrup."

"That's from a cactus, agave syrup."

"I know. One green chili. A small bunch of fresh basil. A small bunch of fresh cilantro. Two tablespoons toasted white or black sesame seeds. A splash of light soy sauce."

Brooke listened through to the end of the salad directions and then told Holly to turn out the lamp and go to sleep.

"I'm not tired."

"Okay, well, I am."

"So, goodnight," Holly said, already looking at her book again. Brooke waited for a minute, thinking of all the bedtimes she'd wasted on impatience when her daughter was young enough to want her to stay. So many nights, lying in the dark, waiting for Holly's breathing to drop into sleep so Brooke could sneak back downstairs to have time for herself, or with Milo, or to do chores. She must have known that sweet dependence wouldn't last forever.

"I'm not a kid anymore," Holly said, as if reading Brooke's mind. "You can tell me the truth."

"About what, Hol?"

"Did you and Dad have a fight?" The sharp planes of her cheekbones. Earnest eyes. "Is that why you're back early?"

"I just wanted to be with you kids."

Holly sighed, as if abandoning a futile task, and returned to her book.

Brooke hesitated, unsure how to tell Holly what she needed to know. It had always been easier to say nothing and believe she was preserving their innocence. But that had been reckless, she saw now. Reckless and selfish.

"You know to be careful around— Like, if anyone ever showed up here, someone you didn't know, you know you should be careful, right?"

"No one comes here, Mom."

"Like today, when Dad and I were gone. If you heard someone outside, or saw someone on the property, you don't have to— If you don't know them, I'd rather you were safe than polite. You could hide. With your sister. You'd be in charge of her, if something like that happened."

"You want us to hide from strangers now?"

"If you don't want to be a kid anymore, I'm going to trust you with some grown-up things."

"Okay."

"Like, there are bad people out there. People who would hurt you."

"Yeah, obviously. I'm not stupid."

Brooke could have told her about the warrant. Holly would have heard of the Cawleys; she wasn't entirely naive. Nonetheless, Brooke held back.

"I know you're not stupid. It's just better to be safe, no matter what. Even if you think it's embarrassing. Just promise me."

"Don't worry, Mom. I'm going to see literally no one, living here."

"But if you did."

"I'll dig myself a hole and hide in it forever."

Holly was looking at her book again when Brooke left the room.

THE SUN CLEARED THE EASTERN WOODS AND THE SKY OPENED UP BLUE. BROOKE heard a door smack and glanced up the hill to the house. She couldn't make anything out at this distance. It would be Milo setting out to clean the shed, letting Holly and Sal sleep in. She doubted he'd locked the door behind him; she stifled the urge to climb back up the hill and check.

Brooke took the thermometer from her backpack and drove the spike deep into the base of the nearest plant. She waited until the machine beeped, and squinted to make out the display: four degrees above freezing. She pulled a cranberry off the plant and rolled it between her fingers. Still a hard, shiny vermillion. The plants at the farther end would be a stage ahead. If it frosted again tonight, they would begin the dry harvest from the south end tomorrow, get through as many plants as possible before the snow came. Once the dry berries were in, they'd flood the bogs with creek water from the reservoir for the wet harvest.

They'd always had horses to draw the harrow and boom and ferry the crop uphill to the rinsing shed. The thought of doing it unassisted was daunting: slogging through frigid water in leaky, duct-taped hip waders, beating the submerged plants, and herding the floating berries into rafts.

It would take all of them working day and night, Brooke thought with a pang of guilt—even Sal. She wished they still had Star.

Brooke remembered the horse's warm coat under her hand

when she'd said goodbye at the harness shop. It seemed to her that she ought to be able to reach out, right now, and take Star back. She forced the thought aside. It was done. Star was gone—some stranger's now. Though she wouldn't have realized it yet, Brooke knew. Star was smart, but she was just a horse. She would still be waiting for Brooke to come back.

Brooke shouldered her pack and moved through the irrigation ditch, checking for gaps in the walls. In the north dike, she found an inch-wide hole below the flood line. She sniffed the edge and caught the distinctive reek of some rodent's fresh marking.

"Come on out," she said, blowing into the tunnel.

There was a hiss from inside: a weasel. It had probably taken the den over from its prey, a mole or mouse whose skin now lined its former home.

"It's for your own good," Brooke said, stabbing her trowel into the tunnel and drawing sharply up, exposing the hole right down to the burrow. The weasel whirled out, a six-inch blur, barking shrilly.

"You're all right," Brooke said. "Settle down."

The weasel backed away from Brooke, her white winter fur conspicuous against the dead ground. There were no kits; she'd find someplace else to live. Slow and watchful, the creature disappeared alone into the cranberry plants.

Brooke filled in the excavated burrow and completed her circuit of the bogs, clearing out two more nests, both empty. It was good to move, good to work, her thoughts absorbed in the tasks ahead. In the farthest bog, as she'd hoped, she found the plants nearly ripe enough to start harvesting.

Brooke wound her way back through the ditches and climbed the hill to the house, peeling off her coat. The grass was dry and brittle and broke under her boots, leaving a trail of splintered ends. When she reached the yard, she noticed with irritation that Milo had left the double doors of the rinsing shed open after cleaning it, and a stirring pole was lying on the ground. He was as messy as the kids sometimes.

As she bent to pick up the pole, Brooke's neck prickled with apprehension.

"Milo, are you in there?" Her voice faltered as she looked through the open doors.

She had been breathing heavily from the hill. Now the air went out of her. She stood frozen for what felt like a long time. In the dimness of the shed was Stephen Cawley, fair-haired, blue-eyed, a scar from his lip to his chin. He was turning toward her. She saw recognition settle on him.

Her mind flew to the house. The kids. Milo.

Run, she thought, panic flooding her body.

Then the muffling calm came back to her, long forgotten but familiar, swallowing her fear. She saw the necessary actions in front of her like a map.

It couldn't have been more than a split second. Stephen Cawley opened his mouth to speak and Brooke lunged, grabbed the rinsing pole from the ground, slammed the doors, and shoved the pole through both handles, trapping him inside. A heartbeat later, the shed shook as Cawley pounded the doors from within, shouting something Brooke couldn't make out. The pole held.

Brooke observed with detachment that there was no vehicle, no horse.

In her mind's eye, she circled the shed. No windows, no other doors. Floorboards he could pry up, packed dirt underneath. He would dig out if he had to, though it was easier to keep ramming the doors until they gave. Which they would. The pole was strong ash, but the doors themselves were only pine; they would break first. Brooke considered fire and discarded the idea. He might plunge through flame-weakened walls and survive.

He was still shouting, and now he began banging at the door

hinges with something heavy. Metal. A shovel, possibly. Brooke had nothing. It was only chance, Milo's carelessness cleaning out the shed, that had given her the pole, and she couldn't use that without opening the doors.

The doorframe was starting to give. She had to be ready. The moment he came through would be her only chance. If she didn't cut him down when she had the advantage, it was done. He was bigger and stronger.

Brooke pressed a hand against her throat. Could she kill him? She'd have to. If she didn't, he would kill her, and then only Milo would stand between Cawley and the kids.

With horror, she realized Cawley might already have found them. Wouldn't he have gone to the house first? Why hadn't anyone appeared to see what the noise was about? She wanted more than anything to call their names, to hear them answer, but she bit back the wish.

Just kill him. Decide how and then do it.

Axes. There were axes twenty feet away, in the woodshed.

Her footsteps over the dry grass were masked by the banging behind her. She leapt onto the chopping block and reached into the rafters for the big axe, the one they used for maple. Hefting it in her hands, she turned back to the rinsing shed.

Halfway there, she saw the top hinge of one door give way and a shovel blade slice down through the opening, hacking at the planks.

It was a mistake. The planks were reinforced by a thick crossbar as well as the pole. Cawley should have been working on the bottom hinge. But to Brooke's surprise, one board snapped and its top half fell to the ground. Three like that and he could climb through, though it would be high and awkward.

If she could get above him, she'd have a clean strike at his head. No, she thought, the roof was sheet aluminum, slippery and noisy, and there wasn't time. She had a minute, maybe less. She would have to stay flush to the side of the shed, take her chances that, in his struggle to get over the bottom half of the door, Cawley wouldn't see her before she swung. He might think she had already run for the house. He might come out ready to chase, not fight.

She raised the axe. She'd have one swing.

There was a crack as two more planks splintered. A shoe appeared over the crossbar. A leg. Now he saw her. As he pulled his other leg through and shifted his weight to raise the shovel overhead, Brooke swung.

She felt the axe pivot in her hands, blunt end forward. A barely conscious choice, mercy sneaking in where it wasn't wanted. Nor had she swung hard enough, she realized now. Too late.

The square face of the axe hit Cawley's kneecap, and his leg caved inward, throwing him off-balance. Seeing him stumble, Brooke kicked hard into the hurt knee and pushed him back. He fell to the ground, the spade of the shovel slicing the necks off a clutch of dry nettles.

Brooke brought the blunt end of the axe down again, this time on the ankle of Cawley's other leg, and felt something give. A grunt escaped his throat. He had the shovel up again and swung hard, forcing Brooke to jump out of the way. At the end of his swing, before he could bring it around again, Brooke threw herself forward, blocking the shovel with one hand and ramming the axe head into Cawley's injured knee with the other. He yelled in pain. Not giving him a chance to recover, she threw the axe behind her, came down with her knees on either side of his chest, and grabbed the shaft of the shovel with both hands, forcing it against his throat.

Cawley thrashed, trying to throw her off. His injuries gave him no leverage. He tore at her, punched her face, her arms, her throat. He clawed for the discarded axe. Brooke locked her elbows and bore down with all her weight. His face turned purple and thick. He tried one more time to heave himself up. She held on with the shovel and kicked down into his injured knee. He choked, his eyes bulging and red, and went limp.

Brooke counted out the seconds in a panted whisper. After a minute, she eased off with the shovel. He was breathing weakly but he didn't move.

She heard a fluttering sound overhead. A flock of snow buntings had landed on the roof of the shed and sat fluffing their feathers and chirping softly to one another.

Cawley lay under her.

Kill him. Like a rooster or a lamb, any animal: fast and without thinking. She stood and retrieved the axe. She ran her hands over the smooth wooden handle, picturing the motion, making it rote, imagining the force it would take for a fatal stroke, so that when she lifted the blade over his exposed neck, her instincts would not betray her again; she would have only to follow the steps and be done.

If she didn't kill him, there was no doubt what would happen. She'd seen him recognize her, and he hadn't looked surprised, either. He'd come here looking for her. Somehow, they'd found her.

Just do it. End it. Get Milo and the kids and run.

If Stephen Cawley knew where to find her, there would be others not far behind.

Run where, though? No horse, no money, no one to trust.

Kill him.

She watched herself step away from Cawley and reach through the broken shed door for the coil of baling twine that hung there.

What are you doing?

Brooke rolled the captive onto his stomach and pulled his wrists together.

2

DEEP DOWN, BROOKE KNEW SHE HAD NO RIGHT TO THIS LIFE. SHE HAD ALLOWED fifteen years' refuge to lull her, telling herself she was no longer in danger, that Milo and the girls didn't need the truth; they were used to Brooke's muteness on the subject of her past, and their conversations flowed around it reflexively, like water around a rock. She'd stopped watching, stopped waiting for it all to be ripped away. But she knew.

She should have run farther in the first place.

She'd arrived in Buxton eighteen years old, scraped raw up one side, and favoring her right shoulder. She'd taken a job at the sawmill, intending to stay only long enough to heal and make a little money, then keep moving in the spring. The mill owner had given her a room above the office, with a window opening onto the stable roof; she could have Star saddled in minutes.

All that long, cold winter, Brooke had kept to herself, sweeping sodden wood chips from the mill floor. The workers got used to the girl who moved like a ghost between machines, her face turned away. She sank into a deep freeze along with the ground—didn't speak, didn't think. If she left the mill at all, it was with a ball cap pulled low over her eyes.

She listened: for names, rumors, bits of news. Once, while she was sleeping in her room over the office, two men with Shaw County accents had visited the mill clerk selling diesel. She woke with the feeling of falling, something not right, fighting her way out of dreams to distinguish the voices coming up through the floor, listening for her name. Panic blurred everything, making her uncertain. When they left, she lay shaking.

She didn't go to the mill floor that day. She sat dressed in everything she owned, ready with the window hasp open in her hand. She didn't eat. Peed in a Tupperware. Night came and she stayed awake. A late harvest moon rose in the sky, big and orange and monstrous. It shrank and whitened as it climbed until it disappeared beyond her window frame, casting its glow down over the silvered roofs of town. That night passed, and the next day, and another night, and still no one came. Brooke's face was stiff and her body felt brittle and dry as an old bone.

Finally, she ventured out. The roar of machinery, calls of the night shift piling lumber. She saw the unswept wood chips piled muddy and thick around the saws. She was dizzy and trembling from hunger. She scooped a mouthful of water from the tap and returned to work, sweeping and oiling and waiting. And no one came.

For fifteen years, no one had come.

Now, Brooke looked down at Stephen Cawley, lying unconscious, bound at the wrists and ankles, where she'd dragged him to an inner room of her rinsing shed. His jacket had yielded a few dollars, an empty key chain, and a baggie dusted with the remnants of chalk, the powerful amphetamine-opioid hybrid that had held sway for as long as Brooke could remember. No needles; he must have been snorting it. She found no gun, no knife. No clue to how Cawley had gotten here. Under his body stink, Brooke could detect neither horse nor diesel.

She closed the door, threw the bolt, and hurried to the house.

Crossing the yard, she listened for voices, movement, any sign of life. Nothing. Then, as she came through the door, she heard music.

Milo was alone in the living room, picking out a tune on the kids' ukulele.

"Where are the girls?" Brooke demanded.

"Outside." He kept playing, didn't look up.

"Where?" she shouted.

Milo flinched, skewing the melody.

"I said they could go." He laid his fingers across the ukulele strings, muting them. "Holly wanted to look for a cell signal. It's okay, I cleaned out the shed."

Brooke remembered teasing Milo at the auction about the frivolous expense of the phone battery. That felt like months ago, not days. She thought quickly. If the girls were looking for a signal, they would have gone north, to the high ground near the road.

"Good," she breathed. "Okay."

"What's up?" Milo asked. "I heard you hammering out there."

Brooke had raced to the house without considering what she would do if they were safe, what she would say. She hesitated. If there was ever a time to be honest, this was it.

A sudden rattle from outside made Brooke jump. The breeze catching a loose flap of siding.

Time was running out. Telling Milo now would mean feelings, and questions, and that would slow them down. As it was, he was unhurt, the girls miraculously hidden at the northern edge of the property. There was still a chance Brooke could get them out of this, if she acted fast.

"Listen," she said, trying to decide how much of the truth she had to include. "There's someone here."

"Who?" He put the ukulele down on the couch next to him. Absently, Brooke picked it up and hung it from its bracket on the wall.

"In the rinsing shed. He's going to wake up soon."

"Someone's sleeping in the shed?" Milo looked more confused than worried.

"It's that man the marshal was looking for in Buxton," she said, the words coming out stilted. "Stephen Cawley. One of the Cawleys from Shaw Station."

"Seriously?"

"I recognized him from the poster," she said. A plan was taking shape in her mind. *Five hundred dollars for information leading to capture*, the marshal had said. *Five thousand for safe delivery.*

"What's he doing here? Are you sure it's him?"

"You have to go. You can get the girls on the way." She cursed herself for selling Star and hobbling them, all for nothing. The Cawleys had found her anyway.

"Go where?"

"To Buxton. Hopefully you'll catch a ride. Get that marshal and send him back here." The marshal would have a vehicle, at least. Feds always did. Once Milo alerted him to Cawley's capture, he'd cover the distance to the farm quickly. If Brooke was lucky, and the other Cawleys hadn't descended yet, she'd claim the bounty, get back to Milo and the kids, and take them as far away as she should have gone in the first place. She rummaged in the desk for the keys to the gun cabinet.

"I don't know, Brooke." Milo was watching her. He hadn't moved from the couch.

"What do you mean, you don't know?" Her hand found the keys in the back of a drawer.

"It's federal business. We don't— What if he's just resting? He might move on."

She kicked a footstool to the base of the bookshelf and reached to unlock the gun cabinet above. "You know who the Cawleys are," she said. "You've heard what they're like." She took down her rifle, a .22 she'd only ever used on gophers.

"What's the gun for?" Milo asked. "You said he was just sleeping."

"I knocked him out."

"What? On purpose?"

"Milo, there's no time. He's dangerous. There are others coming. You have to get the kids out of here."

"What others?"

"Cawley said more of them are on the way to the farm," she lied, more easily now.

"Why? I mean, why here?"

"It doesn't matter!" Brooke's voice rose to a shout. "Cawley's here, and he's not alone, and it's fucking dangerous. How are you still sitting on the goddamn couch?"

Milo stood up.

"You have to go," Brooke said. "Now. Get the marshal. Send him here."

"But, Brooke, that marshal's not in Buxton anymore."

"What?"

"He's gone. He left after the auction. He had a Jeep."

"Shit." The marshal could be anywhere. No knowing how long it would take to bring him back to the area. Brooke's fantasy—that she could still be standing when the marshal showed up—evaporated. Cawley would free himself in that time, or be freed.

Brooke took a deep breath. "Go anyway. Use the satellite phone in town. Call the marshals, tell them where Cawley is, see if you can get the information bounty off them, and then take the kids somewhere safe. Get as far away as you can."

"Aren't you coming?"

"I can't leave Cawley alone here. He'll get out."

Milo drew his eyebrows together, as if trying to solve a riddle. "Then I should stay, if someone has to."

"What? No. You can't use the gun," Brooke said flatly. Milo couldn't even fish, wouldn't hook a worm.

Milo picked up the box of shells from where Brooke had placed it on the coffee table. He read the lettering on the side, put it down again.

"Fine."

"You need to be gone, Milo. You have to go now."

"I said fine," he said. "I'll go."

The gun in Brooke's hands felt suddenly heavier. He was only agreeing to what she'd asked him to do, but it still stung. He really would leave her.

"Go, then," she said, turning to the closet for one of the big backpacks. "Take warm clothes, one change each. Otherwise, the bag will be too heavy."

Milo took the pack, dropped in Sal's boots from the floor.

"We could bring him," Milo said.

"What?"

"Bring Cawley with us to Buxton. Then you wouldn't have to stay and keep an eye on him, and there would be two of us in case . . . I don't know, in case whatever." He gestured vaguely.

"With the kids?"

"It's better than leaving you here, if these people are so dangerous. We'll take him to Buxton, call the outpost at Shaw Station, and stay until the marshals come. People will help us."

Brooke considered it. What hope did she have, alone, of surviving whatever was on its way to the farm even now, out of the south? What hope that she would ever see Milo and the girls again, or be there to protect them?

"Get another backpack, then," she said. "And a rope."

IT WAS STILL EARLY, BARELY MID-MORNING. BROOKE AND MILO LEANED THEIR backpacks against the porch and crossed the yard to the rinsing shed. Brooke listened: crows calling, wind in dry oak leaves, the layered songs of late-season crickets and grasshoppers starting and stopping and starting again.

For a mad second, Brooke wondered if she could have imagined her fight with Cawley. She observed the broken door of the rinsing shed hanging wide, the kicked-up ground in front. There could be another explanation for these things.

Then there came a thud from the shed. Cawley was awake.

Brooke double-checked the safety on her rifle. If she were just willing to shoot him, it would be simpler. She had a gun and he didn't; it wouldn't take more than a couple of shots, no matter how awake he was. But there was no point debating what her hands had decided as they swung the axe: she couldn't kill Cawley. If she did, none of it would mean anything.

Instead, Brooke would have to stand guard with the gun while Milo extracted Cawley from the shed and made sure he was safely bound. If Milo made a mistake and Cawley overpowered him, things could go wrong fast. And even if things didn't go wrong, there was still the greater challenge of moving through open country with a prisoner. Cawley would need his legs free. What if he couldn't walk after the blows Brooke had landed to his knee and ankle? And how would she keep him moving while staying safely out of reach with the gun?

"If he's worked his way out of the ropes, he'll try to grab you," she whispered to Milo, repeating what she'd already explained in the house. "There could have been a razor or something on him I didn't find. Just do it the way I told you."

Milo nodded.

"Stand to the left of the inside door, where the seed calendar is. You have to be totally silent. If you put weight on that—"

"I know," he said, squeezing her hand. "It's okay, Brooke."

She took her position with the rifle as Milo crept into the shed. She saw right away that he was going to put his weight on the soft board, but it was too late to stop him. The board creaked loudly. Milo froze.

The thumping stopped. Brooke sighted the rifle at the closed door.

She wished she could split herself in half. If she were standing where Milo was, she could decipher, from the smallest of sounds, Cawley's position beyond the door. She snapped her fingers. Milo didn't hear. He was watching the door. She snapped again, louder. He turned to look and she signaled for him to unlock the door.

He took a deep breath and reached out, withdrew the bolt, and stood back, waiting. The door didn't move. Milo inched forward, pulled it open.

Brooke couldn't see much in the darkness beyond the threshold. Bars of broken light fell between the wall boards into deep shadow. She could just make out a form—Cawley, low against the back wall. He was lying on his back. A wider gap of light showed where he'd almost kicked through one board. He must be high to the point of numbness if he could kick that hard injured. Chalk was an upper and a downer in one. It made you invincible without the jitters, euphoric without the lethargy. No knowing what Cawley was capable of if he was beyond pain.

Milo stood to the side of the open door, looking in.

"Check his ties," Brooke reminded him. "You have to go in to check."

"Right," he said.

She watched Milo move into the inner room. She had talked him through it: he needed to make sure the baling twine had held, then move Cawley into the yard, where they would adjust his bonds for the walk to the road.

There was a sudden scrape.

"He's bound." Milo appeared again, eyes wide. "He tried to kick my legs out."

"Did you check the twine? Did you feel it?"

"No."

"Check it, then. He could be faking."

"But . . ."

It wasn't in Milo to do this. Brooke had never intended to put him in this position. But gentle as he was—exasperatingly, endearingly—she needed his help; she had no one else.

"I can't put the gun down until you're sure," Brooke said. "Try not to think. Just follow the plan. I've got you."

Milo nodded, took another deep breath. He crept back in, slowly, half crouching, as if approaching an animal.

Shuffling, a shout, grunts. Something falling.

"Milo?" she called.

"I'll break his neck," called a low, phlegmy voice, not Milo's. "Old bitch, you know I damn will."

Brooke was in the shed before she knew it, the floor creaking under her boots. In the inner room, Cawley was on his side, his hands still tied behind his back and his ankles bound. He had knocked Milo down and somehow managed to catch Milo's head between his knees, choking him. Milo was struggling, kicking out. Cawley didn't slacken his grip even when a heel caught him in the cheek.

Brooke stepped forward, where Cawley could see the gun. "Let him go!" she shouted.

"The fuck you thinking, coming at me here?" Cawley slurred his words. "Don't you know when to quit?"

"Let him go," she repeated.

"Fuck you," he spat, and squeezed Milo's neck so hard that his eyes bulged.

Brooke took two long steps, pointed the gun at the ground next to Cawley's head, and fired.

Roaring in her ears. She saw Robin's small form in the narrow alley. A siren wailing. *Run*, she'd screamed, again and again. Too late. She saw Robin flying into the air. Pain ripped through her. She saw him fall.

She stepped back from Cawley, her heart beating so hard she thought she might be sick. She forced herself to breathe.

"Fucking do it, then!" Cawley yelled.

How long until the girls came back and found them like this? How long until she heard hooves or engines from the south?

"Let him go," Brooke said, "or I'll shoot your hands."

She saw Cawley's fingers twitch involuntarily as he pulled against the wrist bindings.

"Take him, then," he said finally, relaxing his legs so that Milo could pull his head back through. "All the good he'll do you. This fucking wuss."

Milo scrambled away from Cawley and lay gasping on the ground.

"Are you all right?" Brooke asked.

He nodded.

"Hitch him in the yard," Brooke said. She stepped back with the gun still trained on Cawley.

"I need a minute."

"Stand up, Milo," Brooke said. "We don't have a minute. Move his hands to the front of his body, attach the lead line, then undo his ankles."

"I'm not sure about this plan anymore." Milo got to his knees, rubbing his throat. "Look what he just did."

"He needs his legs to walk."

"I'm not walking anywhere," Cawley said.

"Shut up," Brooke said. "Do it, Milo."

Milo stood, glancing doubtfully at Brooke. He approached Cawley with tentative steps, got him by the armpits, and pulled him out through the shed. Brooke noticed that Cawley let out a grunt of pain when his boot heel caught on the doorstep. He could feel something, then.

Brooke kept the rifle up and ready as Milo cut the baling twine from Cawley's wrists. When the bonds fell, Milo quickly withdrew out of reach, but Cawley only moved his free hands robotically to the front of his body and held his wrists together in front of his chest. Milo moved in and cinched them together with one of the plastic zip ties they kept for small repairs.

Milo secured Cawley to a long nylon rope. Then he cut the baling twine from Cawley's legs and backed away again.

"This is definitely the guy they're looking for?" Milo asked.

"The scar," Brooke said. "I recognize it from the warrant."

A puckered line ran just off-center from Cawley's bottom lip to the crease in his chin; it was old, knotted, dull purple. There were other marks, too, beyond the fresh red welt on his throat where Brooke had choked him into unconsciousness. A split lip from some recent fight, half healed. A swollen eye. Cawley was younger than Brooke—*old bitch*, he'd called her—but he looked worse; he'd been living hard.

"How are we going to get him all the way to Buxton?" Milo asked nervously. "What if he lashes out like that again?"

"You think I should just shoot him?"

"Of course not. God, Brooke. I'm just saying—"

"We just have to make it to town. If we get a ride, we'll be there this afternoon."

"Brooke?" Milo sought her gaze. "Can we talk about this? You don't seem . . . like you."

Brooke looked away, swallowing her guilt. The time to speak had passed. She was well aware that this cold, hard figure wasn't the person Milo knew, the one who'd gotten comfortable, let her guard down, started believing in the life she'd stumbled into. A loving home. A family.

Brooke longed to be that person, but her longing was like grief. The person Milo knew wasn't the one who could save them. It was another, older self, whose skin Brooke had slipped back into all too easily, that they needed now.

"Let's get the bags." She flicked the safety back on the rifle and slung it over her right shoulder. "It's time to go."

3

THAT FIRST WINTER, WHEN BROOKE LAY HIDDEN IN THE BUXTON MILL, HER nightmares receded until there were some nights she slept right through. When spring came, her shoulder was as healed as it was going to get, and she had a wallet full of earnings. She would have moved on then if it wasn't for Milo.

She came outside to feed Star one morning when the sun was shining and the thick winter ice had shrunk back in the mill yard, runnels of meltwater carving paths like veins through its softened surface. The uncommon sound of children's voices caught Brooke's attention. Across the yard, half a dozen kids were standing on the rail platform with a young man. A teacher, Brooke guessed. He was slightly built, and his wool coat looked soft, well made. His face, listening to the students' questions, was kind. He had black hair, olive skin, eyebrows like ink brushstrokes—features that people in Buxton called "exotic," if they were being polite. Brooke had been raised with other words; it embarrassed her to think of them.

The class was watching a forklift shift two-by-sixes onto a flat-bed. One of the children said something, and the teacher laughed, a sudden glow of warmth that reached right into Brooke's body, waking her up to the potent smell of the forest breathing off skids of fresh logs, the velvet touch of the breeze brushing her skin. She stood shivering in the shadow of the mill, watching until he left.

The next time Brooke saw Milo, he was alone, walking on the main street in town. When he entered a store, she sat on the bench out front. She could think of nothing to do or say to catch his attention, and she felt foolish for being there. Nonetheless, she waited.

When Milo came outside, he stood for a moment in the warm sun, seemingly just for the pleasure of it. The collar of his coat was open, and Brooke felt a strong desire to slip her hand inside, under the fabric.

"It feels good," Brooke said, surprising herself.

"Hm?" Milo turned. His eyes were hazel, flecked with gold. There were creases at the corners when he smiled.

"The sun," Brooke said.

Love was like a levee breaking, two bodies rushing in to meet each other. It surprised them both. Milo was as different from Brooke as she imagined it was possible to be. She knew what her parents would think of him: raised by a foreign, city-born mother who hung strange art on her walls and kept a collection of unfamous, subtitled movies. Milo was well liked in Buxton, for the most part. He held soft views on immigration and gun control, but he was wise enough to keep quiet about it in public; along with his mother's complexion, he had inherited her sociability, her patience, her gentle charm. Still, even friends called him an outsider.

"Does that bother you?" Brooke asked him once.

"Of course it does," he said. "I was born here."

"But you never say anything." Brooke was taken aback.

"I'm tired of having to," he said.

Brooke couldn't guess what Milo saw in her. She was secretive and prickly. She told him early on she was from no place he knew, that she had no family, that there were things she would not discuss.

He accepted this. He loved her. He loved just to be near her. And when he touched her, that hum resonated in her bones, making all the panic and the roaring go quiet.

She did want to tell Milo, after a while. They had become close. She thought it would be a relief. But it was hard to reverse, embarrassing to admit her lie. She told herself that he was better off not knowing. She tried to forget. She started using his last name, never having offered another.

She didn't leave Buxton in the spring, or in the summer, and by fall, she was pregnant with Holly.

Through the years that followed, memories would sometimes surface, and Brooke could feel the old fear hounding her: shots, screams, darkness, running. In those moments, she was hard and distant with Milo, and he treated her carefully.

It never stopped feeling wrong to lie to Milo, but somehow her pull to him only grew stronger. All the drudgery of farm work and the relentlessness of parenting, irritations and disappointments, moments they almost hated each other—there was thing after thing to figure out, not knowing what they were doing, terrified of failing; Milo's mother got old and needed care, and then died; their isolation grew; the farm lost money—and yet the feeling was always there, wildly alive, astonishing her. They fell into bed at the end of the endless days, and Brooke wrapped her hands around Milo's wrists, pushing him into the pillow, biting his lips, hungering for him to bite back. Afterward, she lay on his chest, empty and mindless, until her weight was too much and he eased her onto the mattress.

In time, the memories came less often. Her life was her own. She cultivated cranberries, she loved a man who could not load a gun if you gave him an hour, and their children grew in peace and safety. Proof enough, Brooke thought, that she had left the past behind.

MILO LED THE WAY UP THE DRIVEWAY TOWARD THE ROAD. IF THE GIRLS WERE looking for a signal, they would be there, at the high point of land. Brooke had known Holly to spend hours holding Milo's old phone skyward in stubborn hope.

Brooke walked last, with the lead rope looped in her left hand, the rifle slung on her right, and Cawley in front of her, where she could see him. His aggression in the rinsing shed had not returned. Now, he drifted in a chalk fugue, muttering to himself, laughing now and then.

Brooke scanned the ground as she walked. The driveway had been gravel at one time, but a dozen seasons of spring runoff had blurred it with creek mud, and grass and weeds had taken root. Brooke could still see Star's hoofprints from four days ago, when she and Milo had ridden to town.

Where the driveway met the road, a sharp rise led up into the woods on their right. There, Brooke tied Cawley's rope off to an old fencepost.

Milo scrambled up the hill, calling out to the girls. Brooke stifled the urge to hush him, to keep Cawley from hearing their names. She checked her knots and added an extra clove hitch to slow Cawley down if he tried to escape. Once she was sure of the rope, she followed Milo, now out of sight over the hill.

Brooke could tell the grass had been recently trod on, but in a few places the blades bent downhill, crushed by feet descending instead of climbing, and by a walker much heavier than an eight- or thirteen-year-old girl. Fearful, Brooke stooped to examine a patch of exposed sand; here were the girls' prints—Sal barefoot despite the season, the scalloped outline of her small toes—but there was the tread of a boot, pointing back to the driveway. To the house.

Brooke hurried after Milo. As she cleared the brow of the hill, she heard voices. Holly and Sal, talking at once.

"Mom, what's the surprise?" Holly asked as Brooke came into

view. Both girls were down to T-shirts in the morning sun, their sweaters and coats strewn on the ground. "We were about to come back and see."

"What on earth did you tell them?" Brooke asked Milo.

"They say a man was here an hour ago," Milo said. Brooke saw the look in his eyes: he was trying to hide his alarm from the kids.

"Your friend," Sal said, hopping excitedly. A blue elastic slouched loose from one of her braids and fell to the ground. She bent to pick it up and twisted it back into her hair. "He said he was going to get the surprise ready and we should come after. Is it a movie like Grandma used to have? Does he have a movie?"

Brooke felt something hot rise in her throat. Cawley had seen them. Spoken to them. Spared them only out of some sick, high freak of fancy.

"What's with the backpacks?" Holly said. "And the gun? And since when do you have friends?"

"What did I tell you, Holly?" Brooke barked. "What did I tell you about strangers?"

"Whoa," Milo said, holding out a hand.

"He was friendly," Holly said. "God, Mom."

Brooke spun around, scanning the trees. From the hilltop, she could see their house and the rosy cranberry bogs below.

"Which way did he come from?"

"The road. I don't know. What's going on?"

"Milo, we need a new plan," Brooke said. "Cawley passed them *here*. He must have come from Buxton."

"Well, yeah. That's where they were looking for him."

Brooke reeled at her mistake. It was just force of habit that had held her attention to the south. Whenever she'd had dreams—nightmares—of being found, the threat had always come that way.

"Cawley?" Holly asked, wide-eyed, recognizing the name from who knew what gossip in town.

"We can't take the road," Brooke said. "The others will be coming that way too, if he did."

"What others?" Holly looked from Brooke to Milo. "What's going on?"

"Let me think." Brooke pressed her fingers into her temples, waiting for the spots in her eyes to clear, the roaring in her ears to die down.

East was Buxton, with the nearest phone signal and plenty of Milo's old friends and students they could turn to for shelter until the marshals came. But if the Cawleys were on that road, they'd never make it that far.

West, there was nothing but sparsely populated prairie and the pipeline tracking south, carrying crude oil to the federal refineries.

North were the mountains. There was only one road through the pass to the tar sands. If no one picked them up, they would be days walking, and they could be run down easily.

South was Shaw County, the last place Brooke wanted to go. But if she got Cawley there, the marshals would put him behind bars and pay her enough to get away and start over.

The creek they used to flood the bogs flowed from high in the mountains south through the foothills. If they kept to the water, they could cut cross-country, leaving no tracks.

"Fine," Brooke said. "We'll take him to Shaw Station ourselves."

"Shaw Station?" Holly's face registered disbelief. "Us?"

"You'll have to walk fast and do what I say. Understand?"

"Brooke, no," Milo said. "That's too far. Shaw Station has got to be a hundred miles."

"How far is a hundred miles?" Sal asked.

"We don't even have a horse," Holly complained.

"Help me, Milo," Brooke said.

"No. I'm sorry. This is crazy. Why would we go to Shaw Station?"

"We have to," she said, trying not to shout. "We just do."

"Isn't anyone going to tell me what's going on?" Holly asked.

"That man, he's not my friend," Brooke said. "He's wanted by the federal marshals in Shaw Station, and we're going to take him there."

"Brooke—" Milo started.

"I swear to god, Milo. We can talk about it later."

Milo looked hard at her for a moment. She held his gaze, willing him to trust her.

"We *are* going to talk about it," he said. "Come on, kids. Mom and I will sort it out. Don't worry."

"Take them to the creek," Brooke said, pointing the way down the opposite side of the hill, away from the driveway. "I'll get him and meet you there."

"I need stuff from the house," Holly said.

"We packed everything you need," Brooke said. "Stay with Dad and head straight for the creek."

"Come on, Hol." Milo turned and started off toward the creek. Sal followed, whacking the tall grass beside the path with her stick. The broken stems sawed over, a glaring record of her passage.

"Don't let her do that with the stick, Milo," Brooke called after him. "And try not to scuff your feet on the ground. You're leaving marks."

He shook his head. She saw him gently take Sal's stick.

Holly hadn't moved. "I want my book," she said.

"No time. Go on, after them."

"Why?" Holly took a step past Brooke, back toward the house. "It'll take five minutes. I can catch up."

"I said no." Brooke caught her daughter's arm. Brooke was taller and stronger, but she doubted she could pick Holly up anymore, or force her to go anywhere she didn't want to.

"Hey!" Holly yanked her arm away, affronted.

Over Holly's shoulder, Brooke thought she saw movement in

an upper window of the house. She held her breath. A crow flapped up from the eaves, its reflection gliding over the glass.

Holly was watching her, the irritation in her face changing to something else.

"Just a bird," Brooke said. "Go on. After your sister."

Holly didn't argue. She followed Sal and Milo down through the trees, twisting to look back over her shoulder for whatever her mother had seen.

CAWLEY WAS SITTING AS BROOKE HAD LEFT HIM, SEVERAL YARDS FROM WHERE the lead rope was knotted to the fencepost. He appeared to have emerged from his fog for the moment; his eyes tracked her as she approached, his face twisted in dislike.

"Yeah, fuck you, too," Brooke said, undoing the clove hitch from the fencepost and loosening the other knots one by one.

As the rope came free, Cawley lunged at Brooke, head down, and rammed her in the chest, knocking the breath from her. She grappled for the fencepost, just managing to stay up.

Cawley was running. He was almost out of reach, up the driveway toward the road. Brooke launched herself at the trailing end of the rope and yanked it taut. Cawley came down hard. Before he could stand up again, Brooke ran the rope around the nearest fencepost and leaned back with all her weight to winch it while she raised the rifle with her right hand.

"Down!" she bellowed.

Cawley had his feet under him. He tried to move, but the winch held. He sank back to the ground, cursing.

"Why are you here?" Brooke demanded, overcome with exasperation. "You could have just left me alone. You know I never did anything to you."

Cawley squinted at her. "Brooke," he said, smirking crookedly. "Brooke Holland."

Brooke started at the sound of the name she'd hidden for so long. It was still hers, after all. It wouldn't matter to anyone what Brooke had or hadn't done; it would only matter who she was.

Cawley was still watching her, that odd smile on his face.

"Walk," she said, gesturing toward the creek.

IF BROOKE HAD TOLD MILO HER NAME ALL THOSE YEARS AGO, SHE KNEW WHAT HE would have thought of her. Her family had been notorious, one way or another, since she was born.

Edmund and Emily Holland were legends of the rural resistance, among the first to take up arms. They had both fought at the Warren River standoff when the feds refused to recognize the secession vote, and there was a much-posted photo of three-year-old Brooke standing in the bed of a gun-mounted pickup truck, flanked by her older siblings, Callum and Anita, with Emily behind them, visibly pregnant, a bandana covering her face, an assault rifle across her chest.

During the fight to sever the rural territories from the federal government, and the years of the short-lived sovereign state that followed, the Hollands' single, stylized *H* had been a popular tattoo. Before she could read, Brooke had known what that letter signified: independence, self-determination, justice.

Edmund and Emily had taught their children that if they were going to live free and thrive, they needed every weapon at hand, every skill that could be learned. It was an enfeebling lie that the system would take care of you. Just look around you: minorities and big corporations treated like royalty while the common people went ignored. If something was worth having, you had to get it for yourself. And the Hollands did. It was how they'd become icons of the movement. A Holland would not abandon the cause, no matter what it demanded, how much damage it inflicted. Regardless of the bleak TV commentary, you only had to look at Edmund's and Emily's faces to know that it wasn't over. It would never be over.

Brooke had been shaped by their force, leaning into it as into a strong wind, never thinking she might someday let go and be blown away, or that her life could take root elsewhere.

After the sovereign state fell, things changed. Not right away, and not all at once, and Brooke was young enough, at first, to believe that her parents could still fix it. She'd kept believing that, even when she was old enough to know better, when their *H* had come to stand for something else and decent people got their tattoos reworked into other shapes. The Holland house had once bustled with friends who worked and fought alongside them through secession and independence; few of those people came anymore, and those that did were on different business. At sixteen, Brooke had followed her family into a chalk war with the Cawleys, still believing that survival was what counted, no matter how ugly.

By the time she met Milo, she'd been glad to be rid of her name. Brooke had never known for certain that anyone was looking for her, only that instinct told her to hide. Buxton wasn't far enough—a scant hundred miles from home—but Milo was there, with his kind heart and warm touch, knowing nothing and loving her. And then came Holly, so steady and serious, and sweet, dreamy Sal.

Brooke had moved them to the farm, kept them hidden, stayed silent. Still, nothing she had done could diminish her guilt: she had risked the ones she loved most, she had brought them into something they were utterly unprepared for, and now they might not survive unless Brooke was very careful, and very lucky.

It didn't matter how the Cawleys had found her, or why they had come now, after so many years. Brooke would find a way to the marshals. She would take their money, and her family, and she would disappear, this time for good.

4

HIGHWAY 12 RAN BETWEEN BUXTON AND SHAW STATION ON A COURSE THAT WAS far to the east of them here. Traveling south cross-country, Brooke didn't expect to meet the road for another twenty miles, until it swung west near a place called Buffalo Cross. That far might take two days. Beyond Buffalo Cross, another fifty miles of country stretched to the Warren River and the edge of Shaw County, and the federal outpost was ten miles past that, in the hills outside Shaw Station. A week's walking at best, slower with the kids.

Brooke ran the rope out between her and Cawley and paced her strides to keep it fully extended as they walked. Cawley stumbled and limped, but the chalk was still working on him; he seemed hardly to feel his injuries.

As they climbed the hill and then started down the path to the creek, Brooke erased their tracks and those left by Milo and the girls, brushing the ground behind her with a soft bough, snapping bent stems off at the root and folding them into her pocket. Someone seeing their footsteps on the driveway might assume they had gone to the road.

They came out of the trees. Milo and the girls were resting at the edge of the creek and didn't notice them at first. Sun glossed the fallen humps of feather grass. Milo had taken off his backpack and was leaning against it, wincing slightly as Sal struggled to weave sprigs of heather into his hair, chatting steadily in her high, light voice as she worked. Holly was lying on her back, eyes closed. They might have been on a picnic.

Brooke realized she was smiling. Her stomach fluttered nervously. Cawley only had to say her name in front of them and the whole thing would fall apart. Milo would be confused, the girls frightened. They might refuse to go with her. Brooke considered gagging Cawley, but Milo's principles probably wouldn't allow it. Cawley couldn't harm them with words, he'd say.

The line that connected Brooke to Cawley snagged on a blackthorn bush. She flicked it free. She'd gag him if she had to.

Now Milo and the girls noticed them. Holly sat up, and Brooke watched both her and Sal take in Cawley's presence, his tied wrists, the rope. Holly's eyes traveled curiously to Brooke at the other end of the rope, holding the rifle. Sal clung shyly to Milo, who stood, careful not to dislodge the heather woven into his hair.

"It's okay, kids," he said, in the slightly lilting tone Brooke thought of as his teacher voice. "This is Stephen Cawley."

Brooke knew he was only demonstrating decency and compassion by introducing their prisoner this way; still, she bristled. "Take off your boots," she said. "We're walking the creek."

"You're not serious," Holly said.

"We have to, Holly."

"But it's freezing."

"Milo?" Brooke prompted, turning to him.

"Maybe if you explained," he said, holding her eye. "They don't understand what's going on."

She heard the unsaid part: *I don't either.*

"Later," Brooke said. Holly and Sal watched disbelieving as she started on her own boots.

"Dad," Holly said. "Tell her this is insane."

"I'm sure you can take one minute to tell us why—"

"No." She tied her laces together and slung the boots around her neck.

For a moment, Milo looked like he was going to argue. Instead, he closed his eyes and took a deep breath. After a second, he opened his eyes and smiled faintly at the girls.

"Listen to your mom," he said, rolling his jeans up as high as they would go and bending to remove his boots. "She wouldn't ask if it wasn't important."

Holly swore, pulling one boot off and throwing it on the grass.

"Dad, I don't have any boots," Sal said.

"It's okay, Salamander. We packed them."

"But I don't want to go in the water," Sal whined.

Milo hoisted his backpack and then lifted Sal into his arms.

"You'll tire yourself out if you carry her like that," Brooke said.

"Wrap like a monkey, Sal," Milo said. He waded into the creek, inhaling sharply as the icy water rose past his ankles.

"This is unbelievable," Holly said. "Unbelievable!"

"Hush," Brooke said. "Keep your voice down."

Holly stormed into the water.

Cawley was watching with a look of amused scorn. He had pried his sneakers off without comment. Brooke gestured for him to step away from them. When he was far enough, she undid the knots in the grimy laces, tied the reeking things together and hung them from her backpack. As much as it might have given her satisfaction to sink Cawley's shoes in the creek and let him walk barefoot to Shaw Station, she could not afford to slow him down.

"Into the water," she said.

Cawley did not roll up his pants before descending the bank. He plunged down the creek, oblivious to the soaked denim that added weight to his legs. Brooke followed him into the frigid water, her feet slipping on the rocky bottom.

Brooke let twenty feet of rope extend between her and Cawley, and kept him back twice as far again from the others. Holly forged ahead in sullen silence. Sal clung to Milo until curiosity overtook her and she reached a toe down to the water, half choking Milo as she dangled from his neck.

"You have to wrap," Brooke heard Milo remind Sal again and again, until finally he put her down. She shrieked, feeling the cold, but soon enough she was splashing ahead, water darkening her clothes to the waist.

They moved south. The water was low this time of year, but bitterly cold. Small river crayfish nipped at Brooke's numbed ankles. Their touch felt distant, as if her limbs belonged to another body. From her remove sixty feet back in the creek, she listened to Milo keeping up a meandering conversation with Sal and a mainly unresponsive Holly. He had always been the easier parent. He played with them, did projects with them, made up silly songs for them. Now, he pointed things out to them in the creek and the foothills around them, distracting them, keeping them moving.

Cawley periodically scanned the horizon. Brooke wondered if their pursuers had reached the house yet. If they'd found her trail into the creek, they might even now be closing in, watching from a distance, waiting for one of the kids to straggle, for Brooke to put the gun down.

Brooke's wet jeans clung to her thighs, pulling with each step. The pack dug into her shoulders. She had smashed a toe between two slippery rocks, and the nail throbbed in spite of the numbing water. Her ribs ached where Cawley had punched her. She imagined bending her knees and sinking into the creek, floating the weight off her hips and back, letting the cold soothe her.

Images of their fight outside the shed flashed in Brooke's mind: Cawley's shovel blade hacking through the shed door, his hand reaching for the axe—how close he'd come to winning.

Brooke shuddered to think what would have happened. Milo and the girls undefended, unaware.

He didn't win, she told herself.

"Brooke?" Milo called. Ahead, he and the girls had stopped.

Brooke looped the rope in her left hand, halting Cawley at a distance from them.

"I have to go to the bathroom," Sal called back.

"Just go on the bank where we can see you," Brooke said.

"I don't want . . ." Sal darted a look at Cawley.

"It's okay, Sal."

"No!" Sal shouted, petulant.

"She wants privacy, Brooke," Milo said.

"Go with her, then, but hurry."

"Holly, will you take your sister, please?" Milo asked. "I need to talk to Mom."

"Fine," Holly grumbled, grabbing Sal's arm. "Come on."

"Not far!" Brooke called. "And don't let her out of your sight!"

The girls clambered up the edge of the creek and over a small rise.

"All right," Milo said when they were out of earshot. His teacher voice was gone now, she noticed. "Taking him to Shaw Station wasn't the plan."

"Buxton isn't safe," Brooke said, watching the place where the girls had disappeared from view. "I told you why."

"The marshals were only looking for *him*. We don't know there are others. He might have said that just to scare you."

Cawley looked up. "Said what?" he asked, his voice still gummy.

"Listen," Brooke said quickly, keeping Milo's attention on her. "We can make it. We'll pass Buffalo Cross by tomorrow, if we hurry."

"Brooke, think about it. Even if we could walk a hundred miles, we're not prepared for camping. We don't have enough food. What if someone gets hurt? We can't do this alone. And what about the harvest? If we're gone for more than a couple days—"

"That doesn't matter," Brooke said, hearing her voice rise. She lowered it again. "We just have to get him to the marshals. That's all."

"Marshals?" Cawley coughed and spat into the water. "Since when do you deal with marshals?"

"Buffalo Cross, though," Milo said, thinking. "They're supposed to have a sheriff."

"So?"

"He might help. He might have a phone. We could meet the marshals there, instead of going all the way to Shaw Station."

Brooke had heard Buffalo Cross was unfriendly, a community that had survived by isolating itself and repelling newcomers. She had imagined bypassing it entirely. Nonetheless, Milo was right that they would need food and water by then. Brooke had packed for only a short journey, grabbing things from the pantry that could be eaten without cooking. She'd stuffed two sleeping bags in the pack as an afterthought, but hadn't even considered the tent, which was heavy.

"Okay," Brooke conceded. "We can try Buffalo Cross."

At that moment, Holly reappeared at the side of the creek, alone.

"I'm hungry," she said.

"Where's your sister?" Brooke asked. "I told you not to leave her alone."

"She's going to the bathroom, Mom, okay? She's right over there."

Just then, Sal's thin, high shriek came from beyond the bank.

Brooke ran past Cawley, forcing him to stumble after her through the water so he wouldn't get dragged under by the rope.

"A mouse ran by me," Sal cried when Brooke cleared the bank and saw her squatting in the brush. "I got pee on my leg."

THEY WALKED THE CREEK ALL DAY WITH NO SIGN OF PURSUIT. THE SUN MOVED slowly left to right, never more than halfway up from the horizon, tracking its oblique late-season course. By late afternoon, Brooke guessed they were five miles from home. The mountains behind them still looked close, but the land was opening up.

Their feet were cut and swollen, their legs ached from trying to balance on uneven ground, and the cold had seeped into every corner of their bodies. Brooke had allowed the girls a small ration of lunch while they walked, but she and Milo had eaten nothing since breakfast.

With early dusk coming down, Brooke directed Holly up the bank into a grassy meadow scabbed with bedrock, where they would have a clear view of the approach from all sides.

Holly and Sal collapsed on the rocks, speechless with exhaustion.

Brooke threw Milo the lead rope and watched as he checked the lock on the zip tie around Cawley's wrists and used an extra length of rope to tie his ankles, then knotted the lead line around the base of a juniper bush. Brooke talked him through the correct knot, and how to check it. She kept a careful distance with the rifle, but Cawley made no attempt to escape this time. He lowered himself to the ground, wincing. Without the cold of the creek to numb the pain, he would be feeling his injuries. That wouldn't be the worst of his discomfort, Brooke knew. His high was wearing off. Coming down from chalk could be as bad as the flu.

Once Cawley was secured, and Milo safely out of his reach, Brooke put the gun down and eased herself out of her pack. The sky was darkening quickly, and she didn't want to risk a fire or lantern. While there was still light to see by, she opened her pack and started pulling things out.

"When are we going to eat?" Sal whined.

"Soon, Salamander," Brooke said. "Get changed first."

"No way am I getting undressed," Holly said. "I'm finally starting to warm up."

"Switching to dry clothes when you stop moving is the best way to keep your body temperature up," Brooke said automatically.

"It's *not* up," Holly groaned.

"Come on, Hol. I promise you'll feel better once you're in dry clothes. Dad packed your red scarf."

"When are we going to get somewhere?" Holly asked. "I'm so tired."

"We're sleeping here tonight," Brooke said.

"*Here?* What, on the ground?"

"It's just for one night."

Brooke turned away from Holly's aggrieved sputtering to evaluate their campsite. Forest on one side, rolling meadow and bedrock everywhere else. The meadow grass would soak the sleeping bags with dew. In the bedrock that broke through the surface, there was a long green seam, four feet wide, where moss and lichen grew. That would be the best place for the sleeping bags. She unstuffed them from her pack and spread them out on the ground.

Milo dug the dry clothes out of his pack. Holly hid behind a juniper bush, but Sal didn't fuss about undressing in front of Cawley this time. Either she'd forgotten he was there, sitting apart—Awake? Asleep? Brooke couldn't tell—or she was too tired to care. Once they'd changed, Milo rubbed Sal's legs to warm them, and she squealed as her numbed skin lit up with fiery pins and needles.

"Shh," Brooke hushed her instinctively.

"What?" Holly asked, wrapping her red knitted scarf around her neck. "Who's going to hear her?"

"No one," Brooke said, turning to her pack. "Nothing. Let's have dinner."

"Is that all we have?" Milo asked, looking at the small collection of knotted plastic bags Brooke took out. Their contents were difficult to distinguish in the gathering dark.

Milo hadn't spoken to Brooke since Sal's shriek cut them off in the creek that afternoon. He'd addressed himself to the kids, receiving Brooke's periodic instructions silently. Now his voice was stiff, restrained.

"I packed for a day or two," Brooke said, passing chestnuts and raw carrots to the girls. "We can make this last until Buffalo Cross."

"I thought we were going to Shaw Station," Holly said, biting into a chestnut.

"Well, Shaw Station is a long way," Brooke said, glancing at Milo. "Buffalo Cross is closer. We'll see if they can help us get Cawley to the marshals."

"Why wouldn't they help?" Sal asked.

"I don't know, Salamander. I've never been there."

"What did he do, anyway?" Holly asked.

"That's none of our business," Milo said.

"Then why are we taking him?"

"He said he knew Mom," Sal added. "He said there was going to be a surprise."

"Hush, Salamander," Brooke said. "Keep your voice down. I don't know why he said that. He's not thinking straight."

"Why not? What's wrong with him?" Sal asked.

"He's sick, honey," Milo said. "You know how we've talked about drugs before?"

"Like the guys in the laundromat," Sal nodded sagely, referring to Buxton's small chalk den.

"But why would he say he knew you?" Holly pressed.

"Oh, I know her." Cawley's voice came through the dusk. They turned to where he was leaning against the rocks. His voice was less garbled now. His eyes were clearer and more focused than they had been all day. He was staring at Brooke. "Me and your mom go way back, *Holly*."

Brooke grabbed the rifle and crossed the distance in a heartbeat. She crouched in front of Cawley, just out of reach, her back to Milo and the girls.

"Shut your mouth," she whispered. "It's not too late for me to shoot you."

"They don't know, do they?" he smirked.

"You don't look at them," she hissed. "You don't speak to them. You speak only to me, only when I say so."

"You're no fun to talk to," he said, tilting his head to one side. "So fucking serious."

"Yeah, I am. I'm deadly serious. And if you speak to them again, I will make you regret it."

"Well, shit," Cawley scoffed. "I wouldn't want to *regret* anything."

Brooke clenched her fist around the rifle. She shouldn't hit him in front of the girls. She turned away.

"You look just like your mother," Cawley mused to her back.

"Don't listen to him," Brooke said, returning to Milo and the girls. "He doesn't know what he's talking about. Just try to pretend he's not there."

There was a yip, far off in the forest, soon answered by another. Coyotes.

"Oh my god, I don't see why we're doing this," Holly said. "I hate it."

"Hate it, then," Brooke said. "As long as you cooperate so we can get it done."

"I *am* cooperating."

"You are," Milo said, with a warning glance at Brooke. "You and Sal are both doing your best, and we appreciate it."

Holly rolled her eyes.

"I'm still hungry," Sal said.

"Here," Brooke said, snapping her carrot in half and splitting it between the girls. She sat, facing away from them, waiting for darkness to hide her completely.

THE GIRLS ZIPPED THEMSELVES INTO THEIR SLEEPING BAGS ON THE MOSSY seam in the rock and were soon asleep, despite Holly's assertion that it was too cold and uncomfortable and creepy to sleep, and Sal's fear, stoked by her sister, that they would be attacked by coyotes.

A bright moon rose, nearly full, and by its light, Brooke could see Milo still sitting where he'd kept the girls company as they fell asleep. There was no reason for him to stay there now, unless he was as reluctant to talk again as Brooke was.

Brooke got out the flashlight and busied herself spreading their wet things over a flat-topped juniper bush. Nothing would really dry overnight, but the airflow might prevent mildew. Then she unpacked and repacked both bags, until she was certain she could find any of their contents by feel in the dark. Finally, there was nothing left for her to do.

She swept the flashlight to find Milo. He was no longer sitting by the girls, but moving toward Cawley with something held out in front of him. Something pointed.

"Are you hungry, Stephen?" she heard him ask.

"What are you doing?" Brooke hissed.

"We have to at least feed him." Now she saw it was a carrot Milo was holding.

"Why?"

"Because, Brooke. Even if he's under citizen's arrest, or whatever this is, he has a right to eat."

"He'll just throw up," Brooke said. "He's coming down."

"Try to eat," Milo said to Cawley, tossing the carrot at his feet. Cawley ignored him.

Brooke shook her head. Let Milo give Cawley a carrot if it made him feel better. She shone the flashlight on Cawley, hunched against his rock. If he was listening to their debate, he gave no sign. He sat grim-faced and still. Or not quite still, Brooke realized. He was shaking, his teeth clattering in his jaw. He was still soaked from the creek. His lips were blue.

"Milo," Brooke said. "Are those the only other pants you brought?" She regretted now that she'd told him to pack only one extra set of clothes for each of them.

"Yeah, why?"

"He can't sit in wet pants all night. He'll get sores. You can share one of the kids' sleeping bags to stay warm."

"Wait. What?"

"He needs dry pants."

"Yeah, but so do I."

"Oh, for—" Brooke fumed. "The one thing you could have done instead of me." She took off her sweatpants and threw them at Milo. The cold bit into her exposed skin.

"The *one* thing?" Milo stared at her.

"Come on," she said, picking up the rifle to cover him. "His knee's probably swollen. If he sits in wet jeans all night, it'll open up. We need him to be able to walk tomorrow."

Milo grabbed the bunched-up pants from the ground. He undid the rope around Cawley's ankles and pulled him up to his feet from behind, undoing his fly as if he were one of their kids. Cawley submitted without comment, shivering as Milo shimmied the damp jeans down over his leg.

Getting Brooke's sweatpants on him proved the harder part. They were a close fit, and Cawley's clammy flesh and knobby, swollen joints caught in the leg holes. He lost his balance, and Milo caught him instinctively.

They might have been laughing about this, Brooke thought. If absolutely everything were different.

When Milo was done and Cawley secured, Brooke sat, pulling her bare legs up inside her coat.

"Which kid do you want to share a sleeping bag with?" Milo asked.

"Go ahead. I'll keep watch."

"You're not going to sleep?"

"I'm not tired. It's fine."

"Come on, Brooke. You're freezing."

"I've got my coat."

With a puff of frustration, Milo took off his own pants. "Here."

"Milo," she said. "I didn't mean there was only one thing you could—"

"I'm tired," he cut her off. "Just put the pants on. Wake me up if you need me."

He shifted Sal over in her bag and climbed in. Sooner than Brooke would have thought possible, his breathing dropped evenly into sleep.

Brooke sat awake, alone. Under the moon, the meadow grew silver with frost. It would be clear tomorrow, Brooke thought, and the berries would be ready for picking. She felt a burst of irritation that the first good day for the harvest would be lost.

Then she remembered: everything would be lost. The house and the crops and the tools, the jars of preserves, pickles, ketchup, plums. Their photographs. The stones and feathers Sal stashed on the windowsills according to some mystical logic all her own. Holly's cookbooks. The ukulele.

Brooke remembered the time, months ago, at the beginning of summer, when the four of them had gone together to move the beehives for pollination. It was a warm evening, one of the first of the year, and they were all giddy with it. A current crackled between Brooke and Milo when she kissed him on the porch.

After dinner, Brooke taught Holly how to lay small squares of screen over the hive entrances and seal the edges with duct tape. Then she and Milo hefted the eighty-pound box into the wheelbarrow and descended the path to the bogs, the girls running ahead like puppies, laughing. Below them, the cranberry blossoms were just opening, their upward-curling petals standing like pink crowns over the vines.

They lifted the hives onto a raised platform at the center of the bogs and climbed up to wait for the bees to settle so they could remove the screens. Holly stretched out, describing a process for making cashew cheese she'd been reading about. The western sky glowed orange, streaked by thin clouds, then turned pale, indigo, black. Milo lit a storm lantern and Sal crept into Brooke's lap. Brooke remembered hugging her tight, looking out on the lamplight spilling across a sea of shiny leaves all around them.

The bees and the plants would go wild without them. Animals would burrow in the dikes.

In the meadow, Brooke watched her family sleep. She shrank from the moment when she would have to tell them they were never going home. If she was lucky, that moment wouldn't come until they reached the marshals, the bounty, and safety. But if Cawley said something, or someone in Buffalo Cross identified her, or Milo simply stopped accepting her weak explanations, it would come sooner. And then Brooke would have to tell them everything, and they would see her, and what she'd done, and how little she deserved them.

The night inched forward. Brooke heard each whisper of sound, each snap in the darkness. The calls of night birds. Rodent feet. Something larger in the woods, a coyote or raccoon.

Every few minutes, Brooke checked the dark shapes of Milo and the girls, burrowed deep in their sleeping bags. They slept on, unaware.

5

BROOKE'S PARENTS HAD BEEN PIPELINE WORKERS. THEY LOST THEIR JOBS IN A downturn, years before secession, and after that they turned to bio-diesel. They brewed fuel from canola bought cheap off the prairies and turned an extra profit demethylating the glycerin layer for soap works. It was hard, dirty work, but they did well by it. Gas prices were set in the city, where people made city wages.

"Never mind they don't even need to fucking drive because our taxes paid for their fucking electric subway," Edmund said, as if he hadn't been evading his own taxes for years.

When the Federal Revenue Services finally came after the re-finery, the unsuspecting auditors arrived at the Hollands' property high in the Shaw County hills only to be turned back at the fence line by Edmund, Emily, and a dozen of their friends, all armed. Later, people would call it the spark that lit the rural resistance.

The Hollands were natural leaders in the growing movement to secede. Edmund was smart, well spoken, uncowed by dire reports of their disappearing rural way of life. If he was a purist, if he could also be cold and forbidding, he was made more likeable by Emily, whose fiery, militant joy in the cause was infectious. Jobs in the refinery saved a number of local families from going broke, and the *H* scored into the Hollands' diesel drums became a symbol almost as powerful as the sovereign flag.

The independence movement gained strength with every wave of layoffs and foreclosures. Edmund and Emily complained of Lands and Resources setting quotas on deer when families couldn't afford groceries; they lamented farms gutted by free trade, foreigners pouring in from every corner of the globe. Rural communities were shrinking, their schools were half empty, and the feds seemed not to know or care. In the city, civil servants were striking for pensions like they were a god-given right.

The Hollands weren't alone in their opinions. Associations were formed. Votes were held. After the referendum to secede, commentators declared that rural voters had been fooled into going against their own interests, that the countryside received more tax aid per capita than anyone, and that smaller government could only hurt them.

"Missing the point, as usual," Edmund laughed, relishing their indignation.

The federal government refused to accept the results of the referendum, and the standoffs began. One, then four, then ten resistance members were killed in the conflict. The name of each was memorialized in black above the broad open doors of the drive shed that housed the Hollands' fleet of vehicles. Meanwhile, the feds sent in soldiers and sustained nothing worse than a few burned blockades. There was a second referendum, even more overwhelming than the first, and the federal government had to concede. They let the sovereign territories go, though they cut a deal for 50 percent ownership of the tar sands, which lay deep in ceded territory, on the basis that the government had built the pipeline in the first place.

"With public dollars and my fucking labor," Edmund grumbled.

Brooke started first grade under the newly minted sovereign state: a different anthem, a different flag. With her elder siblings, Callum and Anita, she waited at the end of the driveway for the yellow school bus to gather them up on its long, winding route through the hills to Shaw Station. Their textbooks had been outdated even before secession. The students drew in the new border by hand every time there was a map exercise, and the teachers were sometimes unsure about whether the book agreed with their rewritten curriculum.

"No, that's wrong," Brooke interrupted her teacher's explanation of the thinning ozone layer. "Fake science. Daddy says so."

Edmund Holland was six foot five and nearly three hundred pounds, with a temper to match. There was a joke around the county that the strong spirits in his blood had thinned like whisky down through his children, from hot-headed Callum to Robin, Brooke's little brother, as close as any Holland ever came to gentle. Edmund and Emily did nothing to discourage this mythology. Of Callum, they said: "You know a fire hose, with no one holding it?" Callum's aggressiveness got him into trouble from the beginning. When Emily was called in to school after Callum had slashed a teacher's tires because she was what he called an "uppity city bitch," Emily accepted her son's suspension as his due, but she was smiling when they left the principal's office, and Callum knew it.

Anita, their elder daughter, was queenly, menacing, relentless as a viper. She ran the schoolyard like a fiefdom, enforcing fealty, issuing decrees. Any perceived slight was a travesty to be met with swift, outsized revenge. "Watch your back," Callum told his friends, not without pride.

Brooke, third in line, was steadier and more disciplined than her older siblings, a natural problem-solver. She did fine at school, but it was the applied lessons described in their books that she was interested in, and the school didn't have the budget for chemistry, or robotics, or engineering. So it was at home that she learned. Her parents showed her how the demethylation condensers in the refinery worked, gave her old appliances to take apart and reassemble, and as she got older, she became their fixer, their eraser: no seeping hole she couldn't mend, no knotted wire she couldn't undo. She could make a wrench out of a T-shirt, a bullet from a dime. "Get Brooke," became the family refrain. "She'll do it."

Robin, the baby, was curious, affectionate, more sensitive than Edmund could abide. "You know bread dough before you punch it down?" Edmund scoffed. "You know a fucking *marshmallow*?"

Robin didn't want to build or make or fix; he wanted to talk. He wanted to know how people felt and why. Edmund scowled at the incessant flow of questions, and Robin studied his expression, asking, "What is that face called?"

At school, where they expected another Callum, Robin provoked confusion and scorn. His teacher gave him extra computer time at recess to spare him the other children's rough taunts, and Robin found a new outlet for his curiosity. There was still broadband in town, and Robin ranged as far online as he could, coming home with ever-expanding knowledge of the world outside Shaw County, celebrity news and pop culture trends that had nothing whatsoever to do with their lives.

The rest of the family was quick to point out that Robin would never survive in Shaw County on his own, and Brooke as quick to answer that he'd never have to. She treasured her little brother. He was miraculous to her, something that shouldn't have been able to exist in their world, and yet did.

Shaw County had never been an easy place. The hills were solid rock, unfarmable, the mines tapped out decades before. Its sharp beauty, and its closeness to the city, had once made the area popular with cottagers, who supported a meager tourism industry, but they had almost all sold after the vote to secede, taking their nonresident taxes with them.

Three years into the sovereign state, crude bottomed out. The state defaulted on their co-share payments for the pipeline and began to go bankrupt on foreign borrowing. There were new layoffs in the tar sands and another round of foreclosures. Chalk was new then—an experimental compound, potent and dangerous—and soon it was everywhere.

Brooke was nine when the state dissolved. The news came over the truck radio when Emily was taking them to town for groceries. "It's okay, Mama," Robin said earnestly when their mother ripped the radio out barehanded and flung it from the window in disgust. "It's not your fault."

Half the population of Shaw County left in the first exodus. Then the border closed in response to what the TV called a refugee crisis. ("Vultures," Emily spat. "You hear how much they're enjoying this?") All around them, families were pulling up stakes and seeking asylum at the border, something the Hollands would never do. Shaw County was hard, but it was home. They kept the refinery open, though they lost most of their workers to the border. When the school year was suspended, Brooke and her siblings filled the empty spots in the production line.

Robin was six. The loud machinery frightened him, and the smell gave him a headache. Edmund told him to toughen up; they had no use for a marshmallow. "Survival of the fittest," he said, shoving a siphon pump into Robin's hand. "That's the law of nature."

Edmund called the fallen sovereign state a failure of imagination, the same shit in a new can. If the resistance had held the pipeline by force instead of capitulating, things would have gone differently. But it was over now. The old world was gone, Edmund declared, the new one unknown. From now on, the Hollands' only sovereignty would be their own, their only loyalty to each other. The public school, which remained on indefinite hiatus, had been a waste of time anyway, Edmund said; they'd learn more at home. Shouting over the steam and clank of the diesel silos, Edmund lectured his children on natural law, the principles of evolution, the value of labor, the individual's right to self-defense. Brooke listened avidly.

"The role of government is to what?" Edmund quizzed her.

"Protect the people's rights."

"And if it doesn't?"

"The people can dissolve it."

"Because why?"

"Its existence isn't justified."

"That's my girl," he smiled.

As Brooke grew up, she navigated her father's expectations with eager dread. When his attention fell on her, she braced herself as for a spring swim; when she withstood his judgment, she sported and shivered, exuberant.

IT WAS CALLUM WHO STARTED THEM RUNNING CHALK. AFTER FIVE STATELESS years, the diesel market had shrunk with the population, and then further as fewer people could afford to maintain engines.

Edmund laughed the first time they saw someone riding horseback on the highway. "Check out Johnny Guitar," he said, gunning his engine to pass.

But the sight grew more common. And as the diesel business contracted, it also got more dangerous. Suppliers of federal-controlled gas didn't bother with the ceded territories anymore, leaving the Hollands one of the last fuel sellers in the area. This made them targets. Twice, Edmund was jacked on deliveries; the second time, he lost truck and cargo both. The pirates had been masked and heavily armed; nonetheless, Edmund insisted they were foreign. "Dark as sin," he claimed of the bits of skin that had showed through the holes in their masks. Brooke wondered passingly how likely that was—Shaw Station had only gotten whiter since secession, and a truckload of diesel hardly seemed worth an outsider's time. But if her father said it, it must be true. Edmund was convinced that no one local would steal from a Holland. Their mark—the single, stylized *H*—was scored into the stolen drums, plain as day.

Edmund started bringing Anita on armed guard when he rode out on deliveries. Brooke watched jealously as her sister climbed into the truck with a handgun strapped to her thigh.

"What about me?" she asked.

"You're fourteen," Edmund said.

"So? Anita's only sixteen."

"Yeah, but she's a stone-cold killer at heart. Aren't you, love?" Anita rolled her eyes.

"Let those black bastards try me now," Edmund grinned.

Callum argued that no matter how well Edmund defended the diesel, there would soon be nowhere to sell it. People were starving out there, he said, but they would always find money to get high.

He had it all figured out. The main chalk suppliers in the county were distant cousins of Edmund's: Frank Cawley Jr. and his sister Delia. Brooke had a vague image of Frank Jr. as a blond, tattooed man her parents' age, with a wispy wife—townies whose sons had been in school with Callum and Anita. Delia was easier to picture, though Brooke had seen her only a handful of times, at political events; she was fair like her brother, but with a striking, disquieting beauty and pale, shrewd eyes.

The Cawleys' dealers were pathetic, Callum said, small-time, mostly junkies themselves. He was convinced the Hollands could push them out of the market in six months.

Edmund refused at first. He didn't like Frank Jr. and Delia, didn't even like the fact—debatable, according to him—of their common ancestry, and he liked chalk even less. If half the county hadn't been functionally disabled by that stuff, Edmund said, sovereignty might have had a chance.

"More than half," Callum said eagerly. "This is what I'm telling you."

Brooke expected her parents to shun this callousness, but Emily surprised her by siding with Callum. She was the one who kept their accounts, and she said they had to do something soon or they'd be going horseback themselves.

"What are you always telling the kids?" she teased her husband with a sad smile. "It's the law of nature. Adapt or die, Edmund."

After that, it was inevitable. Edmund abhorred chalk, and the weakness it represented, but he trusted Emily's judgment, if anything, more than his own.

"All right," he glared. "I'll be damned if we're going extinct."

Having agreed, Edmund set himself to the chalk trade with the same force he brought to everything else. Chalk was an easy sell, as the first stable pre-blend of an accelerant and a tranquilizer—a poor man's speedball. Though it was known to be difficult and dangerous to prepare, Edmund successfully taught himself the chemistry in a matter of weeks. Callum sourced the supplies, and soon they had laid in a store of product, ready to go.

Callum took it on himself to manage the front end, operating out of his girlfriend Pauline's place in town. Anita was tasked with enlisting the local dealers, most of whom had until now worked directly or indirectly for Frank Jr. and Delia. The Cawleys had operated unchallenged for years and were said to be stingy with their runners; still, despite nearly universal discontent, Anita found their workforce hard to influence, at first. Delia, as the Cawleys' enforcer, brutally punished dealers who defected, inspiring a terrified loyalty in those that remained. She was said to have crushed someone's windpipe with a snow shovel.

"Fine," Anita said. "If that's how it is." She started coming home with bruised fists and empty cartridges, and soon the Hollands had a dozen new employees.

Brooke wasn't needed for the new venture at first. She stayed busy at the refinery, helping Emily keep up minimal production and finding jobs to occupy twelve-year-old Robin. Other than his skill with computers—he was the only one who could fix their old machine when it froze—he was of negligible value to their parents. Brooke knew it was only a matter of time before she herself was called into service with Callum and Anita, and she feared what use her parents would find for Robin when she wasn't around, so she took up Edmund's abandoned effort to toughen up the marshmallow.

"Did you even try?" Brooke asked on a day when she had Robin cleaning equipment. She gestured at the scrub assembly that Robin had worked barely halfway through a length of plastic tube. "You can't run a diesel processor without clean tubing."

"I don't want to run a diesel processor," he said petulantly, throwing the tube down.

"Don't give up just because it's hard," Brooke said. She picked up the tube and began moving the scrub through it correctly.

"It's always hard." Robin folded in on himself, sulking. He was wearing Edmund's old sovereign flag T-shirt; it hung like a curtain on his slight form. He tried to fit in, dressing like their father, mimicking his gestures and curses, but Brooke could always see the doubt in his eyes. His once talkative nature had lately become muted, wary.

The perimeter alarm rang. Brooke put aside the tubing and rose, hooking a walkie-talkie to her belt. Robin trailed her out to the yard, where they found a pearly blue SUV parked next to the house. A man leaned against it, silver-haired, lightly tanned, smiling. Brooke was aware of how filthy she and Robin were, reeking of diesel, their eyes red from the fumes.

"I'm looking for Hollands'," the man said, making it sound like a store.

"That's us," Robin said, before Brooke could hush him. He was too quick, always, with outsiders, and this man was as glaring an outsider as Brooke had seen in years, from his TV haircut to his toothpaste-colored car.

"I need to buy gas," the man said, still smiling. "Is this the right place?"

This time Brooke caught Robin's wrist before he could answer.

"We only do wholesale," Brooke lied. Emily always blew off city customers on principle. *Those people*, she said. *They'd spread us on their toast.*

"Well, I'm in a bind. I came up to check on the cottage, and it seems that the extra gas cans I was keeping up here have walked off on their own. Along with a few other things. I don't have enough to drive back to the city."

The cottage: a turn of phrase Brooke had always hated. As if everyone owned a second home, as if having a cottage was a foregone conclusion.

"You can't put diesel in that." Brooke nodded at the car. "It's the wrong kind of engine."

"This is a diesel hybrid, actually. Runs on just about anything. Convertible all-wheel drive. You probably haven't seen this generation of vehicles out here."

Brooke lifted her walkie-talkie and pressed the button. "Mama," she said flatly. "Some cottager wants gas."

"Fucking sell him some, then. I don't care," came Emily's tinny response.

Brooke masked her surprise.

"I'll get it," Robin offered, taking a step back toward the refinery.

"Get two jerrys," Brooke said.

"What do I owe you?" the man asked.

"One-twenty," Brooke suggested, randomly.

"Fair enough," the man said, taking out his wallet.

Brooke watched him count the money loosely with his thumb. Four times what they would charge a local, and he hadn't even blinked.

"Great view you have up here," the man said, handing her the cash.

Brooke folded the bills into her pocket without comment.

"Must get lonely, though." The man bounced on the balls of his feet as he surveyed the hills. "Way out here. My daughters would implode."

Robin reappeared, pulling two jerry cans. "How long is the drive to the city?" he asked, fitting a plastic nozzle onto the first can.

The cottager helped him lift and empty the gas into the tank. "Four hours. Bit more. It used to be faster, but the roads out here are even worse than before. And they were never great."

The man laughed, and Robin smiled. Brooke's stomach burned as she imagined her brother riding away in the shiny leather interior of the cottager's car.

When both cans were empty, the man reached into his glove compartment for a package of wet wipes. "Thanks for your help," he said, offering the package to Robin.

"Where's your cottage?" Brooke asked, trying to match the man's light tone. "*The* cottage."

"Down on Diamond Lake. You want to keep an eye on it for me? The front gate says Twin Pines."

"South side of the lake or north?" Brooke asked, amazed to find a grown man so gullible.

"North. Nice rustic place on the bay. Cedar deck. I used to time-share it with my brother, but I bought him out. Got too rough for him." The man winked, opening the door of his car. "Sure is beautiful, though. No place like it. It's too bad I'm the only one who gets to see it anymore."

The next day, Brooke took Robin to the north shore of Diamond Lake on an ATV. It was easy to follow the tracks of the man's car in the gravel road. No other vehicle had been this way in a season. She pulled up outside a gate where lettering had recently been painted a glossy forest green: TWIN PINES. She got a drill from her backpack, unscrewed the cane bolt from the lock, and swung the gate wide, propping it open with a rock. She climbed back on the ATV in front of Robin and drove through.

It was just as the man had described. The deck of the big, old-fashioned cottage had been swept clear of fallen leaves and pine needles, and a wooden lounge chair sat looking out over the lake. Through the trees, the surface of the water shivered with overlapping arcs of breeze. At an inlet across the bay, there was a collection of gray wood where floating docks, detached from their moorings, had drifted.

Too bad I'm the only one who gets to see it, the cottager had said.

Brooke started with the garage. Whoever had made off with the man's gas cans hadn't taken much else, by the look of it. There was still a wall of peg-mounted tools, a charcoal barbecue, a chest cooler, two kids' bikes with blue and purple streamers on the handlebars.

Brooke took a fifty-foot coil of grounded extension cord from a hook on the pegboard and dropped it in the cargo box of the ATV.

"We said we'd keep an eye on it for him," Robin said.

"No, we didn't," Brooke said. She knew Robin had kept the wet wipe. She'd seen it in his drawer, folded carefully, feather dry and spotless.

"You're just going to take his stuff?"

"*We* are going to take his stuff and sell it," Brooke said, climbing the deck to examine the front door of the cottage. "Did you notice how quick Mama was to sell that asshole gas? We need money. And you need a job."

She had thought about it. Salvaging required strength, independence, and ruthlessness: all the toughening up Robin needed. If she could teach him this, he might be all right without her.

"He wasn't an asshole," Robin objected.

"He didn't even argue about paying a hundred and twenty for two cans of gas. He's rich."

"So what?"

"So, he's de facto an asshole. This isn't even his home, Rob. He has this place just for relaxing."

Brooke wrenched the door open with a crowbar. Inside, they found a bookshelf stuffed with dusty paperback novels and magazines, board games, plaid upholstery, wicker baskets, antique kitchen implements.

"What is it about a cottage that makes people think they're living in the past?" Brooke asked. She swung the crowbar into a wall. Robin flinched as the brittle plasterboard crumbled.

"Copper," Brooke told him, reeling wire from the ruined wall. "Ten dollars for thirty feet."

"I don't want to do this," he said. "I don't want to wreck things. I don't want a job. I want to go to school."

"There is no school, Rob. You know that. That world is gone."

"It's not gone," Robin said quietly, lifting a small porcelain figure of a Dalmatian from the bookshelf. "It's only four hours away."

"Put that down," she snapped. "It's worthless."

Tears sprang to Robin's eyes. Brooke never shouted at him.

"You have to take this seriously," she said, holding out the coiled wire. "It's for your own good. Please."

He wiped his tear-darkened lashes and moved to help her, slipping the little Dalmatian into his pocket.

Brooke drove them into Shaw Station with the stuff from the man's cottage. The hardware store bought the satellite dish, extension cord, boat motor, and floodlight system, along with the copper wire, for two hundred dollars.

"Hide this," Brooke told Robin, handing him fifty from the salvage money, plus twenty more from the cottager's cash. The rest she brought to Emily at dinner that night.

"How much gas did that jackass buy?" her mother asked, riffling the stack of bills.

"A hundred. The rest came from salvage. Robin's got a new project."

Emily held Brooke's eye for a moment, appraisingly. "Good for him," she said.

After that, every day they could be spared from the refinery, Brooke and Robin sifted through cottages and boathouses for things to sell: floodlights left in brackets, copper wire snug in walls. Brooke moved like a machine, weighing the price of everything she saw against the effort of carrying it out. Robin gravitated to all the wrong things: photo albums, handmade crafts, quilts—objects with no worth—amassing a collection of junk in his closet at home. Brooke didn't have the heart to stop him. He still salvaged enough to make a profit, and he was back to something like his old, chatty self, speculating about the cottagers who had left these things behind, what they'd been like, why they'd spent their summers here, what they must miss.

Brooke didn't know if people had meant to come back for all the things they'd left—toasters, mini blenders, lawnmowers, weed trimmers, chainsaws, cedar-strip canoes, stereos—or if they just didn't care. Then there were the things that rich cottagers would never have thought to take: electrical wire, brass fittings, glass fuses, fiberglass insulation, water tanks.

The main part of their earnings went to Emily, but Robin's secret savings grew steadily.

Callum laughed at the scavenging operation, calling them scrappers and grubbers, but as long as they were earning, it was tolerated. Callum had been living in town with Pauline, and he was often away now, developing new contacts. He wanted to press further, beyond the local trade, into the city. The border was more permeable all the time, and there were networks on the other side who were interested in cheap chalk from the country. The Hollands could hold that market unopposed, he said, if Anita could just get the Cawleys out of the field.

Anita had been doing her best, though the Cawleys were less disorganized than Callum had originally supposed. Where the Hollands took over their territory, Delia and Frank Jr. hit back. Anita got better guns. Edmund and Emily brought in cameras, trip wires, dogs—Rottweiler crosses that they kept hungry and anchored to old tractor wheels at the edge of the property.

Edmund said it was a sign they were succeeding; the Cawleys, like any animals, would lash out when threatened. Emily said the Cawleys were doomed to fail. Trash like them would take chalk as well as sell it, and this would make them sloppy, lacking in self-discipline.

Brooke wondered whether her mother didn't see Callum's and Anita's red eyes and worsening teeth, or notice their paranoia, the unpredictable edge to their anger. Brooke had watched them change. They had been so many things to her over the years: competitors, comrades, confidantes; they shared a galaxy of memories, unspoken understandings, jokes that were meaningless beyond themselves. Now Callum and Anita were just one thing, the same boring, hollow thing, and Brooke hated it.

It was what happened to everyone—Callum had been right about that much. Chalk clung to the county like a hand over a mouth. Brooke dreaded the day when it would close over her, too.

6

DAWN CREPT OVER THE MEADOW. NO ONE HAD COME IN THE NIGHT. BROOKE
began to nurture a cautious hope that they had evaded their pursuers. If the Cawleys hadn't found the tracks leading into the
creek, their search was unlikely to bring them here. It should be
safe, now, to continue over land.

Brooke stood stiffly and crept over to the sleeping bags where
Milo and the girls slept. Crouching, she laid a hand on the night-
damp fabric.

"Hm?" Milo lifted his head, blinking at Brooke.

"Morning," she said. "Time to get up."

"No," Sal muttered, burrowing into Milo. "Warm."

"Come on, guys," Brooke tried again. "Let's go."

Holly grunted, twisting deeper into her sleeping bag.

"Hey, can you hear me?" Impatience edged into Brooke's voice.

Milo pulled himself, bare-legged, out of the sleeping bag. Sal
curled up like a caterpillar and rolled against her sister, eliciting
another grunt.

"Girls," Brooke said sharply.

"I've got it," Milo said, rubbing his face awake. "You make
breakfast. Just give me my pants back."

Brooke's jeans were damp and chilly against her skin when she pulled them from the juniper bush, but she told herself they'd be moving again soon enough. She rifled in her pack for something to feed them. Even if they stretched the food another day, they'd be arriving hungry in Buffalo Cross. She added a careful measure of powdered milk and quick oats to a half-full bottle of water and shook: a cloudy, foaming swirl.

She poured a small amount into a second bottle and threw it within Cawley's reach. He stared at it, blinking. He looked rough this morning: hollow-eyed, with dark, cadaverous shadows around his mouth. The carrot from the night before lay uneaten on the ground. He reached out for the bottle, unscrewed the lid awkwardly with his bound hands, and took a small sip. Instantly, he spat it out and retched into the grass.

This looked like more than just coming down, Brooke thought. Cawley must be in full-blown withdrawal. In that state he risked heart attack, coma—though perhaps those dangers were past if he'd made it through the night. Still, Brooke would have to watch him even more closely than before. A serious addict was desperate, unpredictable.

Brooke's thoughts were interrupted by the sound of Sal's giggle. Milo was at the sleeping bags, talking softly to the girls, coaxing them out. Holly emerged, looking around with the scrunched-up expression she had woken up with since she was little. Sal finger-combed her shiny dark hair, which had come loose in the night. She redid her braids, fastening each with a blue elastic.

"Stay over there," Brooke said, carrying their breakfast as far as possible from Cawley.

Holly and Sal settled themselves cross-legged on the lichen-bloomed rocks and passed the cold oat mixture between them, trading escalating descriptions of how disgusting it was. Around them, ground frost steamed under the morning sun, wrapping the meadow in wisps of vapor. As she and Milo packed the bags, Brooke kept Cawley in the corner of her eye. He made no further attempt to eat, though he retched a few more times and coughed phlegm onto the ground.

When they were ready to go, Brooke watched with the rifle as Milo untied Cawley's ankles and detached the lead rope from the juniper bush. Cawley was a shivering ball against the rocks. Brooke saw him wince when Sal shouted to Holly in her high-pitched voice as they ranged around, inspecting the meadow.

"Girls," Brooke said, pointing to an opening in the trees to the south. "You first. Keep straight as you can in that direction."

"I could hold the rope today," Milo said, as Holly led Sal from the meadow. "Share things a bit?"

"I'd better," Brooke said, reaching out her hand for the rope. With his kinder impulses, Milo could not be trusted to contain Cawley if he took a notion to run. "Just make sure you stay between him and the girls," she said. "I don't want him close to them."

"We're doing this together, you know," Milo said. "All of us."

"I know," Brooke said. "But hurry up, they're way ahead."

Milo blew out his cheeks and turned to follow the girls into the trees. Cawley went next, limping slowly, chin on chest. Brooke was last, and she brushed away the signs of their campsite behind her.

The sun shone in a royal blue autumn sky. They walked with their wet things drying from the top straps of the packs. Deer runs and the well-worn paths of smaller animals crisscrossed the woods. Their progress was slower than Brooke had hoped. Raspberry canes caught their pant legs and scratched their hands. The girls were in front, with Milo as a buffer between them and Cawley, and this meant they set the pace. The underbrush was heavy in places. Several times, they had to retrace their steps and detour around some impassable feature in the landscape. Cawley was excruciatingly slow, stumbling and swearing at every obstacle in his path.

"Hang on," Brooke called forward to Milo after they had lost a half hour getting back on course because Holly had veered too far east. "I can't steer from the back like this. Not while I'm dealing with him. We're losing a ton of time."

"It's not my fault," Holly objected. "I don't know where we're going."

"Here," Brooke said, throwing the rope to Milo and kicking forward through the underbrush to Holly. "We're going south. Show me south."

Holly lifted a questioning eyebrow and pointed into the trees.

"Just about." Brooke held Holly's wrist to adjust her bearing. "All you have to do is find three landmarks on that line. So, the boulder, there. Then that broken-off birch farther on, see? Hanging down? And what's another one?"

Holly stared into the forest for a moment. "The porcupine?"

Brooke squinted, searching in the distance until she found the dark ball sleeping high up in a spindly tamarack.

"Good. So, when you get to the boulder, you square up the birch with the porcupine and find a new third mark on the same line. See?"

"How does that—" Holly broke off as understanding dawned. "Oh, I get it."

"Get what?" Sal asked, staring into the distance. "Where's the porcupine?"

"It's like a slide ladder," Holly said.

"Yeah," Brooke said. "Exactly."

"Where's the porcupine?" Sal repeated, louder.

Holly was already walking. She moved faster now, more confidently. "I'll show you when we get there. Come on."

In this way, they kept southward, Holly taking bearings and announcing each new mark to Sal, who relayed the information to her parents, puffed up with her own importance.

The day grew warm. Brooke meted water out in sips. There was a bottle and a half left. Not much, considering she couldn't be sure how much longer it would take to reach Buffalo Cross. They were still west of Highway 12, somewhere between the foothills and the ranch land farther south; more than that, Brooke could only guess.

At midday, they paused in an ironwood grove carpeted by fallen leaves. Brooke directed Milo to tie Cawley at the far edge of the grove. Once that was done, she put down the gun and gratefully eased her pack off, shaking out the stiffness in her bad shoulder.

"How much farther is it?" Sal asked, slouching against a tree trunk next to Holly.

"I'm not sure," Brooke said. "We made it about five miles in the creek, and probably another five this morning. We might be halfway there?"

"Is that all there is?" Holly asked, watching Brooke pull two small bags of food from her pack.

"For now." Brooke passed them each a couple strips of dried sweet potato and a handful of soy nuts. Milo took an extra piece of sweet potato from the bag and carried it to Cawley on the other side of the grove. Brooke chewed her soy nuts and said nothing.

"Where did you learn that trick?" Milo asked, returning and lying down with his backpack for a pillow. "With the landmarks."

"I don't know," Brooke said, caught off guard.

"You don't know?" He raised an eyebrow.

It was Emily, of course, the practical counterpart to Edmund's lectures; Emily had taught Brooke to swim, drive, sink a fence post, and Brooke had taken to each new skill just as she'd seen Holly do this afternoon, keen for her mother's praise. But for the most part, Brooke had chosen not to pass this knowledge on to her daughters. It was too hard to know where some of Emily's lessons ended and others began: how to track and evade, how to shoot, how to survive, how to withstand pain, how to cause it.

Sal made an unintelligible sound through her mouthful of food.

"Chew, doofus," Holly said.

"I said, will there be movies in Buffalo Cross?"

Brooke was relieved to have the subject changed. "We're not going for movies, Salamander. We're just getting Cawley to the marshals."

"Your friend?"

"He's not my friend."

"Then who is he?"

Across the grove, Cawley was holding the strip of sweet potato in front of him, his bound hands striped bloody from raspberry canes. He had looked up at his name. Brooke saw a spark of clarity in his eyes, a new energy. The worst of his withdrawal was ending. He might be less of a hindrance walking, but he would also be more dangerous.

"It doesn't matter," Brooke said, meeting his gaze. "He's no one."

IN THE AFTERNOON, THEY CAME TO AN OLD PAVED ROAD RUNNING SOUTH-southwest. It could only be Highway 12, which meant they had drifted too far east and hit the road sooner than Brooke had meant to.

"Let's stay in the bush," she called to Milo, even as the girls were crying out in triumph, running onto the pavement.

"That's crazy," Milo said, bending forward to relieve the weight of his backpack. "The road is faster. We need to get to Buffalo Cross. We're running out of food."

"If they don't find us at the farm, they could be going back south, traveling this road."

"They who, Brooke?" Milo asked, exasperated.

"Yeah," Cawley mumbled. "They who?" He was leaning against a guardrail post at the edge of the road.

The girls were now a distance ahead, Holly's red scarf swinging with her skipping steps.

"All right, the road," Brooke said. "But catch up with the girls. They're too far away."

"Brooke, I know you're stressed," Milo said, straightening up. "Don't forget Stephen was high when he told you there were more people coming. It's possible you're worried about nothing."

Milo moved off after the girls. Cawley was still leaning on the post, watching Brooke.

"I'd be fucking worried if I was you." He drew phlegm noisily back into his throat, coughed it into his mouth, and spat on the ground between them. Then he stood and hobbled on.

THE HIGHWAY SURFACE WAS IN DECENT REPAIR. BROOKE SPARED A GRATEFUL thought for the long-ago road crew that had blasted a smooth passage through these hills. After the woods, their progress felt like flying, even at Cawley's limping pace. They passed half a dozen homes, all abandoned, the lawns armpit-deep in grass and weeds. Most people preferred the security of towns now, unless, like Brooke, they had some reason to seek solitude.

The sky stayed clear, a blue so deep it looked painted. Birds scattered from the trees ahead of them. Wind ruffled the branches. Brooke heard coyotes bark and cry in the distance, and knew they must still be some distance from Buffalo Cross; coyotes would hunt in the daytime only if there were no humans living nearby.

They walked the highway until dusk with no sign of Buffalo Cross. Brooke resisted the temptation to push on; arriving in a new town at night was unwise. They followed an overgrown driveway to a gravel pad where there must once have been a mobile home.

It was gone, carried off by whoever had lived here; only the porch stoop with its iron railing remained, and a garage built of cinder blocks with a poured concrete floor.

When Brooke pried the garage door open, she found it dry inside. Now she faced a dilemma: keep Cawley closer to them than she'd yet allowed—the garage was a standard twenty-four feet to a side—or tie him outdoors, in which case she'd have to stay out all night too, to watch him. She thought she could manage the lack of sleep, but it was cold, and she'd eaten almost nothing, saving the food for Milo and the kids; she'd started shivering as soon as they stopped moving.

"Tie him to that for now," Brooke told Milo, gesturing at the steel track that ran along the inside of the automatic door.

Once Cawley was secured, the girls came in and poked curiously through what the people who lived here had left behind.

"Check it out." Holly held up a small aluminum saucepan from a bin of odds and ends.

"Tea," mumbled Brooke, sitting down with the rifle in her lap. Hot, strong tea might take the edge off the hunger and fatigue that had been combining into a headache all afternoon. The building was far enough off the road that they could probably chance a fire.

Holly opened Brooke's backpack and pulled things out, studying each with the flashlight.

"Sweet potato, cranberries. What's this? Peanut butter? Oh, miso paste. Oats. There's a recipe for savory oatmeal I could do, only we don't have the walnuts and spinach. But at least it would be hot."

"That's all our food," Brooke said.

"Brooke," Milo said under his breath. "Let her."

"I wish I had my books." Holly opened the miso paste to sniff it.

Brooke was too tired to argue. She closed her eyes. She would open them again in a minute, to keep an eye on Cawley while Milo made a fire. She listened to him and the girls leaving the garage, gathering brush outside, talking. It was time to lift her eyelids, but they were so heavy.

She heard a familiar melody. Outside, Milo was singing the girls a song they liked, a long-ago dance hit about breaking up. Brooke doubted Holly and Sal had ever heard the original song; they only knew Milo's version, peppered with blank spots where he'd forgotten the lyrics. Brooke remembered the video. Robin had showed it to her: a young woman, thin arms overhead, shaking impossibly lavender hair.

ROBIN HAD NEVER STOPPED GOING ONLINE EVERY CHANCE HE GOT, PIRATING Wi-Fi from the exchange station or the hospital when they were in town. Brooke didn't know what he used it for, but his facility had proved helpful. When, in defiance of their parents' scorn, they bought the sweet-eyed foal Star—because it had become too cumbersome chainsawing through overgrown cottage roads to make way for a vehicle—neither of them knew how to ride, so Robin had found them an online tutorial.

Brooke remembered sitting under the awning of the Shaw Station hospital with her brother, watching the Hollands' aging laptop slowly buffer the riding video while Star grazed on a nearby median. Robin flipped to another window, and Brooke recognized his e-mail account. They'd all had them in school—the teachers had made them memorize their passwords. Brooke hadn't thought about hers since. It probably still existed somewhere on the Internet, though there wouldn't have been anything more in it than the first few childish messages she and her siblings had sent each other in class. (*Hi! What's new? This is cool! See you at home!*)

Robin's inbox, on the other hand, was full.

"Who's writing to you?" Brooke asked.

"People," he said. He quickly scanned the list of messages, then switched back to the riding video.

"What people?"

"Just people." He hit play on the video.

"Robin," Brooke said, reaching out to pause it. "What people?"

It turned out Robin had been photographing the keepsakes he rescued from the cottages and posting them to an online list. Sometimes the buyers were the original owners, or claimed to be, but his biggest customer was a kitsch dealer who drove out monthly from the city to pick up entire lots. Brooke had noticed that the pile of curiosities in Robin's closet had stopped expanding, but she'd assumed he was finally throwing some of it out.

"What in the fuck is a kitsch dealer?" she asked.

"She has a store. She loves anything from here. Especially if it's old or unusual, or corny. Like anything with a saying on it. Mugs, hats, whatever. She calls them artifacts."

"*Artifacts?*"

"I know, I know," Robin blushed.

Brooke was dumbfounded when Robin told her how much the kitsch dealer would pay for what was essentially garbage. He was making ten times more from porcelain Dalmatians and novelty hats than from salvage. It bothered Brooke that her brother was having regular contact with someone from the city—she hadn't forgotten the way he'd fawned over the cottager with the toothpaste-colored car—still, she had to admit she was impressed. Maybe Robin hadn't toughened up the way Edmund wanted him to, but maybe he didn't need to; he'd found another way to survive.

BROOKE WOKE UP IN THE DARK, BLINKING HER WATERY EYES. MILO AND THE girls were talking somewhere in the distance. She saw the flickering orange light of a fire through the garage door. They had let her sleep.

She could just make out Cawley's shape where he was tie[d]
the steel track. He had been sitting before; now he was stand[ing.]
What was he doing with his hands? He'd better not be pis[sing]
inside, Brooke thought foggily. They'd be stuck with the reel[all]
night.

Then her ears registered the grating sound: plastic against [s]

She felt for the rifle in her lap and struggled to her feet, li[ght]
with head rush.

"Stop," she said. Her mouth was still asleep and it cam[e out]
barely audible.

Cawley turned as she got within reach of him. He made [a sud]-
den movement, holding his arms up in front of his face and [then]
bringing them down, fast, toward his body. It was a bald, [brute]
move: he was trying to break the lock of the zip tie with sheer [force.]
Had he worn it some of the way through with friction on th[e]
door runner? Brooke couldn't see.

"Milo!" she called, but her voice was still stuck in her t[hroat,]
too quiet.

She couldn't restrain Cawley and hold the gun at the [same]
time. She checked that the rifle's safety was on and mov[ed the]
sling across her chest to the other shoulder. Hands free, she [went]
for Cawley's wrists. He jabbed forward with the knuckles [of his]
hands and caught her in the nose, stunning her. She tasted [blood]
in the back of her throat. At least she knew his wrists we[re still]
tied. His ankles, too: he was teetering to stay upright. [Brooke]
grabbed the lead rope that connected him to the wall and t[ried to]
pull him down. Cawley fell back against the garage door [with a]
crash but managed to stay upright. Again, he lifted his ar[ms and]
brought them down fast. This time, Brooke heard the tie s[nap.]

His arms were free.

He grabbed at her, trying to reach the gun. Brooke dodg[ed,]
shrugged out of the sling and caught the rifle by the barrel[, swung]
hard, and hit him full in the jaw with the wooden stock.

was knocked sideways and, tripped up by his bound ankles, landed hard on one elbow, shouting in pain. Brooke straddled him and tried to loop the lead rope around his wrists to replace the plastic tie. He thrashed from side to side, preventing her from getting a hold, and threw her off him. She kicked him in the injured knee, climbed onto him again, and this time passed the rope around his elbows. She looped and cinched it tight, hauling back against the elbow he'd smashed on the concrete floor.

"Bitch," he spat. "Lay the fuck off! I'll tell them, I swear!"

Only now did Brooke realize that she could see. The garage wasn't dark anymore. A flashlight illuminated her and Cawley, casting their steep, garish shadows up against the wall.

"Help her," a tense voice said. Holly.

Then Milo was next to Brooke, kneeling with a length of insulated wire from one of the piles near the door. He wrapped Cawley's wrists tight with the wire, knotted and double-knotted it, and then got a new zip tie from Brooke's bag.

Milo's fingers were shaking, Brooke noticed. She took the slim strip of plastic from him and held it around Cawley's wrists, which were pink and raw from the bond he'd just broken. She fed the tapered end of the new tie into its mouth and locked it.

"We heard the noise," Milo said, still kneeling next to Brooke. "Are you hurt?"

"I'm fine," she said, wondering how long they'd been standing there, how much they'd seen. Brooke wiped blood from her upper lip.

Both girls were plastered against the wall beams of the garage, wide-eyed.

"Take your sister outside," Brooke told Holly.

"Right," Holly said, pulling Sal by the sleeve. "Come, Salamander."

"What happened?" Milo asked.

"He broke his zip tie," Brooke said, eyeing the sharp edge of

the door runner where Cawley must have managed to weaken the plastic. "We can't keep him in here overnight. It's too dangerous. He'll have to sleep outside."

Milo didn't move. He was staring at her. He looked almost frightened.

"What?" She checked her nose with a sleeve. The bleeding had stopped. "What's wrong?"

"What did he mean? Who was he going to tell what?"

"Please don't ask me," Brooke said, holding Milo's gaze.

"Brooke, you can trust me. Whatever it is. You know you can."

Milo had forgiven a lot, over the years. Harsh words, cruel silences, storms of anguish that she'd never explained. Once, when Brooke had been whimpering in her sleep, he'd taken hold of her shoulder to wake her and she'd punched him, hard, before she was properly awake. He'd never asked her to explain these things, and once the shadow passed, he never brought it up again. Every time she'd lashed out at him, or let a black mood overtake her, she had shrunk from the reprisal she was certain must come, and every time, his forgiveness had surprised her. It was as if he'd never learned to hold a grudge.

But this would be too much. It had to be. She felt tears sting and blinked them back.

"Please," she said again. She gathered the rope and led Cawley outside.

ONE NIGHT, WHEN BROOKE HANDED OVER HER AND ROBIN'S SALVAGE EARNINGS to Emily, her mother informed her that Anita needed help the next day. Callum couldn't do it—Pauline was newly pregnant and he had to take her to a clinic near the border for an ultrasound.

"Rob's still stripping a place on Lake Clear," Brooke said before Emily could suggest anything else for him. Robin was thirteen; his voice was just changing.

Emily waved her hand, unconcerned. It wasn't Robin she wanted.

The next morning, Brooke joined her sister.

A local dealer—a legal secretary in her former existence—was claiming for the second time to have been robbed, and had nothing to cover her debt.

In the past month, Callum had brought in a partner, a soap factory near the border where the Hollands had sold glycerin for years. The factory owner had agreed to be a transfer point for bulk shipments to Callum's new contacts in the city. In response, Frank Jr. and Delia were trying to consolidate their hold on the market in town, bringing in new and younger dealers, and terrorizing anyone who worked for the Hollands. Anita suspected the legal secretary of defecting.

Brooke and Anita rolled up the woman's driveway in Anita's hatchback. Anita laid on the horn. The house was two stories, with pale gray vinyl siding. A woman in her early forties came out onto the lawn. Two children peeked out after her from behind a glass-covered screen door. The younger one was a toddler, Brooke saw, the older maybe eight.

"Hold the door," Anita told Brooke, nodding at the house.

Brooke climbed the steps to open the door for the kids. She had her hand on the latch when she heard something behind her. It sounded like the air going out of a cushion.

She turned. Anita had a length of pipe in one hand and the dealer was sprawled on the lawn. The woman was coughing, trying to speak. Anita raised the pipe and brought it down on her back. Brooke was too stunned to move until the latch jiggling in her hand and the squeak of a hinge beginning to open brought her back to her senses. She realized all at once what Anita had meant when she told Brooke to hold the door.

Brooke tightened her grip on the latch and pushed the door

closed. The children cried out, wild-eyed, the toddler sobbing with fear. Their hands pounded the glass, but Brooke held firm. Anita hit the woman again with the pipe, and again, and Brooke braced her leg against the porch railing, pushing with all her strength to stop the children from getting through the door to their mother.

Brooke came home that day gray-faced and silent. The others treated her solicitously; when she pushed her dinner away, Emily said, "The first time's never easy." As if Brooke was the victim, and the beaten woman her affliction.

That first night, when Brooke was so sick and bewildered, Robin told her about the calm place. He'd read about it online; he said it had been taught to kids in war zones, to help them cope with trauma.

"I'm not a kid in a war zone," Brooke said, affronted.

"It can be anything," he said. "Just close your eyes and picture a calm place."

Robin was looking at her expectantly, and she was tired, so Brooke closed her eyes. She pictured green woods, gray mist. After a moment, whether it was working or it was just a relief to have her eyes closed, she did feel a bit better. Something in her spine settled and released with a soft crack.

After that, Brooke was appointed Anita's right hand in the growing turf war with the Cawleys. She did what her family told her to do—she kicked in doors, shot locks, shouted down hallways. She blackened eyes. She cracked ribs. "Get Brooke," they said, and Brooke came: she fixed; she erased. But the calm place protected her; she saw what she had to do through soft gray mist, each task a series of actions that did not connect to her or to her life. She could do it, and not feel it.

The days passed. Robin was making money, so Edmund and Emily left him alone, and Brooke was satisfied. Some days were easy, even happy. Other days, she returned from the calm place and found her life so mean and ugly and sad that she was sure she could never belong anywhere decent; she would ruin whatever she touched.

ONCE MILO HAD TIED CAWLEY'S LEAD ROPE TO THE FRONT STEPS OF THE ABSENT house and Brooke had made sure there was no rough edge he might use to break his bonds again, they joined the girls at the fire.

Holly and Sal had been talking, but as their parents approached, they descended into a wary silence. Brooke saw a glance pass between them.

"Sorry you had to see that," Brooke said.

"Why were you brushing our tracks when we left our campsite this morning?" Holly asked.

Sal lifted a hand to rub the base of her thumb against her closed lips, a trick Milo had taught her when her adult teeth started coming in and she was too old to keep sucking it.

"I don't know," Brooke said, straight-faced. "Just habit."

"Like how you don't remember learning the thing with the landmarks?"

"Let's not give Mom the gears tonight, okay, Hol?" Milo said. "She needs a break."

But Milo didn't argue when Brooke said she would take the watch again. He led the girls into the garage. Brooke stayed at the fire, adding wood to the embers and listening as her family settled down to sleep. The flashlight in the garage turned off, their voices continued quietly for a little longer, and then it was silent.

Once or twice in the night, Brooke nodded off. Each time she woke, the darkness beyond the fire was quiet and still. Clouds advanced from the north, a soft blackness overtaking the stars one by one, winking them out.

7

IN THE MORNING, THEY WALKED THE HIGHWAY UNDER GRAY CLOUDS. BROOKE
could see her breath. They had finished Holly's oatmeal concoction
and the last of their water. The girls whined: they were hungry; they
were cold; they were sick of walking. Rather than trying to cheer
or distract them, today Milo was in a sour mood, complaining of
weeping blisters on his feet and a pinch in his back that sent flashes
of pain down his leg every few steps.

Only Cawley was quiet, limping feebly along, looking sick.

Toward midday, clearing a low rise, they saw a sprawl of buildings, bleakly still under the dull sky. It had probably held a few
thousand people at its peak. The edges were decaying now in patchy
lots of brush. Brooke had heard Buffalo Cross called unfriendly, but
there was no fence or obvious patrol, as Buxton had. She wondered
if people here were beyond caring, or so well defended that they
didn't need to show it; either possibility was cause for concern.

Brooke instructed Milo to add a second rope to Cawley's ankle
and hold it himself, so that Cawley was doubly tethered and could
be pulled to the ground at need. Milo took the rope from his pack
and attached it to Cawley's leg with the knots Brooke had shown

him. When it was done, Brooke looked up to realize that Holly and Sal had not waited for them and were already coming even with the first houses.

Brooke shouted after them, and Holly turned to look over her shoulder as Sal ran ahead.

"Damn it," Brooke cursed, waving at Milo to hurry.

"Hold up," Cawley said as he skipped after Milo, trying not to be pulled down by the rope on his leg.

Sal had disappeared around the corner of the nearest house, where woodsmoke hovered over the roof.

"I told her to stay," Holly muttered as Brooke and Milo caught up with her in the road.

Sal was squatting in the front yard of a house, next to a woman in a plastic chair. The woman was fifty or so, tall and strong, and looked healthy enough; sober, anyway. She was shelling pole beans into a bucket. Sal had gathered a handful of the empty pods from the ground and was trying to stack them, lining up the bulging depressions left by the plucked beans. The toughness of the late-season plants made them rigid and uncooperative, and the pile kept toppling.

"Sal, get over here," Brooke said.

Sal didn't look up, her brow wrinkled in concentration.

"It's all right, Mom," the woman said. "Nothing to fear. Your kid was just curious."

"Is this Buffalo Cross?" Brooke asked. "I heard you have a sheriff."

"Which one's Dad?" the woman asked with wry amusement. "The one tied up or the one holding the rope?"

"That's my dad," Sal said, looking up from her stack and pointing.

Brooke watched the woman's gaze pass over Milo, taking in his complexion, his sharp features. Her expression was unreadable.

"And the other one?" The woman shifted her gaze to Cawley.

"He's a criminal," Sal said, acting nonchalant. "On drugs."

The woman raised her eyebrows and kept shelling. "What do you want the sheriff for?"

"We need a phone," Brooke said. "We're trying to reach the federal marshals."

"You want to bring the feds here? I don't think so. Even if there was a phone, which there isn't."

"Like I said, we need the sheriff. You know where I can find him?"

"I'm him. Lynn Maxwell. Pleased to meet you. I think I can ask a few questions, seeing as you're in my town with a so-called criminal, and who knows what else." Her eyes flicked back to Milo.

"I need to speak to you privately, Sheriff," Brooke said.

"Private how?" The beans continued to fall into the bucket with a soft tapping sound.

"Is there somewhere safe the kids can wait?"

"This whole town's safe."

"Somewhere separate, then."

"You girls run on down to that house," the sheriff said. Brooke could hear it now, the casual authority in her voice. "The last one before the bend. With the brown truck in the yard. You ask Lorne to come back here with you. He's my deputy."

"Don't go inside," Brooke warned Holly. "Stay where I can see you. And keep—"

"I know. Keep Sal with me."

"I can't right now," Sal said, intent on her stack of shells. "I'm busy."

"Go on," Maxwell said, handing her a full bean. "You can take this."

Sal got up and followed Holly slowly, twisting the ends of the long reddish bean, trying to open it.

The sheriff gestured at Brooke's rifle.

"You carrying any firearms besides the .22, Mom? Any alcohol or drugs?"

"Excuse me?"

"I've got a right to ask."

"We don't have anything."

"And what's the story with your criminal friend here?"

The girls were halfway to the brown truck, gawking at everything they passed.

"He killed an agent," Brooke said. "There was a marshal in Buxton with the warrant."

"So you have it on hearsay." Maxwell let a handful of beans fall through her fingers into the bucket.

"He's a Cawley," Brooke said coolly, staring at the fallen stack of bean shells Sal had abandoned. "Stephen Cawley."

"Oh?" Maxwell shucked the last bean and stood up, looking closer at the captive. "That'd be something. Cawleys in Buxton? What, did they run out of kids to bleed in Shaw County?"

"Fuck you, fat-ass," Cawley grumbled. "This bitch is no better, you know. She came at me with an axe."

"I just need to reach the outpost at Shaw Station," Brooke spoke over Cawley. "If you don't have a phone, then loan us horses, or that truck, if it works. And we need food and water."

"Quite the list," Maxwell said, sitting back down. "You should have taken him to Buxton, if that's where they're after him. They've got phones, and they don't like chalkheads any more than I do. Though maybe that's changed, if they're letting marshals in. Feds and chalk never seem to be far apart, somehow."

"Are you going to help us or not, Sheriff?"

"No, thanks. I don't want anything to do with those animals, Cawleys, Hollands, whatever. You're mixed up with gang shit, you can move right on through. This town's dry. We don't let drugs in and we don't tolerate people who deal in them."

"We're not involved," Milo said. "We're just doing a public service."

Holly and Sal were returning now. With them was a young man in a plaid fleece jacket.

"Lorne," Maxwell called out as the man stepped into the yard, trailed by the girls. He was younger than Maxwell, equally tall. He wore a revolver in a low-slung hip holster, like a movie cowboy.

"Hi, folks." He nodded to Brooke and Milo, took in the roped figure between them.

"This man in the ropes is supposedly a Cawley out of Shaw County," Maxwell said. "Mom and Dad want to get him to the fed outpost down there, but they don't have any way to move him."

"Could be," Lorne said, looking Cawley over. "There's bound to be some of them still creeping around."

Brooke watched Cawley's face harden under the scrutiny. She knew the impulse he would be feeling, how gladly he would have wiped that disparaging leer off the deputy's face.

"Mom here says there's a warrant," Maxwell said.

"Any bounty on it?"

"Five thousand dollars," Milo said before Brooke could stop him.

Lorne whistled. "That's a nice payday for you folks. I'd bring him in for that."

"Except you don't work for the feds," Maxwell said sharply. "You work for me."

"We're not asking you to take him," Brooke said.

"No," Maxwell said. "You're just asking for a phone and a truck, and food for the lot of you."

"Five grand, though—" Lorne began.

The sheriff exhaled noisily. "This one could be a Cawley herself, for all we know. I've got no proof he did anything. What if he's the marshal? You want to ride him into the outpost on those terms?"

"We're not giving him over," Brooke said, louder.

"Brooke," Milo broke in. "If they'll take him, we should let them."

"I thought they would have killed each other off by now," Lorne said to Maxwell.

"Who?" Sal whispered to Holly.

"Well, Sheriff?" Brooke broke in.

"Fact is, Mom," Maxwell said, "you've got no witness, I haven't seen this warrant, and I don't know you. You've restrained a man, who may or may not be a chalk dealer, and you're asking me to help you convey him to a federal outpost, where I could just as easily be accused of kidnapping and unlawful confinement if what you've told me isn't true. I don't live out here so I can get tangled up in chalk wars or fed shit. I could untie him now and let you sort your differences out your own selves—"

"I told you, he's—" Brooke cut in.

"However, that seems to be what you've already done, and whether he's guilty or not has nothing to do with my town, so I'll respect your right to freedom of movement and let you pass through if you're not going to make any trouble for people here."

"What kind of law is that?"

"I don't arrest folks on your say-so, Mom. You want a different kind of law, go live in the city."

"What about food?" Milo asked. "The kids haven't eaten since last night."

Maxwell approached him. Brooke tightened her grip on the rifle. The sheriff reached over Milo's shoulder to where yesterday's knee socks were tied drying from the top strap of his pack. Unknotting one long gray sock, Maxwell returned to her lawn chair and filled the sock with beans from toe to heel.

"Fair's fair," she said, knotting the end and tossing it back to Milo. "Your kid helped shell. I'd recommend boiling them, though."

CLOUDS WERE MASSING, DARKENING THE LANDSCAPE AS MAXWELL AND THE deputy led them along the main street through town, ostensibly to show them to the town's central well, where they could fill their bottles. It was clear that Brooke and Milo would not be left unescorted as long as they were in Buffalo Cross. Maxwell walked a little ahead of them, carrying a medium-gauge shotgun she had retrieved from her house. Lorne kept to their other side, one hand resting on his revolver.

They saw no one else until they'd passed the yard with the brown truck—Brooke saw now that it didn't have wheels, much less gas. There, they turned down a residential street where most of the houses looked occupied. A row of recycling bins lined up on the traffic median spilled wide green leaves and the papery golden blossoms of late-season pepper squash. At one house, a pair of children were pulling dead morning glories down from the porch trellis. Flowers grown for pleasure, children doing chores. Maxwell's town was, if not thriving, at least functioning.

The street led to a public square. Two old women and one man were sitting on the raised concrete edge of an empty fountain basin in the middle of the square. Behind them was a Legion hall, a church, a boarded-up bank. In the churchyard stood a fifty-foot pole, still flying the sovereign flag.

"Help yourself," Maxwell said. Brooke saw a tap in the center of the basin, mounted on the elevated pipe that had once fed a decorative fountain. Holly and Sal climbed over the basin's edge with the water bottles while Brooke and Milo stood a short distance away, holding Cawley's ropes.

"It's safe?" Brooke asked, skeptical. Even Buxton had trouble keeping their water clean.

"Straight from a well." Maxwell leaned against the concrete with the old people, making no move to introduce the visitors.

There was a stack of baskets next to one of the women, eggs in one, more pole beans in another.

"Do you think you could spare some of those eggs?" Milo asked, introducing himself to the old people.

"A dollar each," the old woman said with a glance at Maxwell. "Or I'd trade for aspirin."

"Arthritis bothering you, Ash?" Maxwell asked.

"In this weather," the woman answered, gesturing up at the darkening sky.

"I've told you that's nonsense," Maxwell said. "Weather can't make your bones hurt."

"We'll take a dozen, if that's okay," Milo said, not bothering to haggle. He dug his money out of the pack. "I'm sorry I don't have any aspirin."

The woman named Ash shrugged her assent. Milo handed over the money and slipped the eggs one by one into the second sock from the pair on his top strap, twisting the wool between each of the eggs to create a cushion. The last three he had to add in with Maxwell's beans.

"We'd buy bread, too, if you have it," he said.

"The Legion might have leftover," Ash said, counting out what Milo had given her. "You ought to think about staying there anyways, with the storm that's coming."

"These folks don't want the Legion," Maxwell said.

"That other lady who came up the highway, she's staying," Ash said, directing her words at Maxwell. "They ought to, Lynn. For the children, at least. I've seen hail this time of year, more than once."

"It'd be up to Cliven," Maxwell said. "I can't say he'd want them."

"What other lady?" Brooke asked. A cold breeze cut through the square, raising goosebumps under her coat.

"No one you'd like to meet." Ash made a face of disgust. "Blond lady covered in burns."

"She's in there now?" Brooke willed her voice not to tremble. "Staying in one of the rooms?"

"Cliven's got plenty of rooms," Ash said. "Don't worry. There's the whole upstairs."

"Mind if I take a look at the Legion, Sheriff?" Brooke asked. "I won't be a minute."

"Why?"

"Just like to see the rooms. If there's weather coming, like she said."

"Unload your rifle. And it'll be up to the Legion owner if you can stay."

Brooke handed Cawley's lead rope to Milo and cracked the rifle, dropping the cartridges out and passing them to him to hold.

She approached the Legion, bypassing the front steps and instead climbing the fire escape that ran up the side of the building and around to the back of the second story. She glanced back to the square and saw Maxwell watching dubiously, her mouth pressed in a thin line.

At the back of the building, the fire escape looked down on a small parking lot. Through the open doors of an outbuilding, Brooke saw the hindquarters of a heavy draft horse, white or light gray.

Ahead of Brooke, a line of windows was set into the brick. She came even with the first and peeked in: a hallway. The second revealed a made-up room, empty. The third was boarded over.

At the fourth window, the curtains were half open. It took Brooke's eyes a moment to adjust to the gloom. Someone was asleep on the bed. A woman, turned on her side, facing away from Brooke, pale hair spilled across the pillow. Brooke's stomach tightened. It was just as she'd feared. The woman on the bed was a bit thin, perhaps, but the right height. Delia. Traveling on horseback on the highway, she could easily have missed them at the farm and still gotten to Buffalo Cross first.

Brooke scoured the room for any identifying detail. Ash had said this woman was blond, with burn marks. Still, Brooke had to be sure. Of all their possible pursuers, Delia was the most terrifying.

The old sash window had been left slightly open. Careful not to make a sound, Brooke retrieved three spare bullets from an inner pocket of her coat and loaded them into the rifle. She reached a hand into the half-inch gap and lifted the window as slowly as she could manage, fearful of the dry wood squealing. It slid on its runners with a soft sigh. The woman on the bed didn't stir. When Brooke had the window open eight inches, she bent to stick her leg through.

Behind her, the metal fire escape jangled. Brooke spun around, gun raised.

"What the hell?" Holly jumped back, watching her mother with alarm. "What are you doing?"

Brooke held a finger to her lips and stood back against the wall, out of view. No sound from the room. Holly was frozen, staring. Brooke chanced a peek through the window. Delia was still sleeping. She eased the window cautiously back down, thinking she was lucky that Holly had interrupted before terror had made her do something foolish. She could neither capture nor harm Delia here; Maxwell would certainly intervene, not to mention Milo and the girls, to whom she could offer no decent explanation.

They'd have to run.

"We can't stay here," Brooke whispered, inching along the fire escape to Holly.

THE HARDEST PART WAS GETTING THE GIRLS TO LEAVE QUIETLY. HOLLY WAS already arguing before they got off the fire escape, and in the square,

Sal started in with questions, shouting to be heard over her sister.

Milo was no help. During Brooke's absence, he'd bought more food from the old people—heavy jars of beets and turnips that would be hell to carry—and he gazed longingly at the Legion. "The kids are tired," he said. "I'm tired. You haven't slept in two days. We should stay here tonight."

"No." Brooke knew passing up warmth and a dry bed was torment—her own stomach was empty and clenching, the rising wind was bitterly cold, her heels were raw in her boots—but Delia was here, the most vicious of all of them. There was no chance that word of their passage would escape her, none at all. Even if Delia slept clear through till tomorrow, they would have a half day's head start at best.

"Daddy," Sal whined, clinging to Milo. "It's not fair. She said they would help."

"What difference can one night make?" he pressed.

"It's not safe," Brooke said. "It's more dangerous than you know, Milo. Please don't make me explain right now." She turned away before he could say anything else and crossed the square to where Maxwell stood watching with Lorne.

"Listen," Brooke said. "If you do have a phone—I know what you said, but if you do—just call the marshals. Tell them we're coming. Tell them we have children. And tell them—" She lowered her voice so that the others would not hear her. "Tell them someone's following us."

"Getting spooked, Mom?" Maxwell asked. Her expression remained flat, uninterested. "You'd better move on if you're hoping to beat this weather."

"Please, Sheriff."

"Get off the road," Lorne interjected, not unkindly. "If you're worried about being followed. Once you're out of town, head south of the 12. It's walkable all the way to the Warren River bridge if you keep east of the swamp."

Brooke checked over her shoulder to see if the others were listening, but Cawley was at the full extent of his rope, leaning against a telephone pole, and Milo was busy trying to calm the girls.

"Is there anything out there?" Brooke asked.

"My dad's duck blind," Lorne said. "That's about it."

"It's not fair," Sal wailed at Milo, louder than ever, her voice echoing in the square.

Brooke stalked back to the girls and forcefully covered Sal's mouth.

"Brooke, no," Milo said, grabbing her arm.

"We're going," Brooke said, pulling free of his grasp. "Bring Cawley." She lifted a writhing Sal and carried her from the square, one hand still clamped over her mouth.

"Wait," Milo pleaded behind her.

When Brooke turned to look over her shoulder, Milo and Holly were following, with Cawley trailing on his rope. The sheriff and her deputy stood with the old people by the fountain, watching them go, as the clouds overhead grew darker.

8

"NO," MILO SAID. "WE'RE NOT GOING ANY FURTHER UNTIL YOU TELL ME WHAT'S going on. What did you say to the sheriff back there?"

They were stopped a quarter mile outside of Buffalo Cross on Highway 12. As soon as Brooke put her down, Sal had run, still crying, to Milo. Ignoring her daughter's tears, Brooke took Cawley's rope back from Milo and stepped off the highway, intending to lead them into the ranch land that stretched south toward distant woods. But none of the others had moved from the road.

"Yeah, Mom, what's going on?" Holly echoed Milo.

"We're going this way," Brooke said. "Come on."

"Why would we go that way?" Milo demanded.

"To get to Shaw Station, like I told you. Let's go."

"But you said—" Holly started.

"Enough," Brooke spoke over her. "All this bitching isn't getting us there faster."

"I'm not bitching," Holly said, indignant.

"Talk to me," Milo said. "Tell me why we're doing this."

"It's serious, okay? Maxwell won't help, and we have to get to Shaw Station, the sooner the better."

"Fine," Milo said slowly, sounding as if it was anything but fine. "Then why not stay on the road? Highway 12 goes all the way to Shaw Station. And there'll be houses. Food. People."

"We'll get back to the road soon," Brooke lied. From here, the highway ran southeast for many miles before veering back southwest. She intended to take them due south and find her way cross-country to the Warren River; once over it, she'd be on familiar ground as far as the outpost. "The highway loops. This is a shortcut."

"I don't think it is," Milo argued. "I drove this way with my mum once. The road doesn't turn west again for a long time."

"I'm not sleeping on the ground again," Cawley said. "It's goddamn cold."

"You don't get a vote," Brooke snapped.

"Do we?" Holly asked.

Brooke looked at them: Holly, stiff-backed and defiant, Sal's eyes swollen from crying, Milo's face pinched with strain. The second Delia heard about travelers leaving Buffalo Cross with Stephen Cawley prisoner, she would be hammering down this highway as fast as that big draft horse could take her. They had to get out of her path.

"Please," Brooke said, looking at Milo and the girls in turn. "You have to trust me. I want to find somewhere to stay as much as you do. I promise this is the right way."

"We do trust you," Milo said, sighing. "Okay? But everyone's tired, and cold, and the weather's getting bad, and this whole plan is seeming like a worse and worse idea."

"Maybe we'll stay ahead of the weather," Brooke said.

Milo stared at the tufty ground south of the road. Finally, he reached down and took Sal's hand. Brooke watched gratefully as they crossed the ditch together. Holly followed, glowering and uncharacteristically silent.

"Good stuff," Cawley said.

"Shut up," Brooke muttered.

They walked through rolling pastures where thick stands of trees grew in the low places. The clouds darkened and the temperature dropped. The air smelled of storm. Behind them, the horizon was blurred. Brooke hoped the rain had reached the spot where they'd left the highway, to obscure their footprints through the ditch.

Two or three miles south of the road, they reached a large swamp where the limbless spikes of dead trees stood out of the water, as if waiting for someone. Brooke turned them east, skirting the marshy ground. She kept an eye out for the duck blind Lorne had mentioned, which might offer some shelter. It was difficult to see far ahead. Milo and the girls were dark shapes in the gloom.

"Where's the highway?" Brooke heard Holly asking up ahead.

"I don't know, Hol," came Milo's answer. "Please stop asking."

Finally, Brooke spied a lean-to off to one side, made of skinned logs and plastic sheeting.

"Stop," Brooke called forward. "We can camp here."

"Here?" Milo turned, incredulous.

"It'll have to do," Brooke said, catching up with them.

"What will?" Milo asked. "There's nothing here."

"She means that," Holly said, pointing with distaste at the rough structure nearly hidden under a carpet of fallen pine needles.

"That's garbage," Milo said. "It's someone's old tarp or something."

"It's a hunting blind," Brooke said, twisting out of her pack.

"This can't be right," Milo said, staring at the heap of logs and plastic in disbelief. "You said this was a shortcut to the highway."

"I guess it's farther than I thought," Brooke said.

"It's not dark yet," Milo said. "We should keep going. I told you, I traveled Highway 12 with my mum once, and there were plenty of houses then. I'm sure someone is still living out here. We need to warm up."

Brooke wondered momentarily what could have brought Milo and his mother this way, but she tucked the question away and reached into her bag for the flashlight. On hands and knees, she drew aside the opening of the duck blind and shone the light in. No animals. Easily big enough for four. A raised platform that would keep the sleeping bags dry, assuming the ceiling didn't leak. Brooke poked up at the milky plastic, dislodging an avalanche of pine needles outside.

"It's fine," she said, backing out of the structure.

"Dad," Sal whined. "You said we would stay somewhere warm."

"We will, we will. We're not staying here. The highway can't be that far."

"I bet we're nowhere near the highway," Holly said. "I bet she took us here on purpose."

"It's just a little farther than we thought," Milo said. "We'll catch it soon, if we keep walking. Right, Brooke?"

"We're staying here," she said. If her image of the countryside was correct, the highway was now miles to the east of them, swinging its slow arc. "It's going to rain soon, and this is shelter. It's good enough."

"It isn't, Brooke," Milo entreated.

"Told you," Holly said.

"Tie him under those black spruces," Brooke said, tossing Cawley's line to Milo.

"No," Milo said.

"You said you trusted me, Milo. So trust that I know what I'm doing."

"How am I supposed to trust you if you won't tell me what's going on?" Milo stammered.

"Okay, fine, you don't trust me. But you've got to see that we don't have time to get anywhere else before the rain starts. So tie Cawley up. Please."

Milo looked up at the darkening clouds and sighed in defeat, easing his pack to the ground.

"This is bullshit," Cawley complained as Milo led him to the ground under the spruces. "It's fucking freezing out here."

"I'll make a fire," Milo said.

"He doesn't need a—" Brooke started.

"For us," Milo cut her off. "The kids are cold."

"That's not a good idea," Brooke objected.

"Sound good?" Milo addressed himself to the girls, ignoring Brooke. "We'll cook those eggs. Fried eggs! Who wants to go look for firewood while Mom and I talk? There ought to be plenty around."

"I'm cold," Sal said. "I want to go home."

Holly sat down with her knees in front of her and glared into her crossed arms.

"All right, I'll do it," Milo said. He shot Brooke a glance. "But we're going to talk when I get back."

Brooke watched him tramp off into the trees. He was going farther than he needed to, she thought. There were enough dry branches nearby.

Sal had started crying again. Brooke wanted to go to her the way she normally would. She hadn't allowed herself to get close to the kids since Cawley arrived.

"It's okay, Salamander," she tried lamely. "In another few days this will all be done."

"Another few *days*?" Sal sobbed.

"Don't you want to check this place out?" Brooke held the front of the duck blind open, trying to mimic Milo's encouraging tone. "It'll be cozy with your sleeping bag."

"What were you doing back there at the Legion?" Holly asked, her voice hard. "Tell me the truth."

"I—" Brooke faltered. "You just surprised me, Hol, that's all. I'm sorry if I scared you."

"Ugh!" Holly growled. "Whatever. I'm going with Dad. Come on, Sal."

Sal stood and wiped her tears with the back of a hand.

"You don't have to go," Brooke said. But they were already moving away. "Don't go far," she called after them. "Stay with Dad!"

Before they disappeared into the trees, Brooke saw Holly wrap her arm around Sal's shoulders.

Trying to ignore the loneliness in her chest, Brooke resumed the job of making camp. She sorted their food into four days of rations, figuring they had another fifty miles to walk. It was scant but sufficient. Water would be the bigger issue. Maybe if she cut a piece of the plastic sheeting and brought it with them, she'd be able to trap rainwater. Inside the hunting blind, she unrolled the musty-smelling sleeping bags. Something tickled her hand and she flicked an earwig away. Holly hated earwigs.

Brooke heard the sound of rope running against the ground and charged out of the blind to see Cawley settling himself at the farthest reach of his tether.

"That's too far," Brooke said.

"Oh, god," Cawley said wearily, shuffling a few steps closer. "When are you going to get this over with? If you're not going to shoot me, just let me go."

"So you can bring the rest of your family down on me? No. Why would I? I'm getting paid and I'm getting the hell away."

"There *is* no rest of them," Cawley said. "Don't you know that? There's no one coming."

"You'd like me to think that," Brooke said.

"Use your brain, you fucking moron. No one's looking for you. No one cares."

"Then how did you find me?"

"I fucking didn't," he said. "I didn't know it was you."

"Bullshit," she said. "You want me to believe you showed up in my shed, down an unmarked driveway in the middle of nowhere, by coincidence?"

"Forget it," Cawley said, laughing humorlessly.

"You just want me to slow down," Brooke said, "get lazy, make it easy for them to catch us."

"Sure," Cawley said, leaning his head back against the rivened bark of the spruce. "Maybe I'm fucking with you. Maybe there's a whole army coming to save me. And maybe you're going to let Milo fry me one of those eggs."

"Enough," Brooke said. "You don't say their names."

Cawley smirked at her. "He's not as dumb as you think, you know. He's not buying it. Neither's Holly. I could tell them, but it's more fun watching them figure it out for themselves that you're just a—"

"Shut up." Brooke cut him off. A chipmunk had scolded in the distance, disturbed by something. Milo and the girls hadn't gone that way. Brooke listened. A moment later, a starling took off from a tree closer by. Distant hoofbeats from back the way they'd come. She picked up the rifle and moved toward the sound. Fifty feet off. Forty. She raised the rifle, sighted the trees. There, from behind a thick spruce, a tall shape. Brooke kept her finger on the trigger. A tall man on a glossy black stallion. Plaid fleece jacket. Brooke recognized Lorne, the young deputy from Buffalo Cross.

"Don't shoot," he called out, showing her an open palm.

"Deputy." She lowered her gun.

"I came to help, ma'am."

"Oh, thank god," Brooke said.

"Glad to see you found the blind." The deputy dismounted. His stallion looked young and healthy enough that it might make Shaw Station in a day, if pushed. Whatever had changed Maxwell's mind and made her send her deputy out to help them, Brooke hoped the town had a few such animals to spare.

"How many horses did you bring?" she asked, hoping he hadn't left them too far off. She stooped to yank the sleeping bags out of the blind.

"Where's your husband at?" Lorne asked.

"He'll be back any minute. We can be ready quick." The kids would fuss, but Milo would manage them. Brooke hastily rolled up the first sleeping bag and stuffed it into her pack.

"Lynn was wrong to turn you away," Lorne said. "Traveling with children and all."

"That's fine," Brooke said, rolling up the second bag. "Where are the other horses?"

"I can get your captive to Shaw Station," Lorne said, ignoring her question. Brooke noticed he was moving closer to the spruces. Cawley sat looking from Brooke to Lorne and back again, an avid glint in his eye.

"Where are the horses, Deputy?" Brooke asked.

"I need to get moving if I'm going to stay ahead of the weather. It's a ways back to the highway."

"What are you saying?" Brooke's relief faded as she began to apprehend Lorne's meaning.

"Ma'am, why don't you let me do my job, and you can get on with caring for your family?"

"I am goddamned caring for my family. What do you think this is? You're here to take him off me? Is that what you call help?"

"If it's the money you're after, I'll see that you get it."

"Like hell you will." Brooke moved toward Cawley.

"Ma'am—" The deputy held a hand out in a calming gesture that she suspected was borrowed from Maxwell.

"I'm delivering this man to the marshals at Shaw Station," Brooke said, taking another step closer to Cawley. "You can help me or not. I'm not giving him over to you."

"Ma'am, I regret this." Lorne unsnapped his holster. "For your own sake and the sake of those kids, I'm taking custody of your prisoner. I suggest you go home."

Brooke tightened her grip on the rifle.

"Don't do anything silly," Lorne said. "You don't want this to get out of hand."

His revolver was aimed at her now.

"Lorne." Brooke breathed deep. Cawley watched them expectantly. She lowered the rifle. "You don't know what you're getting into. Please."

Lorne holstered his revolver and bent to pull Cawley up from the ground. "I will say you did a real thorough job on those bindings," he chuckled, plucking at the insulated wire and the plastic ties at Cawley's wrists. He undid Cawley's ankle bindings and freed the lead rope from the spruces.

Brooke watched helplessly as Lorne negotiated the bound prisoner onto the stallion. Cawley's knee must have been hurt by the rough movements required to get him onto the horse, but he only grunted.

"Don't keep him that close to you," Brooke warned as Lorne mounted behind Cawley.

"I can handle him," Lorne said with a placating smile.

"Tie his hands down to the saddle, at least."

"Don't worry, ma'am. You take care now, and get your family back home. If you leave an address with the Legion, I'll see you get your bounty. Fifty-fifty."

The deputy flicked his reins and the horse bounded north into the trees, back toward the road.

"He'll kill you," Brooke shouted.

Cawley twisted around in the saddle to look back at her. "Take care of that family, now," he shouted. Brooke was sure she saw a smile of victory on his face as he disappeared from view.

AT FIRST, AFTER LORNE RODE OFF WITH CAWLEY, BROOKE CHASED THEM THROUGH the woods, sprinting, frantic, but they were out of hearing in minutes. She turned back, sharply aware of leaving Milo and the kids exposed. It wasn't just Delia they had to fear now. Cawley would get loose; Brooke was sure of it. He would outsmart Lorne, who was only thinking of the money. A payday, he'd called it.

It was nearly dark and the first drops of icy rain were falling by the time Milo and the girls returned. When she told them that Cawley was gone in the charge of the deputy, they broke into smiles of relief.

"Thank god," Holly sighed, pushing Sal ahead of her into the hunting blind, out of the rain. Inside, the flashlight came on, lighting up the plastic like a milky jewel in the darkness. "Where are the dry clothes?"

"We have to get out of here," Brooke told Milo. "They might stop for the night. If we move fast, there's still a chance we can catch them."

"What?" Milo was sifting through the twigs and birch bark he'd collected to make a fire. "What are you talking about?"

"Don't bother with the fire. Help the kids pack."

Holly laughed from behind the plastic sheet. "Mom, are you joking?"

"Do I sound like I'm goddamn joking?" Brooke snapped. "Get your sister ready."

"Brooke." Milo put the twigs down. "Can you even hear yourself?"

"How many times do I have to say it? Let's go. Now."

"Stop," Milo said, gentler now. "You're not making sense."

"What's wrong with Mom?" Brooke heard Sal ask inside the shelter.

"Listen," Milo said. Brooke felt his hands on her shoulders.

He turned her toward him, and for a moment, the panic beating in her temples slowed. "Something's happened. You're not yourself. You're not well. If you were thinking clearly, you'd see it. We couldn't catch Lorne even if we wanted to. He's on a horse."

"He won't be for long," Brooke said.

"There's nothing we can do," Milo said. "The deputy knows what he's doing. If he needed our help, he would have asked for it. You need to eat, and you need to rest."

"No," Brooke said, breaking away from him.

Then, with a gust of wind blowing down from the treetops, it began to pour. Brooke cursed. They couldn't travel in this. They'd have to wait. At least the weather might slow Lorne down too. He would know of places to take cover. Or he might take Cawley back to Buffalo Cross. Straight to Delia.

"We did our best," Milo said. "We can go home." He ducked under the cover of the spruces, where the ground was almost dry, and attempted to prepare a fire, stacking now-damp birch bark and small twigs for tinder and overlaying that with a tent of larger sticks.

"No fire," Brooke said, kicking the pile apart. "It's too dangerous."

"What the hell, Brooke?" Milo shouted. "What's wrong with you?"

"First break in the rain, we're going," she said, turning to the shelter. "No fire."

She lifted the front sheet of the blind and crawled inside. The girls stared at her silently.

Brooke reached into her pack for the tin mug that was the closest thing they had to a bowl and handed it to Holly with the two socks Milo had filled in Buffalo Cross. "Hurry and eat so we can turn the light off."

"Dad?" Holly called out. "Mom is telling us to eat raw eggs."

Milo pulled the plastic aside and crawled into the shelter. "I can't get the fire started. Sorry. Everything's too wet now."

"We're going home, right?" Sal asked.

"We can't go anywhere tonight," Milo said. "It's pouring. We'll have to leave in the morning."

"You're just going to do what she wants," Holly said bitterly. "You always do."

"That's not true," Milo said. "We're all on the same team, you guys. Tell them, Brooke."

Brooke took the cup back from Holly and cracked an egg into it.

"Mom?" Sal ventured. "I thought it was over."

"No," Brooke said, lifting the cup to her mouth and shuddering involuntarily as she swallowed the cold, viscous egg. "It's never over."

9

THINGS WITH THE CAWLEYS CAME TO A HEAD THE SUMMER BROOKE WAS eighteen. She had been working alongside Anita for more than a year, and in that time, Delia had intensified her attacks. Finally, one of their dealers—an old friend of Anita's named Vicky—was found dead, run over outside her house.

"Was it an accident?" Robin asked.

"Of course it wasn't an accident," Edmund said darkly. "Wake the fuck up, marshmallow."

Anita painted Vicky's name up on the drive shed, alongside the ten resistance fighters who'd been martyred during secession. Brooke felt a conflicting mix of guilt and pride seeing Vicky up there among the names she had grown up venerating. Vicky had taught Brooke to shallow dive at the lake when she was a kid.

Competition between the Hollands and the Cawleys had turned Shaw County's already bad chalk problem into an epidemic. A dozen teens in town had overdosed during the winter, and the community's goodwill toward Brooke's family was gone. The Hollands had new friends—people Edmund wouldn't have stooped to know, once—while others with whom they'd been close for years dropped away. Pauline had tried to join a local playgroup with her and Callum's infant son, Aaron, only to be frosted out by the other mothers, and the hardware store would no longer buy salvage from fifteen-year-old Robin, even though he had no more to do with the chalk trade than Pauline did.

Robin's sideline in cottage memorabilia was still strong, though, and he'd mostly managed to avoid his parents' interest. There had been one bad moment when Edmund got wind that Robin was corresponding with a boy who had left for the city after a disagreement with his parents. Edmund ranted furiously about the kind of miserable rat who would abandon home and family for a life like that.

Brooke wished Robin would stick up for his friend, whom she knew as a smart and creative boy who had been bullied mercilessly at home. Edmund seemed to have grown more oppressive of late. Brooke was certain that, in the past, his judgments had been harsh but fair, based on merit, not just loyalty. But whatever she thought of Edmund's diatribe, she knew better than to disagree with him. Robin knew better too, of course. That was why he sat so quietly, shoulders hunched, waiting for it to be over.

Callum had managed to scale up their operation to supply major chalk networks in the city. This success gave the Hollands a substantial edge over the Cawleys, and rumors began circulating around town that some kind of retaliation was planned. At the peak of summer, Edmund asked Brooke and Anita to provide extra security for a delivery to the soap factory.

It was a humid evening, the roadsides singing with chorus frogs. Edmund and Callum rolled up to the factory gate in Edmund's truck, with Brooke and Anita behind them in the hatchback. Brooke had her window down, a rifle across her lap. She was calm, suspended in the state of vague detachment that she occupied more and more lately.

When the gate didn't open for Edmund's horn, Brooke raised her walkie-talkie to ask if he wanted her to go find someone. Before she was able to speak, there was a soft pop and Edmund's windshield shattered. Anita pulled her down against the console between the seats. The walkie-talkie gave a short burst of static and then cut out.

Brooke felt adrenaline rush into her blood. She stared at the vinyl console, her heart pounding painfully in her chest, pulse ticking at her wrists, her temples. She noticed absently that the frogs were still singing.

Another pop, and the hatchback listed as its front passenger tire deflated.

The shots were coming from Brooke's side of the car. She tried to remember what she'd seen out her window. Storage units, an old parking lot. She thought back to the moments before the first shot, but her eyes had been on the gate ahead of them, not to the side.

"This way." Anita opened the driver's door and slithered out, pulling her handgun from under the seat. Brooke followed, staying as low as she could. They crawled to Edmund's truck behind the cover of the vehicles.

Another pop, and another of Anita's tires went flat. The factory gate remained closed.

Brooke could see Edmund, still in the driver's seat of his truck, shooting through the shattered windshield. Anita let down the tailgate and climbed into the truck bed, scrambling ahead to the cab, where she raised herself and began shooting over the roof. She was aiming for one of the storage units; she must have seen something.

Brooke crept forward and opened Edmund's door.

"Get in," he said, dropping to the ground outside to let Brooke up into the cab.

Brooke climbed into the footwell, and it was then she noticed that Callum was slumped in his seat against the side door, his T-shirt dark with blood; he was trying to lift his gun, wincing with every movement. A shot thudded into the side of the truck. Brooke shimmied closer to help Callum, expecting her father to get in after her, but instead, he slammed the door from outside, shouting, "Drive!"

Brooke crouched low in front of the steering wheel, thinking her father was planning to ride in the back of the truck with Anita. She heard the drone of a motor. She peeked over the dash and saw the factory gate opening.

"Daddy?" Brooke cried.

"I can hold them for a minute," he called. "Go!"

A Jeep was coming through the gate now, and Brooke saw men in fatigues alongside it, advancing with guns raised: members of the volunteer militia from Shaw Station.

It was an ambush, Brooke realized. They'd been trapped.

Brooke felt for the keys in the ignition, trying to stay calm, trying not to look at Callum, who was groaning, no longer trying to raise his gun.

Edmund stepped into the road, aiming his semiautomatic at the volunteers coming through the gate.

"Daddy, get in!" Brooke called.

"Go!" Edmund shouted. "Get them out of here!"

Brooke hesitated. She didn't want to leave him there, but Callum's color was fading, sweat beading on his pale, waxy face.

"Go!" Edmund bellowed.

Brooke hauled the steering wheel to the side and floored the gas pedal, spinning into a turn that toppled Anita in the truck bed. In the rearview mirror, she saw her father in front of the gate with his gun in the air, swarmed by volunteers. She realized she was shaking.

ONE OF THEIR FIRST-TIER DEALERS, JAY, BROUGHT WORD TO THE HOUSE THAT Edmund was being held at the Shaw Station courthouse. A cousin who worked in the building told Jay the town was charging the Hollands for the so-called attack on the soap factory. The factory owner had been tipped off that the Hollands were turning on him and timing an assault with their next delivery, so he'd made a deal with the town council for protection. The volunteer militia had been waiting inside the gate when the Hollands arrived. As soon as they heard shots outside, they moved.

The factory owner realized his mistake as soon as he saw the Hollands' shot-up vehicles; the tip about the planned attack had been a setup, traced with little difficulty to the Cawleys. He refused to stand witness, terrified of reprisal from the Hollands, and even the volunteers who'd arrested Edmund washed their hands of it once they understood what had happened. If it was a war between families, they said, let them fight it out themselves. They had better reasons than that to make themselves targets. But the town had Edmund, and they were under considerable pressure to do something about the growing toll of the chalk trade, so they held him.

Anita wanted to go after the Cawleys right away. She was livid: the perfidy of the soap factory owner, the gutless volunteers—who had taken Edmund only by outnumbering him twenty to one—the cowardly, sanctimonious town council. And, above all, the shooter perched behind a storage unit, who'd vanished as soon as the factory gate opened.

"It was Delia," Anita spat. "I saw her."

"He needs the hospital," Robin spoke up. Callum was burning with fever on the bed in his old room. The wound was near his armpit; the bullet had missed his lung and was stuck in his ribs, a visible lump under the skin. He was semiconscious, breathless with pain.

"They'll kill him," Emily said, shaking her head.

Brooke didn't know whether she meant the Cawleys would kill Callum or the hospital would. Anything seemed possible. The county had turned against them.

"I'm going after her," Anita said again.

"No," Emily said, her voice flinty. "You're going to work. Daddy's not here to run the lab, so you have to. We can't stop. That's what they want. They think we're vulnerable. They think they've got an opening."

"Please, Mama," Robin begged. "Callum needs a doctor."

"Jay will find someone," Emily said with a wave. "And get Pauline and Aaron out here. They ought to be with him."

Brooke was the only one at the house when Jay returned later with another of his cousins, this one a nurse. He'd paid her to come; she was clearly unhappy to be there. She was no older than Callum, but she'd trained at the hospital. She brought sterilized tools, still in their plastic sleeves.

The nurse lifted Callum's T-shirt up, prying it gently where clotted blood had glued the fabric to his skin. Callum whimpered through gritted teeth. She sprayed some kind of anesthetic into the hole in Callum's chest and injected him with a syringe of oxy. The wound was badly swollen, and the nurse had to dig her way in with the forceps to extract the bullet. Callum's body bucked, and he uttered a high, thin scream like a baby's.

"You have to hold him," the nurse said to Brooke.

Brooke held her brother against the bed with all her strength, but he outweighed her by half, and every time the nurse probed in after the bullet, he thrashed out of Brooke's grasp, causing the nurse to pull the forceps back out again.

"Just do it," Brooke said. "The longer you take, the more pain he's in."

"I can't. He's moving too much. I could puncture something.

There's an artery right there. He should be under proper anesthetic. This isn't right. You have to take him to the hospital."

"Fuck," Brooke said. "You hold him, then."

"What?" The young woman backed away.

"I'll fucking do it. Just hold him still."

The young woman held up her hands in refusal, shaking her head.

"Callum," Brooke said, holding her brother's face in her hands, staring into his eyes. "You have to stay still. I'm going to help you, but you have to stay still. Just pretend I'm Daddy, okay? I'm Daddy and I will kick your ass if you move. Understand?" She pulled a leather sandal off the floor and stuck it in her brother's mouth. He bit down, nodding.

Brooke took the forceps from the nurse's limp fingers.

"You can't just—" the girl objected.

"Where's the artery?" Brooke asked.

Wide-eyed, the nurse leaned forward and traced a line against Callum's armpit.

Brooke closed her eyes and summoned the calm place: cool humidity, a misty forest. All that lay in front of her was a series of actions. She would perform them carefully and well. She pictured her way through to the end. She opened her eyes, calm, held Callum's shoulder firmly with her left hand, and guided the forceps into the mess of dark blood and glistening red flesh. Callum squirmed but Brooke did not withdraw, instead moving with him until he was still enough for her to continue. His cheeks blew round and he screamed into the leather.

Brooke narrowed her vision to Callum's skin, the line the nurse had traced, the hump of the bullet pushing against his ribs. She was up to her knuckles. She felt metal touch metal. She had to grip the bullet between the tiny rubber pads at the tip of the forceps. She tried once, twice, and then she had the bullet. Squeezing tight, she pulled. It didn't move. It was caught against the bone. Callum's scream soared high and spit foamed from the corners of his mouth.

"Daddy!" Brooke shouted in his face. He stilled, holding her eye.

She gripped again and pulled. The bullet moved. She held it steady and withdrew the forceps. There it was, a chunk of bloody steel the size of a child's fingertip.

Callum let the spit-soaked sandal fall from his mouth. He was crying, moaning, twisting in pain.

"Clean him up," Brooke said to the nurse.

Then she slammed out of the room, overwhelmed with a fury so sudden and strong it tasted like iron in her mouth. How had this happened? Callum should never have had to bite a shoe in his childhood bedroom while his little sister pulled a bullet from his chest. Her calm had left her, but it was a relief to finally feel what she was supposed to: misery, injury, and blinding, incandescent rage.

She found Anita in the lab, scowling behind safety glasses as she tried to follow Edmund's complex recipe.

"Where's Delia?" Brooke asked, laying her rifle on the counter.

"Sister," Anita grinned. "Fucking bring it."

THEY PARKED NEAR DELIA'S HOUSE AFTER DARK AND CREPT IN THROUGH THE backyard. Anita climbed frog-legged onto the back porch and Brooke followed, keeping her head below the level of the bay window. Someone was talking inside. Together, they rose up just enough to look in.

Delia was at the sink in a frilly apron, fair hair tucked behind her ears, her forearms slick with suds. Even washing dishes, Brooke thought, she was imposing. She had a wind-up radio playing on the counter next to her. She shook her head in irritation at something and reached for the radio. The plastic switch slipped under her soapy fingers and Delia had to wipe her hand on her jeans to try again. The talking voice stopped.

Brooke and Anita dropped back down.

"Can't get in through here," Anita whispered. The window was caged by bars that had been anchored in poured concrete bases.

Brooke crept on her knees to examine the back door. It was locked, top and bottom, with in-facing plates that she couldn't dismantle quietly. Even from inside, those locks wouldn't be quick to undo.

Anita pointed her gun at the doorknob and lifted an eyebrow. Brooke shook her head. The whole door was steel, even the frame. No way to shoot through.

"Hang on," Brooke whispered.

She dropped down into the yard and crept around the side of the house. The cellar door had been covered with a corrugated iron sheet that also locked from inside. The front door was the same as the one in back: steel, with a steel frame, in-facing lock plates. The whole house had been reinforced like a safe room. Brooke picked up the black gleam of cameras under the eaves and shrank back the way she'd come.

"This place is a fortress," she whispered when she got back to Anita.

Her sister was bent over the edge of the porch, shaking something against its wooden lattice base. Brooke smelled the tang of lighter fluid and realized what she was doing. Anita shook more fluid across the siding, around the door.

"Anita, wait." Brooke held out a hand, her resolve faltering. It was the barred window, the reinforced door. Delia would burn alive before this house let her out.

"You want to do it?" Anita held out an old cardboard book of matches.

Brooke took the matches from her sister. Edmund would do it.

He would expect her to do it. She pictured Callum contorted with pain. Delia would come after them again. She wouldn't stop coming.

Brooke tore a match off and struck it, held it to the siding.

"There," Anita said, as the wood caught.

The fire spread like a blush.

EMILY TOLD THEM THEY'D BEEN FOOLISH. THERE WOULD BE NO MYSTERY ABOUT who had set fire to Delia Cawley's home with her in it. The town could use this fresh violence as an excuse to hold Edmund even longer. Callum, on the other hand, was moved to the point of tears, grinning wetly up at them from his bed.

"That's just the oxy," Anita said.

That night, Brooke didn't sleep. She paced the property, checking the trip wires, making sure the cameras on the perimeter were broadcasting to the old smartphone Robin had rigged for the purpose. She moved the Rottweilers close to the house and sat on the porch with a handgun, watching the phone obsessively.

Brooke had done what loyalty required of her. She had honored Edmund's trust. So why was she sick with shame, gnawed by images of Delia burning in her house? Such weakness could serve no purpose other than to distress her. Better she should return to the calm place, or else the mindless anger that had propelled her to Delia's in the first place. But neither calm nor anger would come. All she felt was trapped.

The Hollands had changed. It had happened so gradually that everything seemed normal, but when Brooke looked at herself now, she saw how survival had warped her—all of them—past sovereignty into something more brutal.

Between the house and the drive shed, Emily's vegetable garden had grown full and high with summer. Lettuce, peas, Swiss chard, beet greens, each leaf with a skin-like sheen, as creased as the palm of an old hand. Brooke loved her family; she couldn't help it. Whatever Edmund and Emily asked of her, she knew she would give.

But not Robin. Sitting in the dark, watching the phone and listening for the dogs, Brooke decided that Robin must not end up trapped, as she was. He wasn't like the rest of them, built to fight. If Edmund could be jailed, if Callum could be gunned down, if Brooke herself could be so twisted up with guilt that she would gladly have sunk beneath the earth in the garden, what odds did her little brother stand?

He could still live a different life. He still had a chance.

THE NEXT AFTERNOON, JAY REPORTED THAT DELIA HAD SURVIVED. SHE'D CLIMBED through an upstairs window and made it out with some bad burns and a fracture. Her house was destroyed, but she was believed to be staying with Frank Jr. and Angeline and their boys across town.

Brooke should have been as disgusted by this news as Anita. Instead, while her sister stormed off to the lab with Jay to conceive new and better ways of disabling the Cawleys, Brooke could barely conceal her relief.

It was a reprieve. She made up her mind not to waste it.

She found Robin sitting on the lawn with Aaron. The little boy was wrapped comfortably around his uncle. It was a hot afternoon, storm clouds crowding in, rolling distant thunder.

"You have to go," Brooke said to Robin, pitching her voice low. Emily and Pauline were in the house, changing Callum's bandages.

"Where?" Robin was only half listening as he bounced Aaron in his lap.

"People are getting through all the time now."

"What do you mean?" He turned to look at her.

"The city, Rob."

He widened his eyes.

"Leave?" he asked in a hushed voice.

"They have school," Brooke said. "And jobs, and proper Internet. Phones that can actually call someone." She twitched the old smartphone in her hand. When the camera stream dropped out, the phone would revert to searching for a cell signal, running out its charge looking for something that wasn't there.

Aaron's attention was caught by the phone and he reached for it. Brooke let him look at the home screen: the famous picture of them at the Warren—Emily in the truck bed with her children around her, Robin present in the shape of her shirt.

"Dad would kill me," Robin said.

"Go before he's out."

Robin's brow furrowed. "Will you come too?"

Brooke shook her head and watched her brother's face fall.

"But you'll be okay," she assured him. "You've got money set aside. You can figure it out. Take a computer, or a phone. You can look up what you need to know."

"Why can't you come?" he asked.

Brooke looked out over the property that had been in the Holland family for generations. The garden's listing scarecrow—a pitchfork dressed every spring in a new set of cast-off clothing—the drive shed with its columns of black names, the line of tall basswood trees that hid the road, the distant miles of blue-green forest threaded by the silver ribbon of the Warren: a landscape so well known to her that it felt like looking in a mirror.

"I can't leave now," Brooke said.

Aaron lost interest in the phone and squirmed out of Robin's arms to stand wobbling on the grass. Robin offered him a hand for balance, but Aaron ignored it, stepping forward with an expression of grim resolve, so much like Callum. He fell back on his diaper-padded bum and looked back at them, as if unsure whether to cry.

"It's okay," Robin said.

Aaron, reassured, got back to his feet. Step, step, fall.

Brooke watched her young nephew toddle awkwardly forward. The thunder rolled closer.

Step, step, step, fall.

10

SOMEONE WAS SHAKING HER. A RED GLARE SWEPT ACROSS HER CLOSED EYELIDS.

"Wake up! Wake up, Brooke!"

"What? What? I'm not asleep."

"They're gone. The kids are gone."

"Where?" Brooke sat up, squinting. The beam of the flashlight jerked away, illuminating the duck blind's plastic sides.

Milo held the flap of the blind open, shining the flashlight out on falling rain. It was still dark. "I don't see any tracks."

"They're outside? They'll get soaked." Brooke moved to the entrance, shoving aside the remains of last night's disgusting dinner. Then she noticed that the sleeping bags were gone. And the girls' boots. And one of the packs.

"They're *gone*, Brooke," Milo repeated.

Brooke grabbed the flashlight from him and searched the shelter. The rifle was there, but the girls had taken the first aid kit, their spare clothes, half the food and water. The rain tapping hollowly on the plastic sheet must have masked the sound of their preparations.

"They can't be gone," Brooke said. "They can't."

"I knew something like this would happen," Milo said.

"Then why didn't you say something?"

"I did! I told you it was a mistake to keep going. They wouldn't have run away if you hadn't—"

"Cawley's out there, Milo."

"No more Cawley! Drop it, Brooke. He's gone. He's halfway to jail by now. It's the kids you have to think about. You scared the shit out of them. Would you snap out of it? Forget about Cawley."

"But, Milo, he'll—"

"They're trying to go home. It's the only thing that makes sense. If we retrace our steps from yesterday, we'll catch up with them."

Milo snatched the flashlight back and pushed out of the shelter with the remaining pack.

Brooke sat paralyzed by panic, watching the flashlight sweep across the darkness outside. She couldn't have lost them. She couldn't. The only thing that mattered, gone while she slept.

They had no idea what they were walking into.

Brooke felt on the platform for the rifle and threw herself out the door of the shelter, following the flashlight that was now bobbing away through the trees.

The heavy rain had erased any tracks the girls might have left. Brooke and Milo didn't speak as they moved north through the trees. The swamp was their only landmark. Brooke prayed that they would catch up with the girls before it curved and they had to decide whether to follow it or set off through undistinguishable forest.

The rain turned to sleet and then snow, cutting their visibility to a few yards. They called out for Holly and Sal as they jogged alongside the swamp. Brooke knew it was reckless to reveal themselves so loudly when Cawley could be anywhere, but the snow was now falling so heavily that they might otherwise pass within twenty feet of the girls and not know it. Anyway, she thought grimly, if Cawley did hear them, at least it would draw his attention away from the kids.

Dawn came, dim and dreary through the snow, and the edge of the swamp curved westward. Here, if Holly had her bearings right, she would have left the swamp behind and struck a path through the forest.

"Sal's so slow, we should have caught up to them by now," Milo said. "I can't see anything in this snow. We should split up so we can cover more ground."

"No," Brooke said, her eyes sweeping the ground in the weak light. She looked for places where trees had sheltered the ground from snow. No footprint. No strand of hair caught by a low branch. "How would we find each other again?"

"We can meet in Buffalo Cross," Milo said. "At the Legion. Whoever finds the girls takes them there and waits for the other."

"And what if Delia's still there?"

"Who?"

"The woman at the Legion. I told you." Though now Brooke couldn't remember actually saying the words out loud.

"You saw someone at the Legion?" Milo squinted through the snow. "Who's Delia?"

"Forget it. We can't split up. If Cawley finds you, and I've got the gun—"

"God, Brooke! Enough about Cawley! That's not going to happen. Do you understand me? That's not real. Something's wrong with you. You should be worrying about finding the girls before they're completely lost. And we stand a better chance of that apart. I'm going this way." He gestured into the trees.

"I can't let you do that." Brooke focused on the ground. She surveyed it inch by inch for a clue. She saw bear scat next to an uprooted stump. Bears would be slow and logy this time of year, heading into hibernation. Bears weren't the threat.

"No one's *letting* anyone do anything, Brooke," Milo said. "I'll see you in Buffalo Cross."

"Shh," Brooke said, holding up a hand. A short distance away, just visible in the increasing light of morning, was a dark heap at the base of a pine tree. The heap wasn't moving; still, Brooke crept toward it with the gun raised.

The boot heels at an awkward angle, the plaid fleece collar collecting snow.

Lorne was face down on the ground with three dark bullet holes through his coat. Brooke reached down to feel for a pulse. The stubbled skin of his throat was already cold.

"Damn it," she said.

"Is that—" Milo broke off.

The deputy had been shot in the back, at close range. The snow had covered all signs of the struggle except one: in a sheltered place below a thick-boughed spruce, Brooke found horse tracks angling north into the trees, toward the highway.

The hip holster where Lorne had worn his revolver was empty.

THEY RAN, SLOWING TO A WALK ONLY WHEN THEIR LUNGS BURNED AND THEN speeding up as soon as they could breathe again. By the time the snow stopped, they were clear of the forest, climbing through open hills where copses of pine stood like dark arrows against the white. They had come this way the day before, but snow had changed the landscape, and Brooke couldn't be sure these were the same hills.

Brooke stopped to take her bearings on a stretch of hillside where a boulder stood in the lea of a bald maple. It was an hour past dawn. There was a brighter patch behind the clouds off to the right: east. That meant they were walking north, as they should be, aiming for the highway. So where were the girls?

"There's someone on that ridge," Milo said.

Brooke turned. Across a wide lap of snow to the west was a

rocky spine that ran down the next hill all the way to the forest; on the ridge, moving south, was a mounted figure. They were too far to see the rider's face, but the horse was big—a draft horse with a pale coat.

Brooke crouched slowly, motioning to Milo to do the same.

"You think it's him?" Milo squinted across the hillside at the rider descending the ridge.

"It's not him," Brooke said. "It's her." She unslung her rifle and sighted. Too far.

She'd be exposed if she crossed the open hillside and came at Delia straight on. Brooke scanned the dark line of trees that curved along the base of the hill all the way to the opposite ridge. Something moved near the base of two tall hemlocks. A bit of red, a shape. A face—two faces.

"It's them!" Brooke gasped. Holly and Sal were right at the edge of the woods. They must have followed the swamp too far west. "There. Those two tall trees at the edge of the forest. See? Holly's red scarf. Can you see them?"

Milo climbed the boulder to get a better view. In a panic, Brooke remembered Delia on the ridge opposite. Before she could warn Milo down from the boulder, a shot split the air and he fell back on the ground.

"Milo!" Brooke dove to where he lay. "Where is it?" Even as she asked him, she could see the hole in his sleeve, blood beginning to stain the snow under his arm. She noted absently that the angle of the shot seemed wrong.

"Something hit me," Milo said, a puzzled look on his face.

"Stay down," Brooke said.

She twisted around. The girls had vanished: where she'd seen them, there were only trees.

No, no, no!

But of course they would have taken cover when they heard

the shot. Brooke marked the two tall hemlocks; she just had to find that spot and follow their trail. She glanced to the opposite ridge, empty now.

She turned quickly back to Milo and opened his jacket. The wound had clipped his forearm. There was an inch-wide crater of missing flesh, but it hadn't hit the bone, and the bleeding would stop with pressure. She noted again the angle of the shot, all wrong for Delia's position. Unzipping her coat, she tore a strip from her T-shirt, wrapped the fabric hastily above Milo's elbow, and yanked tight.

"Pack it with snow," she said. "Put pressure on it."

"Did someone shoot me?"

"Listen, Milo: the kids. If I don't come back, you have to get the kids."

"You're leaving me?"

"I'm going after them. If something happens—Do you understand? Get the kids if I don't come back. You saw where they were. Take them to Maxwell."

Milo tried to say something. Brooke turned away. There was no time. She shimmied away from the crest of the hill to avoid being seen and sprinted toward the woods. After thirty or forty yards, she crept back to look again.

The snowy slope was empty and trackless. Delia had not reappeared on the other ridge. She considered the direction of the shot that had hit Milo; it could only have come from the forest. There was someone else here: Cawley.

Brooke burst from her hiding place and ran, crossing the exposed flank of the hill in plain view. If he was in there, she needed to know where.

The first shot came in seconds, disappearing in a puff of snow a few feet ahead of her. Now she knew his position: this side of the hemlocks, at least a quarter mile closer than Holly and Sal. Brooke ran faster, making steadily for the trees. Two shots, three, four. A bullet grazed her pant leg, missing the flesh.

The shots stopped as she entered the forest and bent her path west toward Cawley. The snow muffled her footsteps, but it also made her unsure of the ground. Twice, she stumbled in an unexpected hole. Zero chance she'd get in a shot with the rifle before he heard her coming. And at this range, the revolver, quick to draw and to fire, would give him the advantage.

She came to a place where the ground was trampled: Cawley had shot from here, and then moved once Brooke reached the woods. Why?

The edge of the forest hid the hemlocks from here, but Cawley would have been able to see Delia. And Delia's trajectory would have sent her far to the other side of the hemlocks. It was possible that neither of them had seen the kids.

The stallion's hoofprints led into the trees. Cawley was luring Brooke in against the swamp, increasing his cover and shrinking her chances of escape while Delia boxed her in from behind.

If Brooke followed, it would mean abandoning Holly and Sal.

But if she went to Holly and Sal now, her trail through the snow would lead anyone else right to them.

For a moment, Brooke was still.

Milo knew where to look. Milo, whom she'd left bleeding and vulnerable in the snow. He just had to stay out of sight until it was safe. If he waited for Delia to pass down the ridge and into the woods before he went to the girls, he could get them to Buffalo Cross and away.

How would he explain why she'd left them?

That didn't matter. As long as he took them north while Brooke moved south, drawing the danger with her.

It felt so wrong to leave them, so unbearably wrong that Brooke moaned, folding in on herself. Their faces. The smell of their hair.

The smell of their hands. Their weight, as babies. As toddlers. Their voices. Their soft touch in the dark a thousand times, when they'd called out and she'd gone to them.

Grief dragged through her body as she thought of all the ways she should have been better, the kind of mother they deserved.

She could see no alternative.

She hoisted her rifle and stepped onto Cawley's trail.

11

THE STALLION'S HOOFPRINTS ENDED HALF A MILE IN, AT THE SWAMP. A LINE OF bent and leaning reeds showed where Cawley had ridden into re-flectionless black water, where Brooke could not follow. She stood looking out at the gray spurs that had once been trees. She would have to circuit the swamp to find Cawley's exit point, and all the while she would be ignorant of his position, whether he'd waded clear through to the other side or circled back to come at her from behind, whether he would go east or west.

One or the other, she told herself. *Just choose.*

Brooke turned east. If nothing else, she might lead Cawley and Delia that much farther from the children.

She kept the edge of the swamp in view, walking in the trees, where she'd have some chance of cover if Cawley came at her from the water. Some way along the broad belly of the swamp, she took note of a granite escarpment that slanted away into the forest. Hardly any snow had settled on the steep rock face. She passed it and, a hundred feet farther on, veered toward the swamp, stepping into the reeds until dark water seeped up in her footprints. Then she walked backwards along her own trail, weighting her steps onto her toes. When she got to the escarpment, she stepped sideways onto a lip of the bare rock.

Carefully, carefully, leaning against the granite with her fingertips, shaping her body so as not to slip and make a mark, Brooke edged her way along until she was well off her original trail. She dropped down into a recently trampled turkey run. A dozen or more birds had passed this way. She kept to their corridor of flattened snow, shuffling her steps roughly, hoping to disguise the direction of her passage from anyone who happened upon her boot prints among the turkeys' scratches.

She hadn't gone far when she became aware of far-off hoofbeats—a rhythm barely perceptible as sound, more felt through the soles of her feet than heard. She ducked into the crotch of a forked cedar and brought the barrel of her rifle up against her cheek, listening. In stillness, she was instantly colder. She tried to control her shivering enough that she could hear.

The horse was coming at a walk from the east. Wrong direction for Delia; it must be Cawley. He had left the swamp and was coming back around for her. Strange that he would announce his presence so plainly and give her the chance at a shot.

But the hoofbeats did not seem to get closer. He was passing north of her, some distance into the bush. She must have stumbled on him in the act of doubling back, before he knew her position.

Fearful of a trap but unwilling to let Cawley get out of reach, Brooke moved as quickly and silently as she could to intercept.

The bush here was healthy spruce and cedar; the snow had barely penetrated and the floor was clear of underbrush. Brooke advanced half-crouched toward the hoofbeats, slipping from one tree to the next like a shadow.

Suddenly, a heavy shape separated itself from the upper branches of a cedar to her left, falling and stumbling through the air until, as it came even with Brooke's head, it unfolded awkward wings and caught lift—a wild turkey, brown and bronze, the size of a piglet; as it ascended, the turkey flushed another from its roost, the two of them beating the air loudly, gaining their clumsy elevation. Brooke listened under their huffing for the sound of the horse and heard nothing. The rider had stopped.

She sank against the tree closest to her and hooked an index finger around the rifle trigger. No mercy now; things had gone too far wrong. If there had ever been another choice, Lorne had taken it from her. She had to be ready to kill Stephen Cawley this time.

A woman's voice spoke before Brooke could move. "I'll give you one chance, whoever you are, to come out with your hands up."

Brooke recognized the sheriff's weary tone.

"Maxwell?" she called out, surprised.

"Step out with your hands over your head. If I see a gun barrel, it's over."

Brooke gripped the rifle at its neck and lifted it overhead as she walked toward the voice. She could see Maxwell now, astride a dark chestnut horse that carried heavy saddlebags across its rump.

"It's just me," Brooke said.

"Place your gun on the ground and lie down over there," Maxwell said. "Over against the stump there."

"Why? What are you—" Brooke was twenty feet from the horse now and finally realized what she was looking at. It wasn't saddlebags slung over the chestnut's back. It was Lorne.

"This is your last warning, Mom."

"I tried to warn him," Brooke said. Maxwell still had the gun aimed at her. "Cawley's got his horse, and his revolver."

"Lorne was my nephew, not that it matters to you. He was a good person."

"It wasn't me," Brooke said, realizing what the sheriff was saying. "Cawley stole his gun and shot him with it."

"That man was tied."

"I don't know how he got loose. I wasn't there. Lorne came and found us and took him off me for the bounty," Brooke said, failing to keep the bitterness from her voice. "Is that the kind of good person he was?"

"Shut your mouth and lay your rifle down, right now."

"My kids—"

"Now!"

"They're alone out there!" Brooke shouted. "Cawley shot Milo!"

"Enough," Maxwell said, leveling her gun. "I warned you."

"For fuck's sake," Brooke said, leaning forward to lay the rifle down. "This is dangerous. I'm telling you, Cawley's out there and he's armed. Please, Sheriff."

Maxwell swung down from her horse, cracked Brooke's rifle, and emptied it of cartridges.

"Over there by the stump and face down, with your hands behind your back."

"What are you doing?"

"Goddamn it." Maxwell came at Brooke, shoving her hard in the chest, throwing her to the ground. "Just do what I tell you."

"My kids are out there, Sheriff!"

"Get over," Maxwell said, a hard scowl on her face. She stuck a boot under Brooke's ribs and tried to flip her onto her front, but Brooke twisted away.

"I swear, I'm not the one who killed your nephew."

"Quit flipping around if you don't want to get shot. I'm arresting you and taking you back to town."

Brooke turned slowly onto her stomach and put her hands behind her back.

"They're in danger," she tried again. "You don't understand."

Maxwell collected Brooke's rifle and strapped it with her own gun to the saddle. Then she approached, pulling old metal handcuffs out of a pocket. Brooke scanned the trees for Cawley. This was when he would attack, if he was watching—neither of them armed, one distracted and the other face down on the ground.

Brooke waited for her moment. She felt cold metal as Maxwell worked the first cuff around her left wrist, cinching it slowly. The sheriff was clumsy with the cuffs, as if she hadn't used them before. Tugging the second cuff toward Brooke's right wrist, she fumbled. Brooke moved fast, yanking her arms free and twisting under Maxwell to punch her in the ribs.

The sheriff's thick coat absorbed most of the hit. She grabbed the open cuff trailing from Brooke's left wrist and tried again to bring it around her right. Brooke kicked the sheriff's leg and pulled away, launching herself toward the horse. It shied out of Brooke's reach, and she felt Maxwell's full weight come down on her back.

"Let me go!" Brooke shouted, her face pressed into cedar needles and snow. Her chin ground painfully against the earth.

Maxwell drove her knee into the small of Brooke's back, preventing her from getting up. She gripped Brooke's uncuffed wrist and wrenched it toward the other one.

Brooke's right shoulder, weakened by its old injury, resisted for a brief moment. She felt it going, and then came the sickening pain. She screamed, vomit rising in her throat.

"What now?" Maxwell asked.

"You pulled my arm out of the socket," Brooke gasped.

"Pain in the ass," Maxwell said, dropping Brooke's dislocated arm without cuffing it. She hiked up her parka and removed the leather belt from her pants.

"What are you doing?"

"Breathe," Maxwell said, kneeling behind Brooke. "No more goddamn screaming."

Brooke breathed. With one expert motion, the sheriff pulled the shoulder forward, up, and back, setting it back in the joint.

Brooke was astonished. She had learned to set her shoulder herself, when she'd pulled it in the past, but it had never gone in that easily.

"Hold that," Maxwell said. Brooke obeyed, using her left hand to brace the numb and throbbing right shoulder while Maxwell ran her belt around Brooke's chest and strapped the injured arm firmly in place. It was more stable than a sling, Brooke realized; her right arm wouldn't move at all this way.

"Now get up," Maxwell said.

"Give me a minute."

"I said get up if you don't want me hauling on that arm again."

Brooke struggled to her knees and stood. The handcuffs still trailed from her left wrist. "I can't mount like this."

"You're not riding." Maxwell ran a rope through the empty cuff and tied it to her saddle horn. Then she climbed atop her horse, careful not to kick Lorne's limp body, and took up the reins.

The rope running from the saddle horn was short. As Maxwell started north, Brooke had no choice but to trot alongside.

Next to her, Lorne's booted feet jerked unnervingly as his body was rocked by the horse's rolling flanks. Brooke jogged to keep up, pain radiating through her shoulder with every step.

They left the forest. Out in the open, the landscape was empty and dull under muted noon light. They passed no one, and saw no tracks.

IN TOWN, SHERIFF MAXWELL LED BROOKE BACK TO THE CENTRAL SQUARE, WHERE she dismounted in front of the Legion. Brooke swayed on her feet, sapped from keeping up with Maxwell, her empty stomach cramping, fatigue graying everything, the cold penetrating deep into her bones. Only the throbbing in her shoulder—so severe now that each pulse felt like an electric shock—and her unrelenting terror about what was happening in the forest kept her from sleeping where she stood.

Maxwell climbed the Legion steps and knocked on the door. A man of about sixty answered. He was husky and red-faced, with an iron-gray walrus mustache. Taking in the heap on Maxwell's horse, the man held his stomach and appeared to shrink into his hulking frame, as if suddenly ill. The sheriff put a steadying hand on his arm. Brooke noticed that they had the same build, the same sloping shoulders and high, wide hips; their faces were similarly broad through the brow and cheekbones, stretched-looking, like pit bulls. A brother, Brooke thought. The deputy's father.

Maxwell and the man spoke. Brooke couldn't make out what they said. They embraced, the man shaking with suppressed sobs. Maxwell beat the man's back sharply a few times until he straightened and separated from her. His gaze fell on Brooke, hard and hateful. Her apprehension quickened. A town this size wouldn't keep a jail. They'd deal with their problems some other way.

The man descended the steps, unhooked her rope from the saddle horn, and let it fall to the snowy street.

"Come on." Maxwell was holding the door of the Legion open, gesturing for Brooke to come. As she climbed the steps, she expected any moment to feel a blow from behind, but none came. When she looked over her shoulder, she saw that the man had gathered up the horse's reins and was leading it, with its rocking cargo, out of the square.

Inside, the Legion hall was an open space with tables and chairs, a bar, and a staircase leading up to the second floor. Maxwell led Brooke to the bottom of the stairs and closed the empty handcuff around the handrail bracket.

"You have no right to do this," Brooke said. "I need my gun back. My kids are in danger."

Maxwell gave no sign of having heard her. She clattered around behind the bar and came back with a freezer bag of ice, which she laid between Brooke's injured shoulder and her coat. Then she left, locking the door behind her.

Brooke shivered violently now. The numbing ice eased some of the pain in her shoulder, but the rest of her was turning numb too; she had no feeling in her feet, and her hands were the blue-gray of a corpse, her thoughts sluggish. The early stages of hypothermia. She stamped her feet, trying to keep blood circulating.

Do something.

The handcuffs were steel. The handrail bracket was steel. The screws that anchored the bracket were stripped. She was chained like a dog to the wall.

She heard a high, thin whine, and realized it was her own voice: a pathetic animal sound escaping her throat.

"Stop," she snapped at herself. "Stop it."

She shivered. She stamped her feet. She waited.

BROOKE DIDN'T KNOW HOW MUCH TIME HAD PASSED WHEN SHE HEARD VOICES, footsteps, and a key in the lock. The windows were brighter. The sky must have cleared. The ice on her shoulder had melted and leaked out of its limp bag, soaking her coat and shirt.

The doors opened; against the double rectangle of light, Brooke saw Maxwell's tall form and another—slighter, so familiar.

"Milo," Brooke rasped, looking past him for Holly and Sal.

Maxwell and Milo came farther into the room and the doors swung closed behind them. They were alone. Milo met Brooke's eyes and looked away. He didn't have the girls.

"He came to my house," the sheriff said. "Looking for you."

"Let us go," Brooke said. "Please. You don't know what you're doing."

The sheriff pulled a chair away from one of the tables and settled Milo into it. Brooke saw now that another set of handcuffs hung from the wrist of his unshot arm. On the other side, the sleeve of his jacket had been removed and the wound bandaged neatly. "Can you reach down, here?" Maxwell asked as she straightened Milo's good arm and cuffed his wrist to the chair's chrome frame.

"At least look for the kids," Brooke begged. "We saw them in the forest. They've been out there for hours."

"I'll tell you the same thing I told your husband: your family is not my concern. My job is to protect this town. Right now that means finding whoever's to blame for what happened to Lorne."

"Cawley killed him," Brooke said, seizing on *finding* and *whoever*. In the forest, Maxwell had been certain that Brooke was responsible. "It was Cawley, and he's still out there."

"Does she ever shut up?" Maxwell asked Milo. She jingled the keys in her pocket as she headed for the door.

"They're children!" Brooke shouted.

The sheriff left, locking the door. Her footsteps echoed on the porch stairs outside and then faded across the square, into silence.

"I looked," Milo said. His voice was reedy, as if he'd shouted himself hoarse. "You didn't come back, so I looked, but I couldn't find them, just a trail. I followed it to town. I thought you must have them."

The pressure was building in Brooke's throat and she feared that awful sound would escape again. She needed to feel nothing. She tried to summon green trees, soft mist, but the calm place would not come.

"What happened, Brooke?" Milo asked. Gently. He could still be gentle with her.

She stared at the dusty floor, the chairs with their chrome legs blooming rust, the walls. Stale old pictures, plaques, and posters. Military portraits of long-dead legionnaires. The sovereign flag. Younger versions of Sheriff Maxwell and her brother laying a giant wreath. Memorials. Trophies.

"Brooke?"

The picture of the Warren River standoff wasn't among these relics. Maxwell had made it plain the Hollands were out of favor here, as everywhere. Brooke thought of Edmund expounding at the kitchen table, shouting above the refinery, banging his steering wheel. All his posturing, his theories, his blame. All for nothing.

"Brooke." Milo's voice was more insistent now. "Look at me."

She looked at Milo. She tried to feel the warmth of him across the cold room and only shivered harder. There was no more avoiding it.

She took a deep breath and told him.

12

BROOKE HAD ALWAYS LED MILO TO BELIEVE THAT HER BAD SHOULDER WAS THE result of a childhood fall. Now she explained that the accident had in fact happened just days before she arrived in Buxton, still healing and intending to stay no more than a season.

"Well, accident. I was thrown in front of a truck."

"What?" Milo said. "Who threw you in front of a truck?"

"My dad," Brooke answered simply.

After Delia survived Brooke and Anita's attack, she and Frank Jr. had stepped up their assault, taking the opportunity to recover some of their one-time territory. Callum was finally out of bed but could barely drive, let alone fight, and Anita was running the lab, so it had fallen to Brooke to keep the dealers in line. Twice, she had been shot at from passing trucks—the second time in broad daylight, right in town, where there was a ban on anyone other than militia volunteers carrying weapons.

Then, in the dregs of summer, Jay brought the news that Shaw Station had finally dropped the charge against Edmund. He was set to be released at one o'clock the next day. It was late in the evening when Jay arrived at the house, and by rare chance they were all there, eating an exhausted meal in the kitchen.

"Everyone goes," Emily said, laying her hands flat on the table. "He should see all of you when he comes through the door. Robin, you too. Everyone."

"It's too risky to all be in the same place," Brooke objected, glancing at Robin. Her anxiety had grown with each day that her brother didn't leave for the city. Now she worried they were out of time. "The Cawleys will try something."

"All the more reason," Emily said. "Let them fucking try."

"Rob and I can go on Star, then," Brooke offered, seizing on an idea. "So you have room for Daddy on the way home."

They'd lost two vehicles at the soap factory—Anita's shot-up hatchback abandoned and Edmund's truck still missing its windshield—leaving only Callum's truck. In the excuse to travel separately, Brooke saw an opening. That night, after Emily was in bed, she cornered Robin.

"It's got to be tomorrow," she said. "It'll only be harder once he's back."

"I know," Robin said, sounding younger than his fifteen years. "Can't you come too?" he asked again.

"Rob, what would I do in the city?"

"Anything," he said, grasping her arm. "You can do anything."

"You can e-mail me," Brooke said, squeezing his hand. Part of her wished he would go, just so she could stop bracing herself for the loss of him. "Tell me everything I'm missing."

In a backpack small enough not to invite questions, they stuffed clothes, a toothbrush, an old phone Robin could use to reach out to the kitsch dealer for help getting settled. His birth certificate was lost, if it had ever existed, and they couldn't ask Emily, so they packed the only official proof of Robin's existence they could find: a first grade report card from his last year of school. They tucked his money into a flat leather bag that would fit under his clothes.

The next morning, they rose early to leave the house. Only Emily was awake, feeding Aaron in his high chair.

"See you in a bit," Brooke said to her mother, herding Robin swiftly through the kitchen.

"One o'clock," Emily said groggily, reaching down for the cup Aaron had dropped on the floor.

Robin turned back at the threshold, but Brooke caught his hand and hauled him outside before Emily could see the sorrow in his expression.

Brooke saddled Star and they rode through the basswoods, passing beyond the Holland property without speaking. The only sounds as they wound through the hills were the thick-grown trees rustling around them, the high drone of summer insects, and Star's shoes on the road. They had discussed whether Robin should take Star with him, but agreed that it would be difficult to stable a horse in the city and she was better off staying with Brooke. Now, Robin rubbed Star's coat steadily as they rode, in a gesture of reassurance that Brooke suspected was as much for himself as for the horse.

They'd worked out the night before that Robin would go as far as Shaw Station with Brooke—if they arrived together, Brooke could claim to have had no knowledge of his plans—and once there, Robin would disappear. By following the river, he could move unseen to Highway 12, hitchhike to the interstate, and then carry on to the city. Brooke would be at the courthouse when the other Hollands arrived to meet Edmund. She would say Robin had gone to check the Internet, that he'd probably lost track of time, that he should be back any minute. Only later, when he was well out of reach, would she find his farewell note in her saddlebags.

It was noon when they stabled Star near the courthouse. This was where they were supposed to say goodbye, but looking at Robin standing next to Star, ghostly pale with his small backpack, Brooke relented.

"I've got an hour," she said. "I'll walk you to the river."

They followed the streets away from downtown, through industrial blocks that deteriorated into rubble reclaim lots.

"Don't let anyone see you," she told him for the fifth or sixth time. "And don't tell anyone your last name. Even in the city. Callum knows people."

"If you change your mind—" Robin started.

"Rob."

"*If* you change your mind. I'll e-mail you where I'm staying. You could still come."

Brooke smiled, hoping he would take this as assent.

As they neared the water, a footpath wove through late-summer grass that grew chest-high along the riverbank. They came out of the grass at a concrete boat landing. The river shone dully under a hot gray sky. The landing was empty, save for what Brooke took at first to be a sandy-colored boulder. Then the boulder rose, resolving into the texture of dirty cotton and a messy mop of hair. A boy was standing up from a crouch, holding a garter snake in his fist. He was blond, blue-eyed, younger than Robin, twelve or thirteen. The snake in his hand wriggled stiffly to be free.

"She was heading for the water," the boy said. "Garters can't swim, can they? It ain't a water snake."

"Careful," Robin said. "They make an oil when they're scared and it's the worst thing I ever smelled." Even as he said this, an acrid stink reached them, worse than bear bait and sewage combined. "You need turpentine to get that off."

"Damn it." The boy dropped the snake to the ground, where it uncurled and slithered into the long grass. "Go on and drown then, dumb baby."

Brooke had been so surprised by the sudden appearance of the boy that for a moment she'd forgotten what she and Robin were doing there. It must be almost one, she thought now.

But the younger boy had set off to follow the snake, and Robin was running after him like a little kid, the bag on his back bouncing.

"Come back!" Brooke shouted, trailing after them.

"Don't step on her," Robin called to the boy.

"You don't," the boy retorted.

They chased the snake's papery movement through the sedge, where only the swishing tips of the grass showed its passage, first parallel to the river, then bending into the reeds. Where the ground gave way to marshy shallows, Robin and the boy kicked their shoes off and hopped onto a broad rock that stood in the water beyond the reed bed.

Brooke knew she should be at the courthouse. But she found herself kicking off her sneakers and following Robin onto the rock. It was dark shale, burning hot from the sun. Brooke arched the tender middles of her feet away from the surface, the heat baking through her calluses.

"There!" the boy shouted, pointing off to the right, and they turned to see a snake swimming out from the reeds into open water, head up, body waving smoothly behind, making for the far bank.

"Did you see?" Robin asked Brooke, excited.

"I never knew they could do that," she said.

A sudden piercing wail came from the direction of downtown. It took Brooke a moment to identify Shaw Station's civil defense siren. She hadn't heard it since her school days, the drills against an armed federal incursion that had never come. These days, the siren was used mainly to call the volunteers to fires and other emergencies.

Brooke saw her alarm reflected in the boys' expressions, and then all three of them were hurrying back to the shore.

"Go." Brooke threw Robin's shoes at him, waving him away from her, in the direction of the highway.

"But what's happening?" he asked. "I can't leave now."

"Yes, you can."

The other boy had vanished. Robin didn't move. The siren wailed.

"They need me," Brooke said. "Please go, Rob. Please."

She turned and ran toward downtown, trying to forget the look of blank despair on Robin's face as she left him.

The defense siren was still howling as Brooke approached the courthouse, a broad gray stone building in the old downtown. Emily had parked Callum's truck right on the sidewalk, at the base of the courthouse steps. She sat on the passenger side with her arm hanging out the window, leaving the driver's seat free for Edmund. Callum and Anita stood lordly in the truck bed, ankle-deep in what looked like Robin's last run of cottage junk: a plaster garden nymph, a patio umbrella, a jumble of old-timey Western gear. Jay and several of their other dealers were there too, forming a small guard between the truck and the dozen volunteers who were circling, all camo pants and beefy arms, guns in the open.

As Brooke had feared, the Hollands weren't the only ones who'd come. Up the block was a huddle of teenagers—runners for the Cawleys, including two of Frank Jr.'s older sons. She stepped into the doorway of a building, out of sight. In the next moment, an e-bike cruised silently from behind the teenagers: Frank Jr., with his wife, Angeline. They glided to the curb and Frank Jr. propped the bike up on its stand.

With a hand shielding his eyes from the sun, Frank Jr. looked up the street, past the Hollands and the courthouse steps. Brooke followed his gaze and saw Delia coming from the other end of the block. She wore a fiberglass brace around one knee, and bandages were plastered down one arm from the collarbone to the wrist. The other arm, which wasn't bandaged, was maroon and leathery with healing burns.

"Shit, shit, shit," Brooke said. The others hadn't seen any of it yet. "Anita!" she shouted from her hiding place in the doorway.

Anita twisted around in the truck bed at the sound of her name. As she took in the Cawleys—Frank Jr. on one side, nearing

the courthouse steps with a reluctant-looking Angeline, and Delia approaching from the other side—her mouth twisted in what
could have been fury or excitement. Brooke knew it was both. She
watched Anita's hand move to hover over a suspicious bulky protru-
sion under her shirt.

At that moment, the courthouse door opened and Edmund
stepped out, alone. Brooke was struck by the sheer immensity of
him. After being separated from her father for weeks, there was
deep comfort, despite everything, in the promise of his protection.

Frank Jr. took advantage of the momentary distraction to make
a rush up the steps. Before anyone had a chance to react, he was
within striking distance of Edmund, and Brooke saw that he had a
six-inch knife in his hand. Frank Jr. darted in, feinted, and darted
again. Edmund must have been caught off guard, because there was
a small red stain on his shirt when Frank Jr. jumped back.

Anita let out a snarl of hatred and pulled the gun from under
her shirt. Callum bent in through the truck window, emerging with
an M4. The volunteers, red and puffy with indignation, moved in
closer, shouting warnings that were drowned out by the defense
siren.

Brooke needed to get to the truck. She swept the block for the
rest of the Cawleys. Angeline was moving haltingly nearer to her
husband, looking frequently behind her, as if waiting for someone.
Delia had almost reached the ring of volunteers. She made no effort
to conceal the chest holster worn over her T-shirt. Her hand was
already on her gun. The Cawley sons and their other dealers had
spread out along the street. Brooke, concealed in her doorway, had
no way through.

The volunteers swung around, unsure who to target. Anita was
aiming at Frank Jr., Callum at Delia. Emily was halfway out of the
truck, eyes fixed on her husband.

Now, Edmund held a hand up peaceably, waving his children's

guns down. Reluctantly, Anita and Callum obeyed. The blood on Edmund's shirt leached slowly outward, though he didn't seem to notice. He turned to Frank Jr. and, with startling velocity for someone so big, launched himself, catching Frank Jr.'s knife hand and slamming it into the steps. The knife skittered to the sidewalk, near the truck. As Frank Jr. scrambled to his feet, cradling a clearly broken wrist, Edmund aimed a short, sharp kick at his temple. Angeline cried out as Frank Jr. fell on his face.

For a moment, nothing happened. Edmund watched his fallen rival casually, as if waiting for him to stand up. Then he raised his boot high and brought it down with all his weight onto Frank Jr.'s skull. Brooke saw one arm jerk and fall limp. A dark stain spread over the seat of Frank Jr.'s pants. When Edmund stepped away, Brooke saw the side of Frank Jr.'s face crushed against the concrete step, blood and jelly running out of the place where his eye and nose should have been.

After that, everything happened at once. Anita and Callum jumped from the back of the truck, and Brooke saw Anita firing on Delia, who shot back from the cover of a statue in front of the courthouse. Emily and Callum abandoned the truck to chase down Frank Jr.'s sons. Edmund, still unarmed, charged the retreating volunteers, roaring like a bull. The siren wailed on.

From her doorway, Brooke saw Angeline Cawley standing still amid the chaos, staring at her husband's form on the steps. She wasn't alone now. At her side, clutching her arm, was the boy from the river, in his sand-colored T-shirt, his eyes wide. Snot and tears ran down his face as his mouth formed the word *Papa* over and over again.

Brooke stepped toward him involuntarily.

Angeline caught the movement and looked up. She screamed Delia's name, pointing at Brooke on the opposite sidewalk. Exposed, Brooke dashed across the street to crouch behind the truck with Anita.

Anita had her gun in one hand and Frank Jr.'s fallen knife in the other.

"You need something?" Anita shouted over the siren. "Here." She thrust Frank Jr.'s knife at Brooke.

Brooke had used a knife hunting, but never to fight. She pulled at the webbing the truck had in place of a tailgate, thinking there might be a cargo box, guns. Her hands were trembling and the webbing wouldn't undo. In frustration, she slashed it with the knife and the nylon straps fell down in ragged shreds. No cargo box, only Robin's unsold cottage stuff. Then Brooke's eye fell on the heap of Western memorabilia; under a billy can and a set of cowboy boot beer cozies, there was a coiled leather bullwhip that must have hung on someone's cottage wall.

"Oh, shit," Anita said. "Delia's running. Come on." She darted around to the truck's cab.

Brooke heard a scream on the other side of the truck. A boy's scream.

"Come on!" Anita shouted, honking impatiently.

The boy screamed again, in terror, or pain, or both.

Brooke pulled the bullwhip from the back of the truck and stepped out onto the sidewalk.

Edmund had the boy from the river by the neck and was punching him so hard it looked as if he intended to kill him. The boy's lip was torn clear down to his chin.

Before Brooke could think better of it, she drew the whip back and struck her father full in the face, striping his skin from cheek to cheek. Surprised, Edmund dropped his victim in the street. Brooke was peripherally aware of the boy scrambling away. She kept her eyes on her father.

"What did you do?" Edmund asked Brooke, touching his cheek. He sounded almost amused.

"You can't kill a child, Daddy. It don't matter who they are."

"It *doesn't* matter," Edmund corrected her. "Don't make your-self sound ignorant." Then he lifted her by the throat and she felt her head caught in his grip like a nail in a hammer claw, the weight of her body pulling her down.

An engine roared. In the corner of her eye, Brooke saw Callum's truck skid forward, the torn tailgate webbing dragging in the street behind it. Anita was driving with her gun out the window, her eyes on Delia, who was getting away up the block. As the truck made a wide U-turn in the street, Edmund threw Brooke hard, straight into its path.

"Daddy!" Brooke screamed as she hit the ground, rolling out of the truck's path just in time. Before she could stand, she was jerked backwards, one arm caught in the trailing webbing. She dropped the whip and tried to free herself, shouting, but Anita couldn't hear her. The truck accelerated. Brooke couldn't get hold of anything. In seconds, the pavement had shredded her T-shirt and peeled her raw up one side.

Brooke grabbed the grate of a sewer cover as it swept by underneath, but her other arm was still entangled, and she felt her shoulder twist too far, pulling out of its socket with a crunch. Pain exploded down her right side. She released the sewer grate and let herself be dragged up the block until, finally, the violent bouncing of the truck knocked her loose.

She lay still in the street, her vision sparking white with every pulse of the pain in her arm.

Edmund walked up to her, ignoring the gunshots around him as though he were bulletproof. Brooke thought he was coming to help her.

"You hit me," he said.

"My arm," Brooke said. The siren, still shrieking, swallowed her words.

"To protect that trash?" Edmund bent toward her.

Brooke gasped, barely able to breathe for the pain.

"I didn't raise any goddamn traitors. You ever try that again, you will live to regret it. Do you hear me? You're better than that bleeding-heart bullshit."

"Daddy," she said, summoning her voice. "I think you broke my arm."

"You broke your own fucking arm," he spat, and turned back to the fight, grabbing the fallen whip from the street as he went.

Brooke sat up, her dislocated shoulder hanging low from the socket. Anita and the truck had disappeared. There was shooting from several directions now as the fight expanded into side streets.

Brooke sat in the street, the siren splitting the air around her.

For protecting a child, her father had nearly killed her. She'd been Edmund's tool, his weapon, but one false step, and he'd dropped her like a broken thing. *Traitor.* She felt the slap of the word with bitter pleasure. The burden of her loyalty finally dissolved under his hand.

Movement across the street caught Brooke's eye. She looked up and saw Robin peeking from behind a dumpster. He had come back. As she spotted him, he emerged, flinching with every gunshot in the distance, running straight for Brooke.

Brooke struggled to her knees, nearly blinded by pain. "What are you doing here?" she panted. "You're supposed to be gone."

"I'm sorry," he said. "I couldn't."

"Never mind. It's fine. I'll go with you."

"Are you okay?" he asked.

The effort of getting to her feet increased Brooke's pain so much she couldn't speak. She nodded toward a narrow passage between buildings. With Robin supporting her, they made their way as quickly as Brooke could bear with her loose, dangling arm.

In the shadow of the alley, Brooke paused for breath. She looked Robin up and down. He was wearing his backpack. She reached out and felt his shirt. He still had his money.

"Good," she said. "We're leaving, Rob."

"Really?" Robin asked. "You'll come?"

"Yeah. Let's get Star and go."

The darkness between the buildings suddenly deepened. Brooke turned to see a form blocking the alley: Delia, standing crooked with her knee brace. Her gun was up, her eyes searching the gloom of the alley. Still dazzled by the glare of daylight from the street, she couldn't make them out, but in a few more seconds she would see them.

Brooke backed quietly away, pushing Robin behind her with her good arm. "Get Star," she whispered.

Delia moved to aim. Her gaze was focused squarely on them now. Robin froze, looking from Delia to Brooke and back again.

"Run!" Brooke screamed.

She lurched to the side, trying to shield Robin with her body, but in the same instant, he dove the other way. Delia fired. The force of the bullet knocked Robin into the air, and he fell on his back in the dust, a still heap.

Brooke reached out for him through the haze of pain from her shoulder.

A second shot startled her and she stumbled and fell. An explosion of pain as her shoulder hit hard pavement, and then nothing.

When she came to, it was eerily quiet.

Brooke looked around her. Robin was gone. Painfully, she crawled to the place where he'd fallen. There was blood, but not much. It was possible he had survived. Brooke got to her feet and hobbled from the alley. Her road rash was as bad as the shoulder now, burning and prickling, the cuts packed with dust and tiny rocks.

The street was empty except for two volunteers, looking in the other direction.

Brooke went straight to the stables. Her last words to Robin had been to get Star. That's where he would wait for her if he'd gotten out of the alley alive. She brushed aside the nagging question of what would have compelled him to leave her in the alley.

Brooke found Star in the stables, a bit jumpy but otherwise fine. There was no sign that Robin had been there. Brooke scoured the building—a converted car wash—as if she might find him hiding somewhere, but the place was empty.

If Robin had made it out of the alley on his own, Brooke was sure he would have come here. If he hadn't come here, that meant someone else had taken him from the alley. And only one person other than Brooke had seen him fall.

Brooke's breath became shallow.

She pictured Robin by the river with his shoes in his hands, unwilling to leave her. The desolation in his face when she'd turned to go.

He'd been so close to getting away.

Brooke closed her eyes. The calm place was waiting for her. And, as if Robin were somehow helping her, the fog that closed around her this time was deeper, thicker—an emptiness and a quiet that erased everything else.

She went north for the simple reason that, if Robin had lived, they would have gone south. It took her and Star three days to reach Buxton.

After that, and for a long time, Milo and the kids and the farm were everything. Her first lie, telling Milo she had no family, had been a simple knee-jerk deflection, the same thing she would have told anyone. Later, when she should have told him the truth, it was harder. The lie had become an aspiration: Brooke had tied the past off tight so it might choke, and wither, and fall away, leaving nothing for her to miss, only an absence she could not describe.

AS BROOKE SPOKE, THE LIGHT IN THE WINDOWS OF THE LEGION HALL TURNED rosy. The sun was setting. Wherever Holly and Sal were, the temperature was dropping.

Milo listened to her chronicle, his expression unreadable.

"Brooke Holland?" he said when she was done. Curiously, as if testing it.

"Yes."

"So Stephen Cawley, he was the boy your father—"

"Yes."

"Did you know all along?" he asked, then shook his head. "Of course you did. His name was on the warrant. You knew from the beginning he was looking for you. That's why you were so sure there would be others."

Brooke nodded weakly.

"The rider we saw?"

"Delia," she croaked. She stopped to clear her dry throat. "I saw her in one of the rooms upstairs when we were here before."

"That's why you wanted to leave."

Brooke nodded again.

"I don't get it. Is it just revenge they're after?"

"Yes."

"What if they find the kids?"

"They'll take them," she whispered, closing her eyes for a moment. She wanted to disappear. She forced herself to open her eyes and look at him. "I don't know what they might . . . They might kill them."

Milo's face flashed a look of shock and disgust. Then he was on his feet, dragging his chair to the locked door.

"Sheriff!" he shouted, kicking the door. "Someone!"

"No one's going to come," Brooke said.

"Do something!" He lifted the chair with his cuffed hand and swung it against the door's window panel. It glanced away from the safety glass with a dull thump. "How can you just sit there?"

"I'm handcuffed to the wall."

"They're just kids, Brooke. They don't have anything to do

with the Cawleys. Why would anyone hurt them? They don't even know about this. They don't even know who you are."

"I'm still me," she said.

"You're a stranger."

Brooke inhaled sharply. There it was: Milo would cut her out of their lives like a bruise from fruit.

"Did you tell Maxwell?" he asked.

"No. She already thinks I killed her nephew."

"But if she knows the whole story—"

"She'll never let us go if she finds out who I am. You heard her yesterday." *I don't want anything to do with those animals.*

Milo sank back onto his chair, defeated. "Why didn't you tell me?"

"Isn't it obvious?" she asked, feeling a twitch of resentment for Milo, with his good job and his good mum.

"I gave up everything for you, Brooke. Just because you asked me to. You didn't think I deserved to know who you were?"

"That's not it," Brooke said. She was uncomfortably aware of the corrections he must already be making, reevaluating everything he felt about her, all their years together.

"They might have come for you any day in the last fifteen years. How could you put Holly and Sal in danger like that?"

"I thought they were safe," Brooke said, knowing as she said it that it wasn't true. "And I didn't want you to know who I . . . who I . . ."

"You should have at least told me when Cawley came. I knew something wasn't right. I asked you so many times, Brooke. Why didn't you tell me?"

"I needed you to—" She broke off, realizing her mistake too late.

"What? What were you going to say?"

"I didn't mean it."

"You needed me to cooperate? Follow instructions? I'm an adult, Brooke. I'm supposed to be your partner."

"You are, but, Milo, we were in danger. I couldn't risk it."

"You don't respect me at all, do you?"

"Yes, I do," she said, frustrated. "I love you, Milo."

"That's not love, Brooke. That's not how you treat someone you love."

"I was trying to protect you and the girls."

"Really? By taking us to Shaw Station? Right into the middle of it?"

Brooke felt her temper rise. "Okay, I needed you to cooperate," she said. "So what? What if I had told you Cawley was there to kill us, that his entire family was chasing us? How would you have saved us?"

"How much worse could I have done?" Milo asked, leaning toward her.

Brooke kicked her boot loose, sending it flying into the side of his face.

Milo fell back. His lip was bleeding. He looked at her like he'd never seen her before.

13

IT WAS FULL DARK WHEN SHERIFF MAXWELL RETURNED TO THE LEGION BEHIND the needling white light of a headlamp.

"Same as I left them," Maxwell said. The headlamp swung away for a moment as she addressed someone coming through the door behind her, and Brooke had a glimpse of the tall, heavyset man with the walrus mustache, the one who had led Lorne's body away. Then the headlamp shone in Brooke's eyes again and abruptly went out.

Brooke blinked away the afterimage. She could hear someone moving around behind the bar. Something heavy slid across wood; there was the ring of glass, a scratch and pop. She smelled sulfur, kerosene. Then a cloth wick sparked as it caught. Against the thin flame of an oil lamp, Brooke watched the man's thick fingers twist a delicate metal wheel to adjust the wick, then lower the glass bell into its brass fitting. A warm yellow glow expanded, lighting their corner of the room and the face of the man behind the bar, who stared at Brooke with a righteous anger she knew all too well.

Maxwell settled herself into a chair that squeaked under her weight.

"So?" Brooke asked. "What are you going to do with us?"

"I want to know what happened," Maxwell said. "Then I'll decide what to do."

"I told you what happened," Brooke said. "Stephen Cawley killed your deputy."

"How?" Maxwell asked, arms crossed. "He was tied and unarmed."

"When I had him, he was. Then Lorne came and took him off me. I don't know what happened after that."

"Bullshit," the man behind the bar said. His voice was a low rumble, almost comically deep.

"This is Cliven Davey," Maxwell said. "Lorne's father."

"Lorne rode out there to help you people," Davey said.

"He wanted the money," Brooke said.

"No!" Davey brought a fist down on the bar, causing the light to flare.

"He lost his son, Brooke," Milo interjected, leaning forward in his chair.

"Lorne was a good man," Davey said, composing himself. There was something rehearsed in his posture, Brooke thought. The hands outspread on the bar, the jaw under the mustache clenched. "Whoever killed him is going to die for it," he said. "I've got the right, Lynn agrees."

It was as Brooke had thought. Summary justice.

"Lorne took Cawley off me at gunpoint," Brooke said evenly. "I told him not to keep Cawley that close. I warned him. He wouldn't listen. Milo and I found him this morning, around dawn. He'd been dead for hours already, and there were hoofprints headed north."

"Why should we believe you?" Maxwell asked.

"Who do you think shot Milo?" Brooke asked. "Was that me, too? You saw his wound, and Lorne's. They were both shot by a revolver, weren't they?"

Maxwell shifted in her chair and Brooke knew she'd guessed right. The sheriff had already concluded that they weren't rifle wounds.

"If Cawley killed Lorne and shot your husband, where is he now?" Davey asked accusingly.

"How should I know? I haven't even seen Cawley since Lorne showed up. After he shot Milo, I followed his trail as far as the swamp. I might have him by now if Maxwell hadn't attacked me. And now, the longer you keep us here, the longer our kids are out there with him."

"How'd Cawley get the kids off you, if you never saw him?" Davey asked.

"He didn't take the kids," Milo said. "They ran away."

"Ran away?" Maxwell drew her brows together. "Why?"

"None of your business," Brooke snapped, flushing. "They're on their own, and Cawley's out there with your deputy's horse and his gun—"

"I've heard enough, Lynn," Davey said. "I can believe Cawley murdered Lorne. These folks aren't killers. They probably got mixed up in something over their heads."

"We don't know that, Cliven," Maxwell said. "We don't know what part they played."

"You said yourself this guy and Lorne were both shot by a 9mm and she only had a .22 rifle."

"That's not proof. They could have taken Lorne's weapon and stashed it." But Brooke heard a note of concession in Maxwell's tone. The sheriff might not trust them, but she was eager to get shed of the inconvenience posed by prisoners.

"I don't want to lose any more time," Davey said. "I've got to leave tonight if I'm going to catch his trail before there's more snow."

"I can bring Cawley in for you," Brooke spoke up. "Just give me my gun, and a horse—"

"You're not in a bargaining position," Maxwell cut her off.

"I don't want him brought," Davey pronounced. "I'm not after any fed bounty. That piece of garbage will be the one to pay for what he did. Just tell me where you lost his trail."

"You've never seen him," Brooke said. "You won't recognize him. I can take you to him. I can identify him."

"You're hurt," Davey said, dubious. "You won't be able to keep my pace."

"I'll manage," Brooke said. "Give me a horse to find my kids, and I'll make sure you get Cawley."

"Both of us," Milo said. "We'll both go."

"Be careful, Cliven," Maxwell said. "You don't know these people."

Brooke saw Davey considering it.

"No one's taking Cawley to the feds," he warned them. "You can say goodbye to that money."

"We just want our kids back," Milo said.

"All right," Davey said, squaring his shoulders. "No one else should have to lose a child. God knows that."

BROOKE AND MILO FOLLOWED ON FOOT THROUGH CURVING RESIDENTIAL BLOCKS as Sheriff Maxwell and Cliven Davey rode ahead on chestnut horses so similar-looking they might also have been siblings.

Milo had neither spoken to nor looked at Brooke since they left the Legion. Now he turned to her. "Don't antagonize these people," he said. "They're helping us."

"I didn't antagonize them."

"Davey was ready to kill us; now he's lending us horses, so try to act grateful."

"Davey's an ass," Brooke scoffed. She'd met men of his sort before, all ego, no spine.

"That doesn't matter. We made a deal. Just cooperate with him. Don't challenge him. Let him feel like he's in charge."

Brooke snorted in disbelief, but Milo just walked ahead, leaving her to gape at no one.

They stopped at a brick home on a corner lot. A wind chime pinged, strung from the eaves by wire. Davey hauled up the door of a double-car garage and turned on an overhead light. He and Maxwell led the twin chestnuts inside, where two more horses—a gray gelding and a roan—were penned between well-stocked utility shelves.

They settled the horses and Davey rapped on an inner door. There was the sound of a deadbolt sliding. A young woman opened the door, looking frightened. She was small and pretty, with just-brushed, shining hair, and she gave off a strong smell of perfume. Brooke took her to be Davey's daughter until she turned her face up for a kiss.

"Come in, come in," the woman said when she saw Brooke and Milo. She gestured them through a gleaming kitchen to a sectional sofa in the adjoining living room. Davey's wife—Brooke swore she heard the woman introduce herself as Chlorine—must have been his second. She was too young to be Lorne's mother; if anything, she looked younger than the deputy.

"I'm going to be away a couple days," Davey told Chlorine solemnly, standing with hands on hips as if addressing a crowd. "These folks are coming with me to try and recover their children. We'll need all three horses. I think you should stay with Lynn until I get back."

Brooke thought she saw a slight wince from Maxwell at this, quickly covered by a nod.

"Cliven's the protective sort," Chlorine smiled shakily at Brooke and Milo.

"You pack us some food," Davey said, turning to rummage in a closet.

"Do you folks take mustard in your sandwiches?" Chlorine asked, moving into the kitchen. "I wish there was fresh bread. That whole wheat kind gets so crumbly when it's more than a day old. It's better if you can toast it. Now, I wouldn't be surprised if Cliven can toast bread on that camp stove of his. It's a marvel what he does with it. Last time we were out hunting, he made me blueberry pancakes! Can you believe it? Blueberry! I hope you'll remind him to eat properly. Lord knows he won't take much rest, he pushes himself so hard."

"It's not a pleasure cruise, honey," Davey said from the closet.

"Still," Chlorine said. Brooke noticed a jumpiness to her movements as she filled the cooler bag. "I don't like you leaving in the night like this, Cliven, without any sleep. It isn't healthy. If Lorne hadn't taken the thermos, I could send you hot coffee for the morning, at least. He was in such a hurry, he just grabbed things on his way out. It keeps things warm longer than you'd think, that thermos! Lynn, I don't suppose he still had it with him? You know the one. Bright green?"

"Be quiet," Maxwell said. "You're acting stupid."

"I'm only trying to help," Chlorine said, her voice quivering.

"Lynn," Davey rebuked.

"Well, god, Cliven. A thermos?"

"Just trying to help," Chlorine said again, sniffing quietly over the sandwich bread.

Davey emerged from the closet with a heavily loaded duffel bag. As he sorted through its contents, Brooke saw a naphtha stove, a small axe, a solar filter. He lifted out a binoculars case that bore a night vision logo, followed by a pair of Teflon shooting grips. Brooke recalled Emily once referring to grips like those as "princess paws."

"You need all that?" she asked, incredulous. When Milo shot her a warning glance, she muttered to him under her breath, "This is taking forever."

"I picked most of it up at military surplus," Davey said proudly. "Same stuff the special forces use overseas."

Chlorine zipped closed the cooler bag and came to the sofa with a basket of tortilla chips. Brooke reached hungrily for a handful.

"Lynn told me that man has your daughters," Chlorine said, perching next to Brooke on the sofa. "I can't imagine—"

"Turns out they just ran away," Maxwell cut in. "Domestic matter, doesn't concern us."

"Oh!" Chlorine held a hand over her heart. "How old are they?"

"Holly's thirteen and Sal's eight," Milo said.

"You're so lucky to have girls!" Chlorine exclaimed, laying a hand on Brooke's knee. "You know what they say: 'A son's a son until he takes a wife, but a daughter's a friend for all your life.'"

"I never heard that," Brooke said, jerking her knee away.

"Where are you folks from, anyway?" Chlorine asked, casting a sideways glance at Milo.

"Buxton," Brooke said, knowing that wasn't what Chlorine meant. She'd heard some version of this question every time Milo met someone new.

"But before that?" Chlorine's gaze was more pointed this time.

"My mum was from the city," Milo answered genially.

"Ah." Chlorine nodded, as if this explained everything. She winked at Brooke. "Your children must be just beautiful. I love mixed babies."

"Do you like them frozen?" Brooke asked, squeezing her tortilla chip so tightly it exploded in a shower of crumbs. She glared irritably at Davey, who was still fussing over his gear. "They've been outside in wet clothes for eighteen hours."

"We only packed one change for them," Milo explained to Chlorine.

"Oh!" Chlorine jumped up. "But Cliven has things left from

when Lorne was little! Would they wear boy things? I know how girls can be with their favorite colors and whatnot."

"Anything would be great." Milo smiled. "Thank you. They won't mind."

Soon Chlorine had pulled plastic bins out of the basement, from which she put together a bag of outerwear to fit Holly and Sal. There was a parka of Lorne's for Milo to wear, and an old snowmobile suit of Chlorine's for Brooke.

Finally, Davey was ready. Outside, Maxwell had saddled the gray gelding and the roan, adding an extra strap to both saddle horns to help Brooke and Milo mount with their injuries.

"Take care of yourself," Chlorine said, embracing Davey. "Don't do anything crazy."

"When have I ever?" he answered in his gravelly baritone. "You sit tight with Lynn till I come home."

Maxwell clasped hands briefly with her brother and gave his horse a pat, but she did not bid them goodbye or good luck, just watched them leave, much as she'd done a day and a half earlier, with her deputy by her side.

14

THE NIGHT WAS CLEAR, BRIGHT WITH STARS AND A FULL MOON. THE TOP LAYER
of snow had melted in the afternoon sun and then frozen again
when the temperature dropped after sunset, leaving a paper-thin
crust of ice coating the surface. The horses' hooves punched cleanly
through, each hoofmark outlined as if cut from glass.

Brooke's shoulder jarred with the gelding's steps. The injury
had gotten worse with each successive dislocation over the years,
and the joint was looser than ever now, more liable to fail. She'd
strapped the rifle on the left side of her saddle; she'd never be able
to lift it, let alone fire, with her right arm. If they found Cawley or
Delia before the girls—or worse, if Cawley and Delia already *had*
the girls—her only option would be a one-armed rifle shot. Left-
handed. In the dark.

They stopped a short distance outside town, where a set of
tracks met the highway from the south: a messy trench through the
snow, clearly visible under the moon.

"That's you," Brooke told Milo, recognizing his gait. "You said
you followed tracks back to town?" She turned to Davey. "If we
retrace his steps, we'll be close to the spot where I saw Cawley. I can
find it from there."

"Hold tight," Davey said, dismounting with his night vision goggles. "I'll take a look."

Brooke twitched her reins with impatience.

"Whose trail was I following, if it wasn't yours?" Milo asked Brooke.

From the gelding's back, Brooke studied the snow. Milo's steps had obscured whatever trail he'd been following almost entirely. Still, she thought she could see something underneath, a separate rhythm.

"Was the trail definitely made by feet?" she asked.

"I thought so," Milo said. "I thought it was you and the girls."

"The drag is straighter with a horse," Brooke said. "Longer."

Milo furrowed his brow in concentration. "They did seem long compared to my tracks, I guess. So it couldn't have been someone walking?"

Brooke shook her head. "And you're positive it led toward town, not away from it?"

Milo threw up his hands in exasperation.

"There would be scatter," Brooke prompted. "Each stride is scooped, like a wave; it's higher on one side. Where the foot steps forward, a bit of snow scatters."

"I don't know," Milo said. "Everything had melted a bit. There might have been little shallow spots, on the higher places."

"Which side of the steps were the shallow bits on? North or south?"

"South, I think."

"Aha!" crowed Davey. He was standing next to a guardrail post, bent double with his goggles. In the lea of the post, Brooke saw a single hoofprint, confirming what Milo had just described to her plainly enough: the trail he'd followed to Buffalo Cross wasn't made by someone walking in front of him, but by a rider who had already passed in the opposite direction, heading for the woods.

"Probably Lynn," Davey said, gratified by his find.

"Right," Brooke said, holding back her irritation. The massive hoofprint didn't belong to Maxwell's chestnut. It could only have been made by a draft horse. "Regardless, Milo's trail comes from the place we're looking for, so can we carry on?"

Davey issued a derisive exhale that riffled his mustache, and led the way off the road.

They followed the trail. Thin shreds of cloud passed like smoke over the moon. Twice, Brooke thought she'd found the slope down to the hemlocks where she'd seen Holly and Sal, only to watch the landscape twist as she passed through it—the forest too small, the hill too steep, the trees wrong.

Finally, as the trail descended a rocky ridge, Milo's tracks branched left, across the open slope, leaving the draft horse's trail clear and open down the ridge ahead of them.

Brooke's pulse beat faster. She searched the horizon. The trees were so dark against the wash of stars they looked like they'd been cut out of the sky. Yes, there: to the east, in the lowest lap of the hillside, two tall hemlocks leaning together. The girls had been right there, before they'd hidden when they heard the shots. Any clues to where they were now would begin there.

"I know where we are, Davey," Brooke said. "Right before Milo was shot, I saw the kids down there, at the edge of the forest. I remember the trees."

"You remember the trees from the day," Davey said, with a mollifying tilt of his head. "Things will tend to look different in the dark."

"Cawley's trail is that way too. This is the place."

"All right," Davey said grimly. "Show me, then."

Brooke led them toward the hemlocks. At the trees, she held her right arm against her chest and gripped tight to the extra saddle strap with her left, making to lower herself down.

"No need," Davey said, swinging to the ground ahead of her.

"This is where the kids were," Brooke objected. "I need to look for their tracks."

"Let me see what the ground has to say," he said, hefting his goggles.

"Don't," Brooke said, dismounting with difficulty. There was no light here, the moon blocked by the edge of the forest; it would be difficult enough to see anything without Davey blundering over the ground.

"What do you mean, 'Don't'?"

"It's not a pissing contest, Davey. I know their tracks. Let me look."

"Excuse me? I'm looking for your children's tracks right now. How about a little gratitude? *Pissing contest.*"

"Easy, Brooke," Milo said. "We know you're worried about the kids. Cliven understands that. It's natural she wants to see their tracks, Cliven."

"She can't be flying into hysterics all the time," Davey said with misgiving. It was exactly as Milo had predicted, Brooke realized. Davey would help only if he was in control.

"I'm sorry," Brooke said through gritted teeth. "I just want one quick look. I'll be careful."

"Make sure that you are," Davey consented, arms crossed. "I can't have you disturbing the ground or there won't be anything to see."

As Brooke moved under the trees, she felt Davey watching her, waiting to have his expertise called on. If there was ever a justification for night vision goggles, this darkness under the trees was it. Nonetheless, Brooke kept her back to him, resting her gaze on the dark bole of a tree trunk until her eyes adjusted fully to the shadows so she could see the ground.

There it was. Snow had drifted over their footprints in places, and the melt and subsequent freeze had rounded the edges, but there was no mistaking it. Brooke thought the trail was fifteen hours old.

From the hemlocks, it led back into the woods, clear as a freight train. The kids had no sense of how to cover their tracks; Brooke had never taught them.

"Southeast," she said, remounting the gelding painfully. "They must have seen me coming after Milo was shot, and tried to find me in the forest."

"Hold up," Davey said, sweeping the ground with his goggles to confirm what she'd found. "We don't know this is going to take us to Cawley's trail."

"It will." Brooke hauled her horse around to follow the girls' trail. "He could have them by now. Let's go!"

Milo cleared his throat and made a gesture of caution behind Davey's back.

"If you agree," Brooke said, gripping the reins until her fingernails dug into her palms. It took every bit of willpower she had to stay still.

Davey sat, huffing like a bull. Brooke counted out the seconds in her head. He would go, she was sure—he wanted Cawley—but he would make her wait.

Fine, Brooke thought. As soon as they had Holly and Sal, she and Milo would make a run for it. If Davey wanted to believe that Brooke was weak, that her purposes came second to his, that she would help him get to Cawley before she carried her own children to safety, or even that he would get his horses back at the end of this, fine. Brooke thought of the grasping deputy riding smugly to his death. If Cliven Davey believed that Brooke and Milo would leave their children in danger one single second longer than they had to, he wasn't any kind of father.

A QUARTER MILE INTO THE WOODS, HOLLY AND SAL'S TRAIL MERGED WITH another: Cawley, mounted, and Brooke on foot, following. Davey led, demolishing the traces of the girls' footsteps. Brooke was quiet, careful not to show him up again. If she kept the gelding to one side and a little behind, she found she could glimpse the ground before he trampled it.

At a break in the canopy where moonlight beamed down on the snow, Brooke scrutinized the melted edges of Holly's boot print inside her own. The girls had not been far behind her. Maybe less than an hour. Had they called out for her? Could she have missed that?

As they rode, Milo drew Davey into conversation, asking questions about the woods, hunting, his tracking equipment. Brooke noticed that the more Davey talked, the less attention he paid to the trail. He was also starting to sound dozy now. It must be well past midnight.

They ate Chlorine's sandwiches on horseback as they pushed deeper and deeper into the woods, where scant patches of moonlight penetrated the trees. Wind knocked in bare branches. Owls sent up their chilly calls. Davey fell out of the lead, muttering something about the trail being obvious enough, and then began to lag behind. He was twice their age, Brooke considered, probably used to early nights and a warm bed, being babied by Chlorine.

When Davey halted so that he could pee under a tree, Brooke brought her horse up close to Milo's and whispered, "The trail's going to split ahead. Cawley took the swamp, but the girls will have followed me east. If Davey wants to follow Cawley, we can't go with him."

"Just take off?" Milo looked doubtful. "He won't go for that. But he's getting pretty sleepy, and he's not as good a tracker as you. Even I can see that. He might miss the split."

"If we're lucky," Brooke said, ashamed of how much this small praise from Milo cheered her. "But if it comes to making a run for it, be ready."

Milo moved apart from her as Davey returned to his horse, and they continued on the trail. The moment, when it came, proved easier than Brooke had feared. By the time they reached the swamp, Davey's eyes were watering from fatigue and he was completely unaware that the stallion's tracks had disappeared into the water as Brooke turned them east.

They moved through the cedars. Brooke watched the ground. No other hoofprints appeared. No indication that Cawley or Delia had found the girls' trail.

They reached the place where Brooke had veered into the swamp and doubled back to lose her pursuers. Now, she read the consequences of that choice on the ground all around her: a desperate jumble of footprints. Holly and Sal had followed Brooke's false trail into the reeds, and there they'd lost her. They'd tried one way and then another, their confused trampling returning again and again to the place where her footsteps vanished.

"It's kicked up an awful lot here," Davey observed with a yawn. "Some kind of scuffle?"

"It must be where—" Brooke grasped for words, crushed by what she'd done.

"Where Maxwell found you?" Milo suggested.

"Right," Brooke said. Never mind the obvious absence of hoofprints leading to this place or away from it. Davey had stopped even trying to read the ground.

There was a flattened patch where Holly and Sal had stopped to rest. They would have been delirious with exhaustion, freezing in their wet clothes. But they had kept moving eventually: one trail resolved from the flattened spot, carrying on southeast, following the bend of the swamp.

"Cawley won't find much that way," Davey said, falling into step behind Brooke. He was more asleep than awake now. "Probably trying to avoid the highway. Knows what's coming for him."

"Why this way?" Milo whispered, when Davey had fallen far

enough behind for Brooke to explain what had happened. "If they lost your trail, why wouldn't they just go back the way they came?"

"I don't know," Brooke answered. "They're lost. They don't know which way anything is."

"No . . ." Milo knitted his brows. "That's not right. That hunting blind is next to this swamp."

"So?"

"We always told them, if we got separated, to go back to the last place we were together."

"You think they're looking for the blind?"

"You know Holly. She wouldn't quit until she came up with something. She would have a plan."

It was true. After a while, only the larger set of prints showed, the heel prints deeper than they had been before. Brooke's heart lurched: Holly was carrying her sister.

THE MOON SET AND THE STARS FADED AHEAD OF THE DAWN. DAVEY SNIFFED awake and fell asleep again every few minutes, but his horse followed the other two faithfully. Brooke and Milo passed a jar of Chlorine's cold coffee back and forth between them. They had left the forest and the swamp behind. If Holly was looking for the hunting blind, she had missed it. In the dark, it would have been easy to lose the branching and uneven edge of the swamp.

The trail now followed a shallow gully through tufty flatland. They were gaining on the girls; the trail here was only eight or ten hours old.

The snow lightened to ash and then glowed blue with oncoming daybreak. Suddenly, without warning, the footprints that had carried on for so many miles with astonishing endurance turned abruptly aside into a tangle of bushes. Another flattened patch, tucked under a shelf of juniper. The girls had hidden here.

"Something scared them," Brooke said. But when she and Milo looked around for the continuation of the trail, they couldn't find it.

"They can't have just disappeared," Milo said.

"Up here," Davey called sleepily. He had ambled on, half-awake, when they stopped to examine the girls' hiding place, and now he gestured to them from a dozen yards up the gully.

Brooke and Milo rode to meet him. He was standing in a horse trail.

"What?" said Brooke, disbelieving. "Whose are these?"

"Cawley's, of course," Davey scoffed, still unaware that they had ever left Cawley's trail.

"But the girls . . ." Milo looked back at the juniper bush.

Brooke dismounted to examine the prints. They could be Cawley's. They looked like the ones she'd followed to the swamp the day before. Brooke tried to gauge the timing of his passage. There were flat, hexagonal snow crystals in the stallion's prints. Brooke hadn't noticed any of those in the girls' trail.

"They missed him," she said with relief. "The kids were here later than Cawley. Not much. Less than an hour, maybe."

"How do you figure that?" Davey asked, skeptical.

But Brooke wasn't listening. Mixed in with the smaller, more delicate steps of the stallion, she had noticed the plate-sized hoofprints of a draft horse, and there were none of the hexagonal flakes in them. Brooke dropped from the saddle and crouched, peering closely at the ground. Where one of the massive prints overlaid the stallion's, it was clear that the first trail had already been frozen: a splinter of ice stood up from the stallion's print where the larger hoof had crushed it.

"Another rider was here after Cawley," Brooke said with a sinking feeling. "Close to the same time as the kids."

"Two riders?" Davey sounded annoyed now. "Where are you getting all this?"

"The prints are completely different sizes," Brooke said, heedless of her tone. "The second one's a draft horse."

"I think she's right," Milo said. "They look different to me."

"Well, now, it could be," Davey said, grinding his eyes between a thumb and forefinger. "That burned-up woman at the Legion. She had a draft horse."

"That's what scared them," Brooke thought aloud. "Holly and Sal were here after Cawley, but then De—the second rider showed up and they hid."

"I forgot all about her," Davey said. "Damn it, I'll bet she's after that bounty. She cleared out quick enough when she heard about Cawley passing through."

"She was here the same time as the kids," Brooke repeated, her voice rising with anxiety.

"Then where are the kids?" Milo blanched. "What happened to their tracks?"

"Maybe she gave them a ride to the highway," Davey said. "That horse of hers could carry an adult and two kids easy."

Brooke turned to hide her face. Holly and Sal had no way of knowing who Delia was. They would have climbed up willingly, glad for warmth and a rest from walking.

She thought of Robin in the alley, lying where he fell. Then she pitched forward and vomited the little that was in her stomach.

"We don't know for sure it's her," Milo said, reaching down from his horse to touch Brooke's back. "Not really."

Brooke stared up at him mutely, feeling the warmth of his hand, letting the din fade in her ears.

"What's the issue?" Davey asked. "You ought to be glad. They'll be warmer on a horse. Plus, the extra weight will slow that woman down. Now let's get a move on. She's not getting Cawley if I can help it."

Brooke stood, wiping her mouth. The kids' footprints were gone. It was the only trail they had.

They rode fast through the morning and into the afternoon. The distance between them and their quarry began to shrink. Cawley and Delia had each been on the trail a full day longer than they had, and it showed, with the draft horse losing speed faster than the stallion—slowed, perhaps, by extra riders.

Their only sign of the girls came when Brooke's eye caught a spot of blue a few yards off the side of the trail.

"It must have blown over there," she said, retrieving Sal's hair elastic, crusted in snow. The ground she had plucked it from was scoured by gusts, as if a small whirlwind had passed over it.

Milo reached out to take the small blue band from Brooke. He looped it around his thumb, without speaking.

They reached Highway 12 with a few hours of daylight left. Surprisingly, a truck had passed by on the road, the asphalt still black where snow had melted under the tires. It could be anyone, Brooke told herself; it could be the marshals. Or, she thought with disquiet, it could be the rest of the Cawleys, reconvening in force on the other side of the river.

Brooke was closer to home than she'd planned ever to get. The highway here ran southwest through open prairie all the way to the Warren River bridge. But Cawley and Delia had not taken the highway. Their tracks crossed straight over the road, continuing south with the constancy of a compass needle, heading for the Shaw County hills that were now just visible on the horizon.

When Brooke moved to follow the trail, Davey stopped her. "Let's take the road," he said.

"What? No. We'll lose them."

"Cawley can't get farther than the Warren that way. Highway 12's the only crossing for fifty miles. He'll have to come back to the bridge. If we go this way, we can cut him off before that woman catches up to him. I didn't come all this way just to let some nobody take Stephen Cawley to the damn feds."

"He won't come back to the bridge," Brooke said.

"Of course he will."

"He'll swim."

"In this temperature?" Davey laughed. "Not a chance."

"Go ahead and take the road if you want to," Brooke said. "I'm not losing the trail."

"You'll go where I say." Davey puffed his chest out. "Those are my horses."

"Guys," Milo said with a tired sigh. "We're on the same side. Calm down."

"Listen," Brooke said, holding Milo's eye, "I know what I'm talking about. The only way we're going to find the girls before they're in some gunned-up compound in Shaw County is to follow these tracks right now."

"What compound?" Davey demanded, looking from Brooke to Milo. "What are you talking about?"

Milo stared out at the highway, the trail, the hills, wrestling with what to do. "Okay," he said finally. "I'm with you."

"You're not taking my horses," Davey growled, moving a hand to his gun.

"What are you going to do?" Brooke asked. "You shoot horse thieves in Buffalo Cross like you shoot killers?"

"I'd be within my rights," Davey said, but she could hear the bluster behind his words. He wouldn't shoot her.

"We have to get to the kids, Cliven," Milo said reasonably. "If Brooke's right, and we take the highway now, we'll lose them. If she's wrong, at least we'll still be on the right trail."

"And if that bounty hunter gets anywhere near Cawley before we do, your kids could end up in the middle of a firefight," Davey argued.

But Brooke didn't stay to hear any more. She turned her back on the highway and dug her heels into the gelding's ribs. She heard Milo's roan close on her heels. Behind them, Davey cursed once, and again, louder, and then the steady beat of his mare's hoofbeats joined their own.

THEY REACHED THE RIVER AS THE SETTING SUN DIPPED BEHIND A BANK OF ADvancing clouds. The trail led straight into the water, and a line of hoofprints was just visible leading up the far bank.

Milo nodded to himself and began rolling up his pant legs with a look of dour determination. He and Brooke had swum horses in the flooded bogs during cranberry harvest enough times to appreciate how cold this crossing would be.

"My horses have never swum," Davey said. "I don't think they'll do it. Not in weather like this."

"They'll do it," Brooke said, lifting one foot in front of her to unlace her boot.

"I doubt Lorne's stallion would have crossed the river," Davey said, ignoring the clear evidence that the stallion had done just that.

"Come on," Brooke said, moving to the other boot. "We're going across."

"I'm telling you, these horses won't swim. We should follow the riverbank back to the bridge. We should have just stayed on the highway in the first place like I told you. We'd be way ahead. That woman's going to get the jump on us now."

"It would take hours to go around, Davey. Which of these horses is likeliest to swim?"

"Chevy here," he said, indicating his chestnut mare. "But listen to me. I'm telling you we could all drown."

"Then Chevy should go first. Let me take her across. The others will go when they see her do it."

"You're not taking Chevy."

"If your horses can't swim, Davey, I'm guessing you can't either."

"Like hell I can't." Davey rode to the edge of the water. "Come on, Chevy. Show her, girl."

"Take your boots off, at least," Brooke called after him, stuffing her own boots inside her snowmobile suit.

Davey stood Chevy on the bank and bent down with difficulty to remove his boots. The long ride was telling on him, or he was stalling. He balled his socks up and stuffed them down in the heels of his boots, tied the laces together, and hung them around his neck. He rolled his jeans up to the knee. Finally, he walked Chevy into the shallows. The horse waded up to her thighs and balked. Davey talked her farther in, but there was fear in his voice and the horse nickered nervously.

"Shit," Brooke said, seeing what was coming.

Milo had his boots off. He met Brooke's eye and, together, they advanced into the shallows.

Davey was twenty feet ahead of them. Brooke saw Chevy lose footing as the river bottom deepened. For a moment, the mare swam forward on instinct, but then Davey gripped her reins too tight in his anxiety, forcing her muzzle down into the water, where she inhaled a nose full of cold water.

Brooke spoke softly to the gelding, urging him forward, forgetting for a moment that it wasn't Star's familiar coat under her hands. The gelding swam poorly, casting and jerking once they moved beyond sure footing. With difficulty, Brooke steered him into the deeper water after Davey, who was in the middle of the channel now, clinging to a panicked Chevy, wrapping himself low against her neck, trying not to get thrown. Both horse and rider stood a better chance if Brooke could separate them. The mare would swim fine on her own, and if Davey cooperated, Brooke could tow him. But Brooke saw that it would be pointless trying to coax Davey off the security of his horse's back, so she brought the gelding around in front and, gripping with her knees, reached her good arm out to grab Chevy's bridle. She'd have to lead them both across.

Chevy calmed when she felt Brooke's grip, but only for a moment. Davey was too high on her neck. The mare tossed her head back again and again as she tried to throw her rider, and got dragged farther down in the process. Her hooves slashed the water. If Brooke couldn't keep her own horse clear of the striking hooves, it, too, would lose faith and begin to panic. Brooke was on the point of giving up and letting Davey founder when she felt a change in the tension on Chevy's bridle. Milo had swum the roan around the other side of Davey and taken hold of the flailing horse.

"We got you," Milo said. There was something strange about his voice; it was too low. Then Brooke realized he was imitating Davey's baritone, the pitch Chevy knew and trusted. He murmured continuously, maintaining the falsely deep pitch, as he and Brooke pulled, urging the three horses onward. "It's going to be fine. We're going across together now."

Chevy snorted, stretching her neck forward under Davey's weight, and swam. Between them, Brooke and Milo pulled the half-suffocated horse forward. A sandbar stuck out into the river on the far side. As soon as the horses' hooves felt solid ground under them, they ran up the bank, shaking their manes and puffing out their cheeks.

Brooke shoved her boots back on hastily and jumped down from the gelding, hopping in place to get warm as the adrenaline left her body.

"Thank you," she said as Milo got down from the roan. "You were great."

Milo nodded, teeth chattering. He took her reins and led their two horses downriver to a weedy maple, out of the wind. A stiff breeze was rising, carrying with it the taste of snow.

Davey was pale. He didn't look at either of them, just rubbed his mare's neck. "Good girl," he said in his low rumble. "Good girl, Chevy. You're okay. You did it."

"There's more snow coming," Brooke said. The stallion's hoof-prints led up the bank, stamped clearly into the mud. "I don't want to lose the trail."

"These horses need rest," Davey said, meeting her gaze with barely concealed hatred. "I won't let you drive them to death."

"Ten minutes, then," she said coldly, and followed Milo down-river to where he'd tied the horses, leaving Davey to nurse his outrage.

To the south, the land rose in a steep range of hills, thickly forested with green so deep it was almost black. Ever since the highway, Brooke had watched those hills get closer. Now they had crossed into Shaw County. She was home.

She'd spent fifteen years less than a hundred miles from here, yet it had felt like another world. Was it inevitable that she would come back? Was there some kind of compulsion in her blood?

Wind brushed her face, smelling of wet earth, pine pitch, new snow. She shivered inside Chlorine's snowmobile suit.

"Brooke," Milo said, as she got near. "Look at this."

He pointed to a set of hoofprints Brooke hadn't noticed, lead-ing out of the water farther downriver: recent, clear, big as plates. The draft horse, bigger and heavier, must have traveled faster in the current and come out separately from the stallion.

Troubled that she had missed these tracks herself but eager for a sign of the girls, Brooke followed the massive hoofprints up the bank with Milo. At an outcropping of limestone, the snow had been brushed away and the ground trampled. Someone had sat here, and there were the dusty leavings of a feedbag.

"What are you looking for?" Milo asked.

"She stopped long enough to feed her horse," Brooke said, crouching to examine the ground. "She would have let the kids down. Their footprints should be here, but I only see hers."

"Then they must have stayed on the horse," Milo said.

"No," Brooke said, rubbing her eyes, willing herself to see. If she wasn't so tired, the marks in the mud would make more sense, but her skull felt compressed by exhaustion. "She's been riding that horse hard for two days, and then a swim in cold water—she wouldn't have left the kids on the horse while she was resting it."

"But we haven't seen their footprints since she picked them up," Milo said, "so they were with her when she went *into* the river."

They looked at each other.

"The river," Brooke said.

They hurried downstream. The light was failing fast now. They squinted through the gathering gloom at every rock and deadhead log on the shore. Twice, Brooke splashed into the shallows to examine a splash of color that could have been a sodden red scarf: a clutch of wet leaves, an old plastic bag.

"The current isn't fast enough to carry anything this far," she said after they'd been looking much longer than the ten minutes she'd given Davey. "We would have seen something by now."

"Where are they?" Milo asked, his eyes twitching frantically over the dark water.

Snow began to fall, gently and then harder, swirling around their faces.

"Maybe I was wrong," Brooke said, trying to believe it. "Maybe Delia kept them on the horse. Or maybe she moved them to Cawley's horse somewhere back there and I didn't realize."

"Where are they?" Milo repeated the question as if he hadn't heard her. He grabbed her arm. "You know how to do this, Brooke. You must know where to look. You have to know."

"I don't," Brooke said, feeling the truth of it. "Either I'm so tired I'm missing things, or there's nothing to see. We'll have to just keep following the trail, or else go back and look again, or . . . I don't know."

Snowflakes swarmed between them as if they were alive: falling, swinging out to the side, rising up, falling again to be swallowed by the river.

"We have to do something," Milo said. "Get help, a phone, something. We can't give up. I'm going to go get the horses."

He turned and set off upriver. Brooke followed, her heart heavy in her chest. The snow was falling so thickly now that she lost sight of Milo ahead of her.

"Milo?" she called.

Just as she thought she could make out his form—a different darkness through the snow—she sensed something move at her back. Pulse quickening, she raised her rifle one-handed.

A shotgun cocked, close to her ear.

"Stay still," a woman's voice said.

Brooke froze. The voice was familiar, snaking out of the past, taking shape. She shifted her weight to the left foot, finding a position from which she could quickly drop and spin.

"Your only way out of this is to set the gun down."

Brooke lowered a knee, laid the gun down in front of her without letting go.

"Now step away."

"All right," Brooke said, unsnapping the safety and bracing her shoulder, preparing to twist and strike up with the butt of the rifle.

"Don't block my sight," the woman said. "You think I don't know that trick?"

Brooke hesitated, confused, memories clamoring.

"Stand down." Davey's deep voice interrupted her thought. Brooke peered up through the screen of her hair. She could just see him through the snow. He'd come up more quietly than she would have given him credit for.

"Why are you following me?" the woman snarled behind Brooke. That voice. It was so familiar, but it wasn't Delia's.

"Ma'am," Davey said, "if you're traveling with a man by the name of Stephen Cawley, you better offer him up if you value your life."

"Cawley?" the woman echoed. Now Brooke twisted around to look up at her. Her face was hard to make out in the dark and the snow, through a screen of pale hair whipping wildly in the wind, but Brooke was no longer in any doubt.

"He's not with her, Davey," Brooke said, straightening up, her heart hammering in her chest.

She was older, thinner, somehow shorter than Brooke remembered, but it was her. She peered at Brooke through the snow, lowering the shotgun.

"It's me," Brooke said.

"Step closer."

Brooke did as she was told. Snow flew into her eyes.

They were face to face now.

"Brooke," Emily breathed.

"Yes, Mama."

"That's impossible."

"No, Mama."

"But you died."

"I didn't die, Mama."

"Goddamn," Emily choked. "Goddammit."

15

THE STORM HAD WHIPPED ITSELF INTO A BLIZZARD. EMILY LED THEM INTO THE hills on her draft horse, barely visible through squalls of white. Their urgent need for shelter had kept conversation by the river mercifully brief. After a long, disbelieving moment, in which unasked questions hung as thick as the flying snow between them, Brooke and Emily had seemed to reach a tacit agreement to start with the more immediate question of survival. All of them, human and horse, were wet and chilled; if they didn't get out of the storm soon, they would freeze.

"Strange coincidence, her turning out to be your mother," Davey had muttered darkly.

It was indeed strange. Emily, who belonged to the past, was here, diminished by time, yet still so much the same, familiar beyond words.

Brooke's tired mind adjusted her understanding, piece by piece, of what had happened since they first reached Buffalo Cross. It must have been Emily, not Delia, that Brooke had seen through the window of the Legion. Emily they'd spotted on the ridge before Milo was shot. Emily's tracks that had followed Cawley's through the gully and all the way to the river.

But Emily hadn't seen any children, much less carried them. She'd picked up Cawley's trail on the far side of the swamp, she said, and chased him all the way to the Warren. The previous evening at dusk, in a dry creek bed, she'd gotten close enough to catch sight of him. She'd taken a shot, but missed.

"A rocky gully?" Brooke pressed. "Open country all around it? Twenty miles north of here?"

Emily nodded. "Coward rode faster, rather than turn and fight. He outstripped me after that."

"That's where we lost their trail," Milo said. "Your shot must have been what scared them."

"I wasn't shooting at *them*," Emily said. "I wouldn't have hurt them."

"They couldn't know that, could they?" Milo asked tersely. His usually friendly manner was strained—influenced, Brooke imagined, by everything he'd learned about Emily so recently. "So they weren't with you, but we know they came this way. The hair tie was miles past that."

Brooke's mind ran in circles, crazed with not knowing. Even if she did know where to look, and she could get the horses away from Davey, and the horses could be driven past exhaustion, there would be nothing to find. The snow was piling up so fast that any tracks would disappear within an hour. Their only option was to take shelter with Emily and wait out the storm.

"Guardrails," Emily called out from the front of the line as the path rose sharply. Brooke slowed the gelding so he could lift his forelegs over the steel cables. They had met the hill road. In one direction lay the federal outpost, Highway 12, and Shaw Station; in the other, her childhood home. Brooke squinted into the trees, trying to guess how close they were to the Holland property, but she struggled to see anything through the snow, and what she could see was overgrown beyond recognition. Emily, on the other hand, navigated with no apparent need for sight, following each curve and twist of the road without hesitation.

They climbed higher into the hills. Snow fell steadily, and the wind drove.

Brooke tried to steel herself. Somewhere through the storm waited Edmund, Anita, Callum—all of them except Robin—along with the questions that had been held in temporary abeyance by the weather. *Traitor.* Brooke remembered Edmund's hand around her throat, how she'd hung in his grip.

She wasn't a child anymore, running scared. She'd built her own life and her own family, on her own terms, since she left. As long as there was still any chance of recovering that life, she told herself, shivering, neither Edmund Holland nor anyone else was going to take it from her.

When, after an hour, Emily's horse turned off the road, Brooke didn't recognize the driveway at first. The fence had fallen—rebar posts stood out of the snow, their barbed wire slouching down like cobwebs. No cameras, no defense. Just a rotted-out doghouse.

Brooke followed her mother with an increasing sense of dissociation; it was the same and not the same. Like Emily, everything seemed to have shrunk. The driveway was shorter than Brooke remembered; much sooner than she expected, they emerged from the basswoods into the yard. Darkness and falling snow hid the buildings, so Brooke didn't see the drive shed until it was right in front of her, gaping quiet and cold.

Milo and Davey caught up to them as Emily dismounted. A motion-sensor light on the drive shed flicked on, illuminating whirling snow in front of the doorway.

Brooke dropped down from the gelding and followed her mother into the building. The long, vaulted shed had once housed half a dozen vehicles; none remained. Emily led the draft horse to a rough stall that had been rigged at one end of the yawning space.

Brooke watched with disbelief as her mother loosened the horse's tackle, undid its girth strap, and removed the saddle. Emily had sneered when Brooke and Robin bought Star. *Walking steak*, she had called the foal. It was Emily who'd insisted on branding Star, like she was one of their diesel drums.

A clatter of hooves announced Milo and Davey behind them.

"This place is a dump," Davey said, looking around the drive shed with distaste.

Emily answered him with a flat look, clapping her gloves together to free them of snow.

When no one else spoke, Davey grabbed the reins from Brooke and Milo and pulled his three horses into a sheltered corner, behind a row of rusted old gas cannisters. "Wait," he said, suddenly rigid. "These drums are marked with an *H*. You're Hollands."

"Yeah?" Brooke and Emily answered at the same time.

Davey turned toward them, chest puffed out, mustache trembling. Brooke watched his face redden as he pieced it together. "This is all a drug war? Lorne's dead over *chalk*?"

"Cool it, Davey," Brooke said. "What difference does it make now?"

"Lorne was decent, if you even know what that means. His life *mattered*."

"I don't know who the hell Lorne is," Emily said, currying her horse down with a rubber brush. "But you want to watch your mouth if you plan to stay here."

"To hell with that. I'm finished with you people. I'm going after Cawley as soon as the snow stops," Davey said. "Alone."

"We need your horses to find the kids," Milo objected.

"Forget it. I've done enough. Hell of a lot more than you deserve."

"I can pay you for the horses," Emily said. She threw a dusty blanket over her horse and closed its stall.

"Pay me with what?" Davey asked snidely. "It doesn't look like chalk has made you too rich."

"I have better than cash," Emily said, waving Davey quiet with one hand, the same simple gesture of authority that had kept four children in line. "You take the first watch and I'll spell you off in a few hours. There's a heater in the corner. Brooke, with me." She didn't address Milo. Brooke was aware that her mother had scarcely acknowledged him since they were introduced at the river.

Brooke and Milo left Davey grumbling and followed Emily out of the drive shed. As they forded through shin-deep drifts toward the house, objects emerged unexpectedly from the darkness, confounding Brooke's sense of direction. Past another pile of rusted diesel drums was the garden—so much closer than she remembered—and the weathered old scarecrow, still leaning, the folds of its faded shirt filling with snow. Brooke peered at it, stepping closer. Reaching out, she pulled the scarecrow's stuffed body toward her. The pitchfork listed over and the fabric parted as easily as tissue, sending its stuffing of wood chips and softened newspaper down over the snow. Brooke unfolded the scrap of cloth in her hand. By the light from the drive shed, she could see what it was they'd stuck up there like a ghost: the old sovereign flag T-shirt that had been Edmund's and then Robin's, worn thin with wear. Brooke shoved the cloth in her pocket and moved past the fallen scarecrow toward the house, preparing to face her family.

As the willow tree next to the house came into view, Brooke saw that it had withered, its fullness gone. And the house itself, she realized, feeling suddenly off balance, was impossibly small, beyond what memory could distort. Only the kitchen, and her parents' bedroom above it, remained. Where the other half of the house should have been, there was nothing.

"Mama," Brooke said, stopping short. The snow in front of the door was bare and unbroken, the woodshed under the eaves nearly empty, the windows dark. "What happened to the house? Where is everyone?"

"You don't know?" Emily spoke lightly, but Brooke heard the dangerous edge underneath. Her mother said nothing else, but climbed the porch and pushed open the door, letting snow spill in over the threshold. A light came on inside the kitchen.

Brooke looked at Milo beside her. "I think this was a mistake," she said.

"We're here now," he said, taking Brooke's arm and drawing her forward. "Might as well go in."

Emily ignored them as she made a fire in the cookstove and then lifted a trapdoor to descend into the root cellar. Milo busied himself hanging his and Brooke's wet things over the stove, casting curious glances around the room. Brooke, feeling unsteady, passed through the kitchen and climbed the stairs to the landing. The house had been built into the hillside, with the kitchen low on the slope, under the willow, and the other rooms above. From the broad landing where Brooke stood, the stairs split: one way led to her parents' room over the kitchen; the other had led to a hallway and the rest of the house—her and her siblings' bedrooms, the living room, the utility room—but now, on that side of the landing, the stairs ended in an opaque sheet of plastic that billowed and slapped in the wind, brushed by pelting snow. Brooke shivered in a draft.

Emily emerged from the root cellar with a dusty jar of something orange, and bent gingerly to lower the trapdoor back into place.

Emily was sixty, Brooke calculated. Her brown hair had gone gray, and then yellowed to the color Ash's old eyes mistook for blond. Her face was lined and dappled by sunspots. She moved with the same strength and agility, though more slowly, as if bearing a greater weight than the quart jar of preserves in her hand. And there were the burns that had made Brooke so certain the woman at the Legion must be Delia. Shiny scrawls traversed Emily's hands, forearms, and face, where they had never been before.

"What happened?" Brooke asked again.

Emily sat down at the table, wiping dust from the jar with her sleeve. "Here," she said. "If you're hungry."

"Where is everyone, Mama?" Brooke stayed where she was on the landing. "Where's the rest of the house?"

"They burned it," Emily said. "Years ago."

"The Cawleys?"

"Who else?" Emily unscrewed the metal ring on the preserves and pried up the rubber seal. "You know," she said with a hollow laugh, "I'm still getting used to the idea you're not dead. Robin *saw* Delia kill you."

"Wait." Brooke's heart banged in her chest. "Robin's alive?"

"There was no body when we went back to get you. Robin kept saying you could have made it somehow, but you never came home, no word, nothing. And you would have come home, wouldn't you?" Emily held Brooke's eye with a hard look.

"Where is he?" Brooke asked. Her heart kept hammering. He was alive. Robin was alive.

"Gone," Emily said, scraping the underside of the lid against the open jar. "Left for the city a few years ago. Took Anita's kids with him, said it was for their own good. I haven't heard from him since. Who'd have thought he'd be the one to survive? He was more help than I would have expected, I'll say that. But he still left."

"What kids?" Brooke asked, confused.

"Anita's girl and boy. They'd be nine and ten now."

"Nine and ten," Brooke echoed. "Then where's Anita?"

Emily sighed wearily. She set the jar down on the table and pushed it away from her. "It was a fucking mess, Brooke," she said. "Delia should have quit the business after Frank Jr. died, but she wouldn't. Kept on trying to fight. The feds got involved. Callum wanted to be done with it. He went after her. He thought he was paying them back for you, on top of it. You'd been gone years by then. Anyway, he didn't make it. Died of gunshot wounds."

"But he was getting better," Brooke said stupidly. Callum couldn't be dead. Aaron fatherless so young. She lowered herself unsteadily to sit on the landing.

"Anita ambushed the lot of them after that," Emily continued. "She had a good plan, smart, caught them at their compound early in the morning and took down a bunch of them. I caught up with Angeline myself a few months later. Just luck; I saw her in town. That should have been the end of it. But then they came and burned this place. Anita died in the fire. She threw the kids out the window, but the roof fell in before she could jump. I tried to get to her, but Robin pulled me out."

"Anita?" Brooke asked, her voice barely audible.

"Edmund went after Frank Jr. and Angeline's sons with Aaron, the night of the fire. Aaron got hit. Edmund was trying to get him in the truck when Stephen Cawley shot your daddy clean in the head. Just like that. Aaron drove himself back here. Lived just long enough to tell me what happened."

"Not Aaron, Mama. Aaron was a toddler."

"He was eleven, and he idolized Edmund. He would have ridden into hell itself to stay near him."

Brooke couldn't comprehend it. Edmund, Anita, Callum, a half-grown Aaron she'd never even known . . .

She was reminded incongruously of the first time she'd driven Anita's hatchback, an automatic transmission, after having learned on a standard: her foot plunging after a clutch that wasn't there, hand swiping for a nonexistent gear shift.

They were all gone.

"Aaron shouldn't have been there, Mama," Brooke said. "He was eleven?"

"Shut your traitor's mouth, Brooke!" Emily whirled on her daughter. "*You* should have been there. If it had been you with Edmund that night instead of a goddamn child, he would have survived. Now I hear you had Stephen Cawley and you *lost* him? Why didn't you shoot him?"

Brooke wondered if she would have shot Cawley if she'd known how much he had taken from her. She looked at Milo, standing next to the stove. He returned her gaze, and she saw there was sympathy in his eyes.

"I'm not like that anymore," Brooke said.

"I can see that," Emily said with disgust.

Brooke hung her head.

Green woods, gray mist. Nothing came.

She felt footsteps on the stairs and then Milo was sitting next to her on the landing. He had something, she saw: the framed picture from the Warren. He had taken it down from its nail next to the stove. He handed it to her wordlessly.

"Who's this mutt you've dragged home, anyway?" Emily asked, watching Brooke and Milo beadily. "Your father wouldn't have let one of them in the house."

"Oh, Mama," Brooke said, feeling sick. Nothing had changed. The better part of their family murdered, and Emily would hold on to her hatred as if life depended on it. As if Milo was some kind of affront. As if killing Cawley would bring any of them back.

"Is this you?" Milo asked Brooke, pointing at the image of her three-year-old self. He had tensed at Emily's words but did nothing to acknowledge them.

Brooke nodded, grateful and embarrassed.

"You look like Holly at that age," Milo said.

"Holly." Emily turned the name over in her mouth. "That's one of your girls? I would have thought they'd come out dark. Ethnic genes usually show through."

"Stop it, Mama," Brooke said, gripping the picture frame harder.

"It's a simple fact."

"Why do you even care?"

"Your father would care."

"Well, he's not here, is he?"

"No," Emily whispered, and Brooke was amazed to hear her mother's voice thickened by tears. Emily had never cried, not once.

"Holly looks like you, too, actually," Milo said. A stiff, conciliatory offering that Emily didn't deserve.

"I'm sorry, Milo," Brooke said. She handed the picture back to him. She couldn't see the resemblance to Holly. "I thought I could keep them safe. I was trying to protect them, but I only put them in worse danger."

"Life is danger," Emily said, with a sad smile, spinning the jar of preserves slowly on the table in front of her. "You think you can protect them, but you can't. Trust me."

EMILY MADE HERSELF UP BLANKETS NEXT TO THE STOVE, PLANNING TO SWITCH with Davey halfway through the night. Brooke and Milo left her to her hateful thoughts and climbed the stairs to the bedroom. Out the upstairs window, Brooke could see a light still shining in the drive shed, where Davey kept watch.

She climbed into the bed beside Milo. The blankets smelled like they always had: dust and wood chips and lavender soap.

The loss of Callum and Anita and Aaron hurt like a hole in her chest. The revelation that Robin was alive was a deep and unexpected comfort, but even if she could tell him how sorry she was for leaving him behind, she felt certain he would never be able to forgive her—what could his life have been like here, without her, watching the rest of their family die?

The only one she couldn't find it in her to miss was Edmund. Knowing he was gone from the earth, relief dwarfed every other feeling. It was like a muscle loosening that she hadn't realized was tensed all these years.

She rolled toward Milo on the bed and felt him twist to look at her. She put her hand under his shirt, reaching up to the springy hair of his chest, needing his warmth, the smell of him, heat and salt, his soft touch.

But the hand that grabbed hers through his shirt wasn't soft. He held her like a spider in a tissue. She froze. Milo, who had loved her, had always forgiven her—he knew the truth now, and it must be sinking in, as she'd feared it would. *You're Hollands*, Davey had said, as if even the name tasted foul.

Brooke shrank back, but when she moved to withdraw her hand, Milo didn't let go. He turned, sinking his face into her hair, his hand holding her injured shoulder still while he pulled himself against her, awkward with his own hurt arm. He kissed her, and there was roughness behind it, and feeling. Brooke could have cried with relief. Desire came, full and ready, and she let it, kissing him back, her good arm around his shoulders, hand running down to the small of his back, drawing him to her, turning to meet his body with hers, kicking the covers down.

They held their voices in, each swallowing the other's breath, desperate. If everything around them was absence and imbalance and mistakes, there was still this, touch speeding on desire, the heat explosive, somehow contained to the outline of their bodies.

Brooke had expected to lie awake, eaten by images of Holly and Sal cold and alone for another night. With Milo's warm hand on her chest, anchoring her to the earth, she felt fatigue overtaking her.

On the edge of sleep, she heard Milo whisper, "I miss them so much, Brooke. I don't think I can stand it."

"No," she murmured. "Me neither."

Her dreams were dark, and she forgot them later.

16

BROOKE COULDN'T TELL AT FIRST WHAT HAD WOKEN HER. IT WAS STILL NIGHT.
Milo snored softly next to her. A golden-orange glow lit the window. As sleep thinned, Brooke became aware of a familiar smell. She struggled upright against leaden fatigue, hoping she was still dreaming.

She staggered to the window, one leg asleep and caving under her.

Outside, the drive shed was burning, flames rising fifty feet into the night sky.

"Wake up," Brooke croaked to Milo, searching for her clothes on the floor. "They're here."

She pulled her pants on as she hurried downstairs. Davey was stretched out under blankets next to the stove. Brooke must have slept through the handoff with Emily; no guessing what time it was. She kicked him as she passed. "Get your gun," she called, grabbing her rifle from the counter.

Brooke threw open the kitchen door. Across the yard, the drive shed was engulfed in fire. There was a steady rushing sound, like water falling through a burst dam. A single figure moved against the glow—Emily.

Brooke scanned the darkness around the fire, trying to figure out which direction the attack had come from. She could only see Emily, running with her shotgun, shouting something Brooke couldn't hear.

"Mama!" Brooke's voice was lost under the roar of the fire.

Tucking the rifle close against her right side, praying her shoulder would hold when she needed it, Brooke darted into the open toward Emily. Only when they were close enough to touch could Brooke make out her mother's words.

"Come and get us!" Emily screamed into the darkness. "You want us, come and get us, coward!"

"Where are they, Mama? Which way?"

"Brooke! You got your rifle? Good." Emily's face was streaked with tears, and her eyes were puffy. Brooke wondered if she'd tried to put the fire out and suffered the effects of smoke. But her clothes didn't look burnt. More as if she'd simply been crying. Crying and crying for hours.

Then Brooke understood.

"Mama, you didn't."

"If Stephen Cawley's anywhere inside of ten miles, he'll see that blaze. We don't have long to wait now."

"Goddamn it, Mama, there could be any number of them out there. Milo can't shoot to save his life, and I'm still hurt."

"There ain't any number, Brooke. There's just one."

"I only saw one, but you know how they are. There's going to be more. That's probably where he went, to get them."

"No, I told you, Stephen Cawley's the last of them. I've been looking for that cowardly, murdering piece of shit for years. The feds posted a warrant for him up north, so I went there to beat them to it. I'll be damned if any Cawley's going to live large in a city prison after what they did to us. I been waiting years for this. You want your girls to grow up safe? This is how you do it."

"He can't be the only one. What about Delia?"

"Haven't you been listening? Anita got her after they killed Callum. Killed her at their own compound. I got Angeline, and Daddy rode the other sons down the night of the fire. All but one. That trash turned tail and ran, only reason he's alive today."

"He was telling the truth," Brooke said, backing away. Ash rained down, freckling the snow. She turned and saw Davey and Milo hurrying from the house.

"My horses are in there!" Davey boomed, jabbing a finger at the burning drive shed.

"I moved them, don't worry," Emily said dismissively. "They're out back, under the willow."

"What happened?" Milo asked.

"She lit the drive shed on fire," Brooke said. "She's bringing Cawley right to us."

At this, Davey drew out his gun, saying, "If he's coming, none of you better get in my way." He crossed the yard into the darkness beyond the burning building.

"Your mother set the fire?" Milo asked, voice still thick with sleep.

"We should never have come here," Brooke said, pulling him toward the house. "I've gotten everything wrong, Milo. We have to get out of here."

Brooke winced as a hand came down on her bad shoulder. She twisted around to see that Emily had followed her.

"Let me go, Mama," Brooke said.

"Don't you dare," Emily said. "Don't you dare leave me again."

"Let go," Milo said, pulling Emily's hand off Brooke.

"Mind your own business!" Emily spat at him.

"You're going to get her killed too," Milo said. "Is that what you want?"

Brooke caught movement at the edge of the yard. Someone was coming through the basswoods.

"Shit," she cursed, struggling to lift the rifle with her aching arm.

"No!" Milo said in a strangled voice. "Don't shoot! Look!"

Brooke hesitated, squinting through the sparks and wavering heat thrown by the fire, trying to discern the shape emerging from the darkness of the trees. Whoever it was had their hands at their sides, no visible weapon. And they were small.

Brooke's heart constricted painfully as they stepped into view, lit by the fire. Holly came first, her dark eyes betraying no fear. The same serious, interrogating look she'd had since she was a baby, calling the world to account. She was holding Sal behind her as she stepped out of the trees, shielding her sister from whatever lay ahead.

"Is that—" Emily began.

Brooke and Milo ran. The distance closed with awful slowness, each second an eternity. Then Brooke's hand closed around Holly's wrist and the kids were in their arms, whole and alive. She dropped the rifle to gather Sal closer.

"Are you okay?" Milo cried.

Holly and Sal collapsed against their parents, both talking at once. Joy knifed through Brooke, so sharp she thought it would rip her in half. They were okay. They were here.

A twist in Brooke's gut told her something was wrong. She had barely registered heavy footfalls and a face materializing from the dark—bloodshot eyes, crooked scar—when Holly screamed and Brooke felt Sal being ripped from her arms.

Holly was the first to leap after Cawley, but Milo caught her, pulling her back.

"Let me go!" Holly railed at Milo, but he wrapped his arms around her and held on tight.

Cawley was half carrying, half dragging Sal toward the burning drive shed. Brooke sprinted after him, leaving the rifle on the ground in her haste. Sal was shrieking, twisting in Cawley's arms, reaching back for Brooke.

A blast from Emily's shotgun and Brooke ducked.

"Don't shoot!" she heard Milo shout. "He has Sal!"

Brooke kept running, getting closer. Cawley was slowed by his injuries and Sal's struggling. Halfway to the drive shed, Brooke reached out with her good arm and caught Sal's hand; now she was running with them, Sal's hand clasped tight in hers. Brooke kicked for Cawley's ankle, but he sensed it coming and skipped over her foot. They were close to the fire now. Heat blew in Brooke's eyes.

"Mom!" Sal cried.

Brooke kicked again, higher this time, and Cawley tripped and fell, Sal still pinned to his side. Brooke's right arm was useless, and the rifle was back where she'd dropped it, but she still had Sal's hand. She kicked Cawley in the back, the ribs. The heat was baking. A flying ember caught Brooke's hair and she reached instinctively to bat the flame, letting go of Sal's hand for an instant—long enough for Cawley to get back on his feet. He looked around him, eyes wild, and then spun sharply, heaving Sal through the open door of the drive shed.

"No!" Brooke screamed.

A shrill cry from inside. Sparks rained down as the roof beam elbowed deeper.

Brooke's mind flooded with fear as she squinted into the flames, desperately seeking a way through. Cawley was between her and the building, barring the way. His mouth chewing nothing, his eyes blurry slits. Wherever he'd been, he'd found more chalk—a lot more. He was muttering, laughing jerkily to himself. He reached for the revolver shoved in the waist of his pants, but before he had it, another shotgun blast sent him diving for cover behind a long pile of rusted oil drums.

The roof of the drive shed was going to let go any second. A massive side beam split and fell in a billow of smoke, blocking half the door. Another cry from inside. Brooke pulled her shirt up over her face, preparing to launch herself through the half-collapsed door. But before she could move, Emily flew past, shoving her shotgun into Brooke's hand and disappearing into the flaming hole.

"Sal!" Brooke cried. She could see nothing in the fire. Then a bullet slammed into the front of the shed, splintering a burning board. Brooke hesitated. If she went after Emily and Sal, Cawley could still shoot any of them. Milo was back where he'd tackled Holly, still struggling to hold her. It had all happened so fast. Where the fuck was Davey when she needed him?

"Get her out of here," Brooke shouted to Milo. "The horses are behind the house. Take the rifle! Run!"

Brooke aimed Emily's heavy shotgun at the oil drums. She was afraid of making the shot with her right arm, but she didn't trust her aim on the left. She gripped her bad shoulder with her good hand, bracing for the recoil, and squeezed the trigger, shooting into the empty barrels. Half the pile toppled: Cawley wasn't there.

She turned back to the drive shed. There was movement inside, behind the broken beam—something lumbering toward her through the wavering heat.

Emily came out, half falling through the flames, hunched over the bundle in her arms. Sal didn't look burned, though she was wheezing and coughing, eyes shut tight. Emily's face, by contrast, was scorched, her brows and lashes gone, her eyes yellow and thick from the heat. She must be blind, or nearly.

"I'm here," Brooke said, running to them and reaching for Sal with her good arm. Sal, feeling Brooke close, climbed onto her instantly, clinging so tight it hurt. "I'm here, Salamander. I'm here."

"Where's Cawley?" Emily rasped. Her eyes roamed, sightless.

"We've got to go, Mama," Brooke said. "Can you follow my voice?"

"Cowards kill children, Cawley!" Emily called in a voice like sandpaper.

"Mama." Brooke was holding Sal against her with her left arm, the shotgun loose on her right. She tried to reach Emily's sleeve, but the gun was heavy; her shoulder quivered on the edge of slipping out of the socket. She dropped the gun and caught her mother's arm.

Emily's damaged gaze had finally landed on something, a burning object close to her feet—it was the pitchfork, Brooke saw, the fallen body of the scarecrow. Emily shook free of Brooke's grasp and reached down to hoist the blazing handle like a torch.

"I know you're out there!" she cried into the darkness. "Trash like the rest of them!"

"Mama, let's go," Brooke tried again. She backed toward the house, holding Sal tightly to her.

Cawley emerged from behind the drums that were still standing. He must have been watching, because he approached unconcerned, as if he knew that Emily couldn't see him, and that Brooke had dropped the shotgun. He walked straight up to Emily, the revolver in his hand.

"He's in front of you!" Brooke shouted.

Emily swung the pitchfork, missing Cawley by a few feet.

"Come on, you coward," Emily wheezed. In her singed face, fury and exhaustion.

"Thinks she's better," Cawley said, glancing at Brooke, addressing her as if they were compatriots. He had been feral, crazed, when he reeled out of the darkness and grabbed Sal, but this was different. His words were still gummy with chalk, but there was purpose behind them. Brooke thought she glimpsed the boy she and Robin had met fifteen years before. He shoved the revolver back in his waistband. "You know she knifed my mom in a public bathroom and left her to die? Took three hours for someone to find her. My mom never hurt anyone. Only thing she did was marry an asshole."

Emily snarled and raised her pitchfork to lunge again. Cawley caught the handle and wrested it from her with one hard yank.

Then he lifted the pitchfork in a slow, elegant arc and drove it down, straight through Emily's chest.

Brooke felt the shock in her own body and stumbled backwards with Sal. Emily sank to her knees, a look of disapproval on her face.

A gunshot cracked. Brooke and Cawley both ducked instinctively. Across the yard, Brooke saw Davey coming, gun raised.

The first shot had missed. Now Davey fired again and Cawley dodged sideways behind a toppled oil drum. The revolver fell from his waistband, skidding toward the door of the flaming drive shed.

He could have run then. If he'd made straight for the woods, he might have escaped. But he made a dash to retrieve his gun. Davey fired a third time and Cawley's body flew into the wall of fire.

Davey was still bearing down on the spot where Cawley had landed, when the shed's main roof beam screeched and folded, and the building fell in on itself in an explosion of sparks and smoke, devouring everything inside.

Davey turned around, fist up in triumph. "I got him!" he shouted. "I got him."

Brooke stood speechless, holding Sal. Emily was leaning forward on her knees in the garden, held up by the burning pitchfork, but Davey couldn't see her. The toppled pile of diesel drums hid her from view.

"Didn't you see I got him?" Davey asked, indignant.

"Go," Brooke said. "Find Milo and the horses."

Davey snorted in disbelief. "They better all be accounted for," he muttered, striding off toward the house.

Sal whimpered, still holding tight to Brooke. Had she seen any of it, or had she kept her eyes closed?

"Don't look, Salamander," Brooke said, tucking her daughter's face against her neck. "It's just a bad dream." She kneeled next to her mother. The pitchfork's wooden handle was driven into the snow, still ablaze, as fire crept closer to the four metal teeth that pierced Emily's chest. The pressure must be excruciating, Brooke thought.

"I can take it out, Mama," she said. "Do you want me to take it out?"

Emily tried to speak. Her voice was garbled, full of holes. She coughed and dark blood sprayed Brooke's face, Sal's hair.

"Should I take it out?" Brooke asked again. "I don't know what to do."

Emily's eyes were unfocused, closing.

"Mama, don't—"

She was still. Brooke watched for breath. There was none. Brooke waited, holding Sal against her. The seconds passed. No breath.

Brooke struggled to her feet, numb with shock. She didn't know what to do. She carried Sal away from the fire, past the house, toward the willow. She found Milo pacing anxiously and Holly perched on the angled door that led down to the root cellar from outside.

"Sal!" Milo cried, rushing to take her from Brooke. "Is she okay? Is she hurt?"

"She breathed in a lot of smoke," Brooke said in a daze.

"Davey said Cawley's dead."

"Yes," Brooke said. "Is he gone?"

"Looking for the horses," Milo said. "They must have bolted. Where's Emily?"

Brooke shook her head, dropping her eyes.

"Oh, no," Milo said.

"Who's Emily?" Holly asked.

"I need you to wait for me in the house," Brooke said, noting absently how calm she sounded, as if all this was normal. Maybe it was.

"Brooke, I'm so sorry," Milo said. "I'll come with you."

"No," Brooke said. "Stay with them. Keep them inside. I can't leave her how she is, but the kids shouldn't see . . . Don't let them look out the window. I'll be there as soon as I can."

Milo nodded, gesturing for Holly to come, but she stayed crouched on the cellar door, watching Brooke with a look of naked pleading.

"What's going on? Who was that woman?"

"Hol," Milo said, reaching stiffly with his shot arm to pull her up. "Mom needs a minute, okay? Let's get your sister inside."

Holly got to her feet, looking confused and defeated.

"Are you sure you don't want help?" Milo asked Brooke. "You don't have to do this alone."

"It's fine," she said. "It's better."

Brooke watched Milo guide the girls inside and waited until the kitchen window lit up. He would take care of them. Build up the fire, pack snow on Sal's singed face, find clothes for them, feed them, comfort them. He would know what they needed.

Fatigue dragged at Brooke's legs as she returned, step by step, to the garden. Close to the fire, the mire of melt and ash made for sloppy, unsteady walking.

Emily was on her knees, eyes closed, head bent. The flames on the pitchfork handle had shrunk to embers.

Brooke shook her sleeve over her good hand to grab the burned handle, set a boot against her mother's chest, and pulled. The pitchfork wrested free. Emily's body fell lifeless on the bloody snow.

Brooke found a shovel under the eaves of the house and chipped away at the cold garden furrows, pain radiating with every stab of the blade. Behind her, the fire fell bit by bit to a flickering pile of coals.

By the time the night sky began to lighten, Brooke had scraped out a shallow grave.

She wondered where the rest of them were buried. There was

no one left to ask. Only Robin, lost to the anonymous city. Had anyone helped him and Emily lay their family to rest? Had anyone mourned with them?

Brooke crouched and threaded her left arm under Emily's ribs. Wasted thin with time, Emily was still too heavy for Brooke to carry one-armed. The best she could do was drag Emily to the hole. There, she fell to her knees and laid her mother down.

The hole wasn't deep enough, but Brooke's muscles were sore and spent, and there was no way to dig around Emily without lifting her again, so Brooke piled the dirt around and over her as well as she could.

The garden was bordered by fieldstones unearthed long ago by Brooke's parents or grandparents, or whoever had lived here before the Hollands. Brooke kicked them free from their earth beds one by one and rolled them across the melted, messy ground to cover the mound of dirt and protect it from scavengers. There was no way to mark the grave. There was no need to mark it. Anyone seeing this heap of stones would know what it was.

17

IN THE THIN LIGHT OF DAWN, THE DRIVE SHED WAS A BLACK SCAR, RINGED IN mud and ash-black snow. Farther out, the snow faded to gray, and beyond the basswoods, it was white. Brooke looked out over the hills, the woods; in the distance, the silver river—so familiar, once, that it had been like looking in a mirror.

She trudged to the house, clawed at the doorknob. Her hand, cramped from shoveling, wouldn't grip.

Milo opened the door, a smoking cast-iron skillet in his hand. Brooke smelled pancakes.

"Brooke—" Milo started.

She held up a hand, not wanting to hear whatever kind thing he had found to say about Emily, and he stood aside to let her into the kitchen.

Holly and Sal were at the table, plates of food in front of them, wet hair combed back against their heads. They had on clean clothes, baggy and rolled up. Emily's things.

"Are you okay?" Brooke asked. The girls shrank from her as she approached.

She looked down at her hands, dark and crusted. Felt the wet, matted hair hanging around her face. The stiffness of dried blood on her clothes, her skin.

"I'm sorry," she said, stepping back. It sounded feeble, even to her. How long had she left them while she buried her mother? Hours? She took in the aluminum washtub next to the stove, half full with cloudy, gray water. Time enough for Milo to heat pot after pot of water on the stove. To clean the soot from Sal's red and tender face. "I had to . . . I couldn't . . ."

Holly and Sal waited, staring. Sal's eyes were puffy and bloodshot. She brought her thumb to her mouth and sucked it, something she hadn't done in over a year.

"It's just me, Salamander," Brooke whispered. "It's okay."

Holly let out a sharp hiss, turning away from Brooke to stare at the wall.

"Are you hurt?" Brooke tried again. "What happened?"

"They're okay," Milo said, guiding Brooke to a chair on the other side of the table. "They have some blisters and scrapes. Sal's got some burns on her fingers, and her throat hurts. But they're okay."

Brooke sank into the chair. Her hope of finding them had been so tangled up with the contrary, pointless effort not to hope. Now, amazingly—improbably—they were here, safe and intact. "How did they . . . Where did they . . . It's been . . . How long has it been?"

"Two days," Holly said to the wall. "Three nights and two days."

A silence, punctuated by sparks in the chimney and Sal's wet, rhythmic thumb-sucking.

"I've got water heated for you," Milo said, clearing his throat. He dragged a stockpot to the edge of the stove and tilted it to pour steaming water into the half-full tub. Then he turned back to Brooke, kneeling to pull off her boots. Holly kept her gaze on the kitchen wall, but Sal watched mutely, thumb in her mouth, as Milo delicately unbuttoned Brooke's shirt and gestured for her to lean so he could ease it off her shoulder. He drew the sleeve carefully over her cracked and swollen hands. Every cut and crease was packed with dirt and blood, the palms stained rusty.

Brooke stood and Milo helped her tug her pants and underwear down. The clothes were unsalvageable. Milo piled them in a heap next to the stove.

With a hand on Brooke's back, Milo led her across the floor and helped her fold herself into the tub. The water could not have been more than lukewarm, but it scalded her chilled skin. Grime swirled from her body. It wasn't just her hands. Her goose-fleshed arms and thighs, her chest, her belly—stretched and doughy from two pregnancies—every part of her was steeped in dirt, sweat, ash, blood.

Something touched her and she looked up. Milo was handing her a washcloth. She recognized the threadbare pattern from childhood: white leaves against faded teal.

The blood and dirt dissolved slowly. Milo used a margarine container to pour water over Brooke's hair. He scrubbed the grit that clung to her scalp, rinsing it again and again. The girls picked at their food. They were more tired than Brooke had ever seen them, drawn and frail. Sal leaned on Holly, her head lolling limply against her sister's arm.

Brooke rose, dripping, to dry herself. The water was cold and murky now, deep brown.

"Here." Milo handed her a stack of clothes. Jeans and a yellow sweatshirt of Emily's. Brooke maneuvered herself into the sweatshirt slowly.

Milo put the skillet back onto the hot part of the stove, greased it, and spooned in batter from a bowl. The faded box of pancake mix stood on the counter. Judging from the table, he had fed Holly and Sal everything he could find: lentils, carrots, blueberry preserves, tea, canned ham.

Milo slid more pancakes onto Sal's plate.

"I'm full." Sal's voice was almost unrecognizable, gravelly from smoke.

"Just one more," Milo said.

"I already had one more."

"Three bites, then."

"Dad," Holly said. "Stop. She'll barf."

"I don't want to barf." Sal's voice broke, on the edge of tears.

"It's okay," Milo said. "You're not going to barf. It's okay."

"It's not okay!" Holly shouted, drawing her knees up in front of her. "Stop saying that! Nothing is okay!"

Milo stood, holding the stack of pancakes. Brooke moved around the table to the girls. Sal was crying now, in hoarse, muted barks. Brooke pulled a chair up next to her, laying a hand on her shoulder. Sal looked at her warily, gulping back a sob, but didn't object, so Brooke gathered her in close, and Sal dissolved against her, gripping a handful of the yellow sweatshirt tightly.

"Did something happen?" Brooke asked. "Did someone hurt you? Milo, do you know where they've been?"

Milo shook his head. "They saw the fire and came toward it. That's all I've gotten."

"Holly?" Brooke asked.

Silence.

"Please," Brooke said. "We need to know. Where have you been? How did you get here?"

"How about where have *you* been?" Holly muttered. "How about what *you* were doing? How about what *we* want to know?"

"We were looking for you," Brooke said.

"*Here?*" Holly spat.

"That's—It's complicated."

"Yeah. It's complicated, we wouldn't understand, you'll explain later, whatever. I don't care. Don't bother."

"Holly—"

"No!" Holly slammed a hand down on the table. "I'm sick of it!" She shoved herself out of her chair and ran up the stairs. The bedroom door slammed.

"Holly, I'm sorry!" Brooke made to stand, but Sal clung to her, crying harder than ever.

"Don't," Milo said. "Give her some space."

Holly kicked something upstairs and then opened the door again just to slam it harder.

They were here, Brooke reminded herself. They were safe. That was enough. She couldn't expect to be forgiven.

"Is there coffee?" she asked, adjusting her position to hold Sal more comfortably.

It took a while, but eventually Sal's sobs abated and, softly, softly, Milo convinced her to tell them what had happened after she and Holly struck out from the hunting blind. The story came out confused and out of order, interrupted by renewed bouts of tears. Milo prodded gently, asking simple questions, and gradually they were able to piece it together.

As Milo had guessed, Holly's first plan had been to lead them to Buffalo Cross and home from there. They had quickly become lost in the dark, and then the snow had started. By the time Brooke had caught sight of them beneath the hemlock trees, Holly had already given up and was trying to get them back to their parents.

Brooke and Milo exchanged a glance. Holly wouldn't abandon even an obviously bad idea once she had set her mind to it unless something stronger overpowered her pride—fear, or hopelessness.

They'd heard shots, Sal said, and saw someone fall on the hillside. From their hiding place in the trees, they couldn't see who it was. Then Brooke had appeared, running for the woods, and they'd set off to find her.

When they lost Brooke's trail at the swamp, they had despaired, until Holly had thought of the hunting shelter, their last common location, recalling that it was also next to the swamp. They changed into their dry clothes for warmth, as Brooke had taught them, and kept moving.

Nothing looked familiar in the snow. The swamp had many inlets and tributaries too wide to cross, and they got off track. Late in the day, they were following a rocky stream when they heard more gunshots and took cover. Holly chanced a peek and saw a rider in the distance. They remembered Brooke referring to "the others," back when they'd first left home, and wondered how many more strangers with guns might be out there.

It was then that Holly remembered watching Brooke brush the tracks from their first campsite. She and Sal searched quietly near their hiding place until they found supple birch boughs to sweep with.

"We stayed on the rocks," Sal explained to Brooke and Milo. "That way, you don't leave tracks. And when we had to walk in the snow, we brushed it."

"You did a good job," Milo said. "Fooled Mom."

Brooke thought she heard a snort from upstairs.

Sal explained how they'd followed the rider, not sure what else to do, hoping at least the trail would lead them to a road or town. They had no sense, anymore, of where to look for their parents. That night, they'd come to the highway and, cold and hungry enough to risk it, followed the light of a storm lantern to where some people were stopped in a covered flatbed truck. The people—a crew just finishing their season as cleaners in the tar sands—had been kind; they'd fed the girls and given them space to sleep. In the morning, Holly had asked about getting back to Buxton, but the people were going the opposite way, south to Shaw Station, and they warned the girls against taking the road north alone. So, having failed to find their parents and unable to get home, Holly and Sal made a new

plan: they would go to the federal marshals Brooke had been trying
to reach.

They rode south in the truck. Beyond the river, where the hill
road branched off from the highway, the people set them down,
pointing the way to the outpost. It wasn't far, they said, but the
road was too rough for the truck. The weather had been clear at
first, and Holly and Sal sang to keep their spirits up as they walked.
But they must have missed the outpost. It got dark. The blizzard
had started when they were walking a stretch of road next to a
lake, with several cottages close together, all seemingly abandoned.
Afraid of losing their way, they'd taken shelter in a place with a
broken lock on the front door. The walls inside were all broken up,
Sal said, with wires and pipes sticking out. They'd changed their
clothes again, slept a little, and waited for a break in the weather.

It was dark when the snow stopped. They were too cold and
hungry to sleep. They decided to keep walking. Late in the night,
they'd seen an orange glow in the distance and thought it was the
outpost. Closer, they'd hesitated, smelling smoke. Then they'd been
spooked by a sound in the woods—someone else approaching—
and hurried forward. They'd come through the trees and heard
Milo shout, and then their parents were running toward them.

Sal stopped talking and closed her eyes. She didn't have to tell
them what had happened after that. Cawley, the burning drive
shed, Emily.

"It's over," Brooke said, stroking Sal's damp hair. "You're safe."

"Can we go home?" Sal whispered.

Brooke hesitated. "I hope so," she said, wishing she had a better answer.

"Time to sleep," Milo said. "Come on, Salamander. There's a
warm, dry bed."

The silence from upstairs was palpable. Brooke knew those
gappy floorboards. Holly would have heard everything.

"I'll stay down here," Brooke said. "I don't want to make it worse."

"It's okay," Milo said. "She'll come around."

"No, I won't!" Holly shouted from upstairs, making Sal flinch.

"Go ahead," Brooke said. "I'll be all right." A tangle of blankets still lay on the floor where Davey had kicked them aside in the night.

"Let me know if you need me," Milo said, kissing her still-damp head. Brooke felt tears spring to her eyes and blinked them away.

Sal leaned away from Brooke into Milo's arms, her thumb in her mouth again. Brooke watched them climb the stairs and listened to their footsteps through the ceiling. Milo's muted voice, an angry whisper that must be Holly, the rustle of blankets, the weight of the bed shifting on the floor, then silence.

Brooke looked around her childhood kitchen. All the details of this place that she'd forgotten: the canvas sling for carrying firewood, hanging from its nail; the strip of mirror that hung over the door, reflecting the rafters and the ceiling fan, except the fan was gone now, a paler circle of wood and three empty screw holes left behind; the little clay pot of toothpicks and medicine droppers by the sink; the yellow plastic basin under the U-shaped pipe; the chipped ceramic knob of the cutlery drawer. She had avoided thinking about home over the years, and when she couldn't help it, there had been certain tokens she returned to. Now she saw how meager those few images had been—flimsy, worn thin.

The framed photograph that Milo had taken off the wall was lying on the table. Holly and Sal must have seen it. Brooke wondered what, if anything, Milo had told them about where they were, and the kind of people who had lived here.

Brooke returned the picture to the wall. She felt a stab of fresh grief, seeing Emily, fierce and pregnant, and Callum and Anita, younger than Sal then, their faces already so recognizably their own. And there was Brooke, staring down the camera, tiny fists at her sides. People had loved that picture: the invincible Hollands. Now, Brooke found it odd that such a young child—barely out of diapers—would have stood in the back of a pickup truck, amid guns and anxiety and cameras, looking so stern and sovereign. Why wasn't she reaching to be picked up?

Brooke set about the familiar task of eating the scraps from her daughters' abandoned plates. What now? She'd told Sal she hoped they could go home, and in one sense there was nothing to stop them from returning to the farm now. Stephen Cawley was dead. All the Cawleys were dead, and Brooke's parents with them, everyone she'd been hiding from for fifteen years. She could move through the world without fear of being hunted.

There were other dangers, however, more mundane but equally real; the cranberries were likely frozen by now, they didn't have the money to wait out another growing season, and the bounty was gone with Cawley under the smoking remains of the drive shed. They would be penniless before spring. Brooke could hunt for food, and she and Milo—even the kids—could hire themselves out if there was work to get, but it was a bleak and perilous way for a family to live. She'd seen it.

She surveyed the kitchen for what might be sold. The most valuable thing, the cookstove, weighed at least nine hundred pounds. She could try pulling it into Shaw Station with Emily's big draft horse, if Davey came back with it, and if she had something to use as a sled. One of the aluminum roof sheets might do. The thought of stripping the roof—leaving the sad remains of her childhood home gap-toothed, open to the rain and snow—gave her pause. Then she shook her head. She should take whatever this house could give. Her family was gone.

Exhausted, Brooke put the empty plates in the sink, spread the blankets out by the stove, and lay down. But when she closed her eyes, she saw Emily on her knees, held up by the pitchfork, and then it was Brooke's own chest that was full of holes, her own body from which breath fled. She jackknifed upright, gasping and reaching reflexively for her rifle. It wasn't in the kitchen; Milo must have brought it upstairs, along with the backpacks.

Better to do something, she decided, folding the blankets away. She pulled open the drawers, putting everything she judged sellable into a pile. Cutlery, rubbing alcohol, mousetraps, glue. She felt through the pockets of Emily's coats and bags, hanging by the door. No wallet, no money. How had her mother planned to get through the winter? But Brooke didn't need the near-empty woodshed outside to tell her that her mother had stopped planning for the future a long time ago.

She moved to the sideboard and found it unexpectedly locked. The latch was an old-fashioned mechanism, simple to pick, and there would be tools in the root cellar, but Brooke didn't want to test her shoulder on the heavy trapdoor. She chose a wire whisk from the pile of salvage, pried one of its loops free, and used it to pop the lock. She opened the sideboard and saw what was inside: a shotgun, two handguns, a semiautomatic assault rifle, and a .303 bear gun.

I have better than cash, Emily had told Davey.

Brooke sat back on her heels. "Thank you, Mama," she breathed.

She slid open an inner drawer and found neatly ranged boxes of ammunition.

Clean and complete, the guns were worth more than Davey's two horses, and if she resold the gelding, they'd have enough to buy a few months of food. A start.

Brooke built up the fire, propped the door open for ventilation, and cleared a space on the table to clean the guns. She wouldn't risk going upstairs for a sheet to work on in case she woke Milo and the girls.

The temperature was dropping again, the house creaking in the cold. Brooke disassembled the guns and brushed and oiled and wiped. Twice, she thought she heard Davey coming with the horses and looked out the window to find the yard empty. It was just the old house constricting, or some part of the wreckage outside collapsing, telegraphing through the ground.

By the time Brooke heard real hoofbeats, it was late in the day. From the window, she watched Davey ride in on Chevy, with four other horses strung behind him: the two Milo and Brooke had ridden from Buffalo Cross, the draft horse, and Lorne's stallion. Davey tied them in the woodshed and came stomping up the steps, loudly knocking snow from his boots.

"They're sleeping," Brooke shushed him, opening the door.

"You're welcome," Davey said. "Your mother's goddamn draft horse led me a two-mile chase. She's lucky I bothered."

The draft horse was Brooke's now, though she didn't plan on telling Davey that Emily was dead. Better he should expect her objectionable mother to walk in at any moment, if it speeded him on his way back to Buffalo Cross.

"I want to keep the gelding and the roan," Brooke said without preamble.

"That's nice," he uttered tonelessly. "But I'm not giving them to you."

"No one's asking you to give anything. Come inside. And be quiet."

Brooke ushered Davey into the kitchen. When he saw the guns, cleaned and arranged on the table, his eyes widened appreciatively.

They negotiated the trade and Davey soon left. He was sore and sleep-deprived, but as Brooke had anticipated, he preferred a cold ride through the night to spending more time in Emily Holland's house.

With a handful of pancakes in his pocket and the guns and ammunition packed on Lorne's horse, he followed the driveway through the basswoods and was gone.

Brooke checked that the gelding, the roan, and the draft horse were settled in the woodshed. Then she unfolded her mother's blankets on the kitchen floor once more, and lay down. This time, she slept.

18

BROOKE STARTLED AWAKE. IT WAS DARK. SHE WAS LYING ON THE FLOOR, wrapped in a familiar-smelling blanket. Bright moonlight picked out grit and debris on the wooden boards in front of her face. Table and chairs. Cookstove.

A sound had woken her. Milo or one of the kids moving around upstairs?

No, that was wrong. It was close by, a heavy scraping.

Brooke began to sit up, but her head hit something; it felt like the corner of a door. She twisted blearily to see what it was, tried again to sit up. Dizziness blurred her vision, and something wet was running into her ear.

Above her, an impossible image took shape: Cawley. Holding a hammer. His hair burned to a singed mat of stubble. A raw section of scalp on one side of his head, like a skinned knee. Wheezing badly. His shirt black with blood.

Brooke's eyes struggled to focus. He'd hit her hard. Behind him, she thought she could see the door of the root cellar yawning wide. He must have gotten in through the outer hatch.

There were sounds of movement from the bedroom.

Brooke tried to stand. The air resisted her. Cawley raised the hammer again. It was coming down. She fell to her knees, and the hammer swung past her.

"Stop!" Milo was there, jumping down the stairs three at a time.

Brooke remembered that the rifle was upstairs. She tried to form words, but her tongue was thick and slow. Tried again to stand, and fell sideways. Hot pain blazed in her ear. She raised her hand, and it came away slick with blood.

Milo was swinging something. The iron skillet. *Pancakes*, she thought. Had she said that out loud? Then she thought, *Brain damage. I have brain damage.*

She registered a sound—metal on metal—and the hammer skidded past her on the floor. It was near her foot. She pictured herself reaching for it, lifting it, but her arms would not obey. Her legs seemed to work, though, so she kicked it and it disappeared down into the open root cellar. *There*, she thought.

A clattering sound. Cawley was rifling in the cutlery drawer. It came too far out and fell.

A frightened yelp from upstairs. The kids.

Brooke crawled toward the stairs, moving more and more slowly, as if against a sucking tide. She reached the cookstove. Her head wouldn't stay up. She kept landing on her face. She turned onto her back and felt for the iron base of the cookstove with her foot.

She saw Milo take another swing with the skillet, but Cawley had a paring knife now and Milo had to jump back, out of the way. Cawley lunged past him, going for Brooke on the floor. He came down with the knife. She blocked him at the wrist, but the deflection was weak and she felt the blade cut deep into her forearm.

The pain gave her a brief rush of energy. As Cawley was recoiling with the knife, she reached up for his remaining stubs of hair, pulled him toward her, and dodged at the last second, letting his skull crack against the floor. He rolled away from her.

She felt again for the leg of the cookstove. If she couldn't walk, she'd have to slide to the stairs. She had to get to the girls, to the rifle.

Her sock foot found purchase on smooth iron. She pushed with all the strength she had, propelling herself across the gritty floor. Then she was falling. She had botched the angle and, instead of hitting the base of the stairs, had sent herself through the open trapdoor. The rungs of the ladder caught her spine, and she slammed against an earthen floor.

Sounds of scraping and crashing from the kitchen above her, and, farther off, a scream from the bedroom.

"Holly," Brooke cried. It came out as a whisper.

She had to get to them. She had to climb.

Instead, somehow, it seemed as if she was sinking farther down. She peered through a narrowing tunnel, darkness creeping in from the corners of her vision, as the moonlit square of the trapdoor got smaller and smaller, receding in the distance.

"Holly—"

It was gone. Darkness. Silence. The texture of the ground underneath her had changed. Instead of cold earth, she was lying on something soft—moss? Impossible. Yet when she put her hands down to push herself up, it was the live springiness of moss that she felt.

She blinked, and gasped. In the instant that her eyes closed, it was as if she'd opened them; the world lit up in front of her—but the wrong world: a green forest, moss under her hands, sunlight, and birdsong.

She opened her eyes and blackness closed around her. She had to wake up, climb the ladder, get to the girls. Brooke closed her eyes again, brushing her eyelashes to be sure, and the strange scene reappeared. She pinched the inside of her arm, and it hurt like a bee sting, but the forest remained.

"I don't want to be here," she said, looking desperately around at the forest as if she might find a doorway back to her life hidden among the trees.

The only thing she saw was a notebook, lying open on the ground.

She leaned closer. The page showed a drawing of a woman lying on moss, under a tree. Brooke recognized herself: tangled hair, blue jeans, yellow sweatshirt. In the drawing, she carried a pistol in a hip holster and her belly was flat, her waist cinched.

Brooke touched her stomach reflexively. It was normal, her same doughy belly. Now she noticed that her pain was gone. The backache from days of walking and riding and carrying a pack, gone. The pain in her ear, where Cawley had struck her, the cut in her arm, her blistered feet, the ache of her separated shoulder, all gone.

"This isn't real," she said. Her mind wasn't working right. She had to wake up. She had to go back. She needed something to hold on to.

She lifted the notebook, and it fell open to a different page. She saw more images of herself. The drawings were sectioned off in squares like a comic book. In the second-to-last drawing, Brooke held a smoking pistol and Cawley lay dead on the ground.

"That isn't what happened," she told the notebook, turning to the front page. There she was, looking out over the cranberry bogs, the morning sky blushing pink. In the next frame, she stood in the door of the washing shed as a hand reached out from the darkness and clamped over her mouth. Her eyes in the drawing were wide with terror.

She flipped the pages: the sheriff, the Legion, the swamp. Some scenes were as they had happened; others were wrong. In the picture of the duck blind, Stephen Cawley sat bound, watching Brooke. Behind his back, he was folding a sharp rock into his palm. She turned the page: Emily, running toward a blazing barn in place of the drive shed, looking shocked, hair in a tidy, maternal bun, no shotgun in her hands. On the next page, Milo and the girls in the yard of the Holland farm, in daylight, the house behind them undamaged.

The texture of the drawings under Brooke's fingers felt real. The paper was waxy and smooth where someone had pressed in with colored pencil. The faces of Holly and Sal, though inexpertly drawn, were Holly's and Sal's faces.

Brooke shook her head. Holly and Sal were in danger. All Cawley had to do was get past Milo and up the stairs. She stood, and her dizziness from the kitchen was gone.

Now she became aware of a house at the edge of the trees. It was gray, sprawling, many-windowed. The door was open, and Brooke could see that the house was shallow: across a single room, a second door stood open on the other side, and someone was sitting there, looking out.

Brooke made her way silently over the mossy forest floor. At the door of the house, she hesitated, unsure why she was reluctant to enter. It was a man, she saw now. An old man, sitting with his back to her. There was an empty chair next to him. Beyond, the lawn dropped away.

No . . . Brooke looked closer: the lawn was dissolving into mist. The house, the grass, the bit of forest Brooke had just come from—she saw now that they comprised an island surrounded by encroaching whiteness. Even as Brooke watched, a willow tree was overtaken, thinned, erased.

She was running out of time. She had to get back. She had to wake up.

She forced herself through the doorway, across the room, toward the man in the chair. Iron-gray hair combed over a thinning patch on top. Wide, heavy shoulders—a body made for movement, conspicuous in its stillness. The size and weight of him in all things.

Laughable to have believed him dead. As likely the earth itself should die.

"Who's that?" Edmund Holland leaned forward and turned to see who was behind him.

He was older. In fact, Brooke realized, he was older than he should have been. He looked to be in his eighties, when he wouldn't yet have reached sixty-five. A child's pack of colored pencils poked from his pocket.

"Did you do the drawings, Daddy?" Brooke asked, hearing how silly it sounded. Edmund's hands had done many things in life—built, worked, wrecked; never drawn.

"It came this morning, all this," Edmund said, forgoing greetings as Brooke had done. He waved at the whiteness beyond the grass. "The dog went into it and didn't come back when I called. She always comes when I call. And then I couldn't remember her name. It's like that with everything. I had a family. Now I can't remember their faces."

"You're dead," Brooke told Edmund. "You're not real."

"Faulty logic," he pronounced. "Which is it?"

"If you're dead, why am I here too?"

"Put it together, daughter. What could that possibly mean?"

"No," Brooke said, shaking her head.

"Death comes to everyone. You know that."

"Milo and the kids are still back there."

"It would seem that such partings are not forever."

Brooke stared out at the mist. If Cawley killed her family, would they come here? Was Emily here somewhere? Anita, Callum, Aaron? Brooke looked out over the lawn, wishing for them to appear and dreading it in equal measure.

The drifting mist was peaceful. The pain was gone. She wasn't waking up.

Brooke sat down in the empty chair, the notebook loose in her hand. The green smell of forest all around her. The wall of nothing had advanced a few more feet across the lawn, bisecting a hedge. There was no sign that another world even existed.

In the drawings in the notebook, Milo and the girls were safe. Brooke had killed Cawley and the story was over. Was that it? Her real life erased, just like that?

"Why did you bring me here?" Brooke asked hopelessly. "What do you want? Do you want me to apologize? You think I'm not sorry for what happened?"

"You had everything you needed," Edmund replied. "We gave you everything you needed. Yet you abandoned us."

"No, Daddy," Brooke said. "You're the ones who disappeared. It's only me who survived."

"Let's not forget the marshmallow," Edmund said, and Brooke saw something, she thought—a glimmer of love, maybe, inside the malice.

Brooke looked at the notebook in her hands. The last drawing was of her in the forest. One blank page remained. Brooke stared at the stippled whiteness of the paper as if there might be some image hidden there, some clue to what was happening in the world she'd disappeared from.

It didn't bear wondering if she was dreaming, stuck unconscious back in that root cellar, dying, dead. She knew she hadn't killed Cawley. The danger was not past.

"Help me, Daddy," she said. "It didn't go like in these pictures. I have to go back. If you brought me here, then whatever you did, undo it. Send me back. Draw a door. Back there in the trees, the same place I came from."

"Ah, yes," Edmund said with contempt. "Back to the old world. Why adapt when you can degrade?"

"I don't want to hear it, Daddy," she said, shoving the notebook into his lap. "My kids are in trouble. Draw the door."

Edmund sighed and took the box of colored pencils from his pocket. Brooke watched him draw.

"It was better the way I had it," he said when the page was done.

Brooke took it from his hands.

"You don't get to decide anymore," she said.

Edmund stared at her for a moment, and then his eyes slipped past her, to the mist.

"Goodbye, Daddy," Brooke said. She passed through the house, over the lawn, back to the woods.

At the place where the door was supposed to be, there was nothing.

Brooke looked at the notebook, checking the drawing. There was the low bush to her left, the two cedar trees beyond that. And where the door in the drawing was . . . Then she understood. The mist had already overtaken it. The place where the door should have been was gone. Or almost gone—Brooke could just see the corner of what could have been a doorframe, planted in the grass at the edge of the whiteness. She had taken it for a branch or a tree root.

She stepped to the threshold, facing nothing.

19

BROOKE SMELLED DIRT. A DEEP CHILL EMANATED FROM THE PACKED-EARTH floor of the root cellar. She lay twisted where she'd fallen at the bottom of the ladder. Above, the trapdoor was a square of moonlight. The pain was back, all of it: spine battered by the fall, ear throbbing where the hammer had landed, a hot sting in her forearm from Cawley's knife, and her shoulder—old, aching companion.

The notebook was still in Brooke's hand. She lifted it, and the trace of light that reached into the cellar showed her only a handful of newsprint, limp and faded.

There was a shout from the kitchen above.

Brooke gripped the first rung of the ladder and began to pull herself up. Her head swam. Everything went black again for a moment. Scuffling feet overhead. Something dragging across the floor.

Her vision cleared and she could see the trapdoor, the kitchen ceiling, the beam missing its fan. She tried to picture the string of actions in front of her, but the images bled together, dilated, splintered. Her head was all wrong. She tried again, caught one image, held it.

Reach.

Her hand closed around the next rung of the ladder. She drew a deep breath and forced her heavy, listing head upright.

Reach.

Her hand found another rung. With every pull, Brooke could see more of the kitchen: stovepipe, top of wall, cupboard.

More crashing in the room above. Another cry, abruptly cut off.

Reach.

Brooke was almost at the top. The commotion from the kitchen stopped, a sudden hush in its place. She heard only the sound of labored breathing.

Reach.

Brooke's eyes cleared the level of the floor. Overturned chairs, cutlery scattered. Cawley was leaning against the table, holding Milo in front of him, the paring knife to his throat. They were both breathing heavily, standing perfectly still, their eyes fixed on a point high up, beyond Brooke.

She turned her head with difficulty. Holly was on the landing of the stairs, holding the rifle.

"Let him go," Holly said.

A whimper from the top of the stairs: Sal, huddled behind the railing.

No one had noticed Brooke. The trapdoor was in the shadow of the staircase. She reached across the floorboards to the newel post at the base of the stairs. Pulled herself forward until her legs were out of the hole.

"You let him go," Holly repeated. "I'll count to three."

"Come on," Cawley said, his voice a ruined croak. "Put that down."

Brooke told her body to stand, but it did not respond. She pictured the movement, piece by piece.

Knee.

She raised her knee in front of her.

Hand.

She gripped her knee.

Up.

She braced herself to rise.

"One," Holly said.

Brooke pushed against her knee and was halfway to her feet when she was caught by another wave of vertigo. She swayed, falling roughly against the bannister.

Now they were all looking at her.

"Holly," Brooke gasped. "Don't do it, honey."

"Listen to your mother," Cawley said, his eyes darting from Brooke to Holly.

"Two," Holly said. "And shut up, Mom."

Brooke clung to the newel post and lurched awkwardly to the bottom step.

"Call her off, Brooke," Cawley rasped. "Or I swear I'll knife him."

"Three." Holly came down a step and leveled the rifle. The safety was off. Her grip was bad, Brooke saw, but not that bad. She might hit one of them.

"Hell," Cawley muttered, ducking behind Milo for cover.

Brooke stabilized herself on hands and knees and climbed the second step.

"I mean it," Holly said.

"Stephen," Brooke begged as she fumbled her way up another step. "Please."

"I never asked for this shit," Cawley said, blinking, his smoke-damaged eyes leaking. "This fucking shit."

"I know." Brooke's vision rocked. She was two steps below Holly. She reached out and touched her daughter's foot. "We were just kids."

Something went out of Cawley then. He closed his eyes and slackened his arm. Milo reached up and moved the knife away from his throat. Cawley sank, knees buckling, and Milo twisted around and caught him, easing him into a chair.

BROOKE HAD A CONCUSSION—HER HEAD ACHED, HER BALANCE PITCHED AND rolled, and she found herself phasing between moments, losing the spaces in between. One minute, she was on the landing with Holly, fumbling with shaky fingers to unload the rifle; the next, she was holding Sal in her lap at the top of the stairs, rocking her like a baby. Now, the girls were both out of reach, watching as Milo shined the flashlight in Brooke's eyes, asking if she knew where she was. She tried to answer, but her lips were wet and blurry; instead of words, tears came. She wiped her cheeks.

"Mom," Holly said, shocked.

"I'm sorry," Brooke gulped.

"Is Mom okay?" Sal whispered.

Brooke's attempts to stand only brought her down with head rush, so Milo helped her to the bed, and there she collapsed. Holly and Sal sat near her, tapping the backs of her hands to keep her awake until dawn lit the frost-feathered window.

Brooke watched daylight grow in her parents' bedroom and puzzled over what had happened to bring her here. Memories of their journey came to her out of order, a spill of images and feelings, terror and raw eggs and blank snow. She couldn't make sense of it. She just knew she was grateful for Holly's and Sal's fingers tapping her hands, and their warm bodies close to hers.

The moments passed less jaggedly as Brooke's brain recovered its fluency, retracing how to think, how to arrange time. Eventually, she could speak again, the sparks cooled in her eyes, her limbs moved as she willed.

Only the tears did not abate. Brooke rose, and dressed, and moved haltingly through the work of getting them ready to leave; she helped the girls pack; she filled their water bottles; she put the disordered kitchen back together; and through it all, with dismaying frequency, she found herself blinking and watery. Milo saw, the kids saw, even Cawley saw, and she could not stop it. Whatever Cawley had knocked loose in her head had uncovered a well of tears that seemed bottomless.

Cawley himself sat, despondent. Milo had tied him to his chair, though it hardly seemed necessary; even if Cawley's injuries hadn't prevented him from escaping, his fight was gone.

They packed the remaining food, some fresh clothes, water, taking only what they needed. Once they had collected the bounty on Cawley, there would be no need to sell mousetraps or rubbing alcohol to survive.

When they were ready—bags packed, horses saddled, fire damped down—Brooke led Milo and the girls to the garden and its pile of stones.

If the Hollands had lived to see it, Emily's funeral would have been an occasion for howling speeches and bloody vows. As it was, Brooke could think of nothing to say. Hands in her pockets, she fingered the shreds of the old T-shirt she'd taken from the scarecrow.

"I thought you didn't have a mom," Holly said.

"I did," Brooke said. "I should have told you."

She would tell them. About her family, and everything they'd taught her.

She pulled the shredded shirt from her pocket and stuffed it down between the stones.

"Goodbye, Mama," she said.

They left the house unlocked. Let anyone seeking refuge here help themselves.

THEY SAW NO OTHER TRAVELERS ON THE ROAD. BIRD CALLS, TREES CREAKING IN the breeze. The morning grew sunny and warm, and the snow sank into itself, pockmarked by clumps that fell from the branches. Descending a switchback against gray cliffs, they passed above a lake, not yet frozen, a black mirror in the snow.

Holly rode the gelding, and Milo carried Sal on the roan, chatting lightly with her. Sal's responses were few. She had been quiet since the fight in the kitchen, sucking her thumb most of the time, folded into herself.

Brooke carried Cawley on Emily's draft horse. The burnt, raw smell of him filled her nose.

The outpost was a mile off the hill road, on the near side of Shaw Station. They arrived in the afternoon. The place had belonged to the national park service once, with a campground and hiking trails. On the old parking barrier, the feds had nailed up signs. FEDERAL PROPERTY. NO UNAUTHORIZED ACCESS BEYOND THIS POINT. TRESPASSERS WILL BE PROSECUTED. NO HUNTING. NO ACCESS.

In the distance was a concrete and steel bunker with a double-high garage on one end. Brooke had never seen the outpost in person. She remembered Callum telling her and Robin that there was a trapdoor in that roof, that the marshals could climb straight out into a waiting helicopter if they were under attack. By the brutal look of this place, Brooke could believe it was true. High in the walls were thick, shatterproof glass windows. Cameras were mounted on steel poles, behind cages. Their approach was being watched, if there was anyone in residence to watch it.

When they were a hundred feet out, a panel in the steel door slid open and a voice shouted, "Dismount and place your weapons on the ground! This is federal property!"

"No shit," Cawley muttered.

"We're here for the warrant on Stephen Cawley," Brooke called out. She couldn't see anything through the speaking panel on the door.

"Place your weapons on the ground and step away! You are on federal property and subject to federal law. We can and will use force if you do not comply!"

"This is Cawley," Brooke called. "We have children here! You show yourself first."

"If you are carrying firearms, place them on the ground and step away or I will shoot! This is your final warning!"

"Who are they going to shoot?" Sal whimpered, her thumb hanging from her lip.

"It's okay," Milo said.

"Mom?" Holly asked. "What should we do?"

"We don't know who's in there, Milo," Brooke said.

"We came to turn Cawley in," Milo said. "This is how it works. They're marshals. They're not going to shoot us." He dismounted and crossed to Brooke's horse, unstrapped the rifle from her saddle, and dropped it on the ground. Brooke worked one leg over the horse, still sore and weak in her movements, and slid down.

Cawley's attention was palpable now, eyes darting between the rifle and the opening door. A marshal emerged from the gloom of the doorway, and then another, their handguns trained on the visitors. For a moment, Cawley seemed about to throw himself off the horse—Brooke could feel the desperation radiating from him in the face of these men, their handguns and their bunker—but then he slumped. It would be pointless, bound as he was.

The marshal in front was the same young man who had stood up at the Buxton auction to announce the warrant. He advanced on Cawley, half-crouched, jaw set, gun raised, backed up by the second marshal, who was paunchy and middle-aged.

"Stephen Cawley?" The young marshal shouted from ten feet away.

Cawley just stared at him.

"I said, are you Stephen Cawley?"

"You know who I am, Jeff," Cawley said wearily.

"Stephen Cawley, you are under arrest for fleeing lawful detention and are hereby remanded to federal custody, where you will be charged with third-degree felony escape in addition to your other charges." The marshal Cawley had called Jeff unhooked a set of nylon restraints from his belt and secured them around Cawley's wrists before taking out a retractable razor and sawing through the rope Brooke had used to tie him to the saddle.

Waste of a good rope, Brooke thought.

"Where'd you pick him up?" Jeff asked Milo.

"Near Buxton," Milo said, lifting Sal down from the roan.

"You brought him all the way from Buxton?" Jeff turned to the older marshal, who had holstered his gun. "I told you it was worth it going up there, Chester."

"He's killed two people," Milo said.

"What?" Chester asked. "There's nothing in the system. We would have seen it."

"Lorne Davey from Buffalo Cross and—"

"Milo," Brooke shook her head. "They don't care."

"Not our jurisdiction," Chester said, with audible relief. "Unless the victims were traveling under federal visas."

"Let's get on with this," Brooke said. "There's five thousand dollars bounty on him, and you'd better have it."

INSIDE, THE BUNKER LOOKED LIKE CALLUM HOLLAND HAD PERSONALLY DECO-rated it. A first-person shooter paused on an old wall screen. A split vinyl sofa with the cushions caved in. Free weights and a bench in the middle of the kitchen. A sink full of dishes. A life-size poster of a naked teenage girl, waxed and bent over the hood of a car. The place stank like rancid oil.

Holly stared at the poster of the naked girl, disgust wrestling with embarrassment in her face.

"Why don't you guys wait outside?" Brooke said.

"Yeah," Milo said, surveying the room. "Come on, Hol. We'll go back outside."

"Dad, why did that girl have her—" Sal's voice was cut off by the heavy steel door closing. An eddy of fresh air moved through the room before the stale stench of the outpost returned.

"Let's do this quick," Brooke said to Jeff. Despite his youth, he seemed to be the one in charge. "Where's the bounty?"

"We don't keep that kind of cash on hand." Jeff took out his phone and started swiping at it. "The goddamn rabbits around here will shoot you for a five-dollar bag."

"Stephen Cawley killed my mother two nights ago. I know you don't care, but you better realize I don't have a drop of patience left for him or for you. If the money's not here, where is it?"

"You'll get it," Jeff said. "Don't worry. I just need authorization so we can print a check."

"A check's no fucking good to me."

"If you want me to cash it for you, I have to charge fifteen percent. That's policy."

"I brought him a hundred miles, right to you."

"It's policy." Jeff shrugged, throwing himself down on the sofa, his eyes still on his phone. "Who do you want it made out to?"

She hesitated. "Brooke Holland," she said.

Jeff looked up, cocking an eyebrow. "They're going to run your name before they authorize the check, you know. I can detain you right here if you have an open record."

"I've never done anything to the feds," she said stonily.

He shrugged again and turned back to his phone, jamming tiny headphones in his ears.

The older marshal, Chester, had to clear piles of junk out of a holding cell before he could put Cawley in it. Then he looked over Cawley's injuries, noting everything down on a form, and pulled out a large first aid kit.

Chester sprayed something over the burns on Cawley's scalp. Cawley closed his eyes and sweated while the marshal cleaned the wound. If it hurt, he made no sound.

The TV screen on the wall turned itself off. Jeff was still on his phone. Brooke combed through the first aid kit, removing gauze patches and antiseptic wipes for the cut on her arm, burn cream for Sal's fingertips, adhesive bandages, sodium pills, petroleum jelly.

If Chester noticed her taking these things, he pretended not to. Brooke watched him wrap Cawley's swollen knee. The feds would take care of Cawley's injuries. They'd probably pay for doctors, rehab, food, books—whatever prisoners were entitled to, whatever was considered humane. Measure his literacy, x-ray his teeth, test his blood, murmur dolefully about the forces that had made him.

Edmund had taught Brooke to think of life as some kind of cage match for the fittest to survive. And she had done it, brought Cawley in, just as she intended. Was she supposed to feel proud? The same forces that made him had made her, after all. Only, she had not killed a federal agent, or stolen from them, or destroyed their things. She had beaten and terrorized people, fractured families, put drugs in the hands of children, sowed despair, ruined lives. Still, the marshals would run her name in a database and see nothing.

"I'm sorry." It was Chester. He was done bandaging the prisoner. "About your mother. I've been stationed here a while, since your family was still in chalk, and the Cawleys. The people that took over after them make Emily Holland look like a freaking saint. I saw her a few times, riding around. She poached a deer I caught once; heard the shot, I guess, finished it off before I could get there."

"No such thing as poaching from a fed," Brooke said automatically.

"Yeah, that's what she said." He nodded sagely.

When Chester left to put away the first aid kit, Brooke approached Cawley's cell. He was lying on his side, facing the wall.

His head was bandaged, and Chester had rolled his pants up to accommodate the plaster wrapped around his knee and ankle. The bruises where the plaster ended were black, already turning green.

"How did you find me?" she asked Cawley's back.

He didn't answer. From the set of his neck, she could tell he wasn't asleep.

"Just tell me, and I'll leave you alone."

Slowly, Cawley turned, easing his burned head down onto the towel they'd given him to lie on, and spoke dreamily to the ceiling. Chester must have given him oxy. "I told you, I wasn't looking for you," he said. "I thought you were her."

"Who?"

"Your mother. She's been after me for years. Like it wasn't enough, what they did. Word travels. If I ever showed up in the county, blah blah. Same old shit."

The scar in his lower lip pulled when he spoke, Brooke noticed. He must feel it all the time.

"Why would you look for her in Buxton?"

"I didn't. I've been running chalk through the tar sands for years with *that* fucking narc." He twitched a finger across the room at Jeff, but the marshal had his headphones in and didn't hear. "Crooked piece of shit. Somebody figured him out and the mother-fucker turned on me, let his fed buddy take a bullet like a fucking pussy. And then they put a bounty on me because they're fucking *feds* and they *shit money*—" Cawley dissolved in a fit of coughing.

"Then what?" Brooke prompted him when he was done.

"I needed a horse. You tried to cover that brand, but I could see it underneath. Seen that goddamn *H* so many times I couldn't miss it if I tried. I thought, *That bitch is coming at me here now?* It wasn't hard to find out where the horse came from. People are friendly in that town. So I went to deal with her."

"But my kids," she prompted him. "Who did you think—"

"I was fucking high. I don't know what I thought." Cawley was quiet for a minute. Then he spoke to the ceiling again. "I forget sometimes, how long it's been. Anyway, I shouldn't have fucking bothered about that horse. I didn't know it was you."

"Well, it was," Brooke said.

"Yeah." Cawley turned to face the wall again. "It was."

20

IT WAS WELL INTO THE AFTERNOON BEFORE THEY LEFT THE OUTPOST WITH A
check for Cawley's bounty. They arrived in Shaw Station as evening
was falling. The hill road descended sharply into the basin of the
Warren River, passing through a narrow latitude of woodsmoke.
The town below was as Brooke remembered it: a sprawl of streets
filling the lowland between hills, as if life had pooled there. She
led Milo and the girls past the east-end mall, which had become
a recycling center. The rest of the suburban commercial zone was
mainly green now, orchards and chicken farms, parking lots made
over to solar panels.

They passed into town proper. Some things had changed; many
more had not. The old trees, the pitted roads, the familiar house
fronts. Brooke realized that part of her was surprised to find it all
still here. Had she expected the entire county to come to ruin along
with her family? That would be Edmund's reasoning. His vision
of survival had been so fraught, so narrow: a single unerring path,
navigated by force of will, and any diversion from it a dead end. A
world that outlived him, that lived without him, was unthinkable.
Brooke was weary of the whole thing. She was weary, especially, of
the idea that her life was a test, to pass or fail.

Holly and Sal took it all in silently. Compared to Buxton, Shaw Station was a metropolis. Block after block of lit windows, strangers' homes, a TV playing news from a pirated signal, children shouting, amplified music, a peal of laughter. Brooke saw curiosity creep into her daughters' faces, a softening of the pinched anxiety that had taken up residence there in the past week.

Brooke led them through the neighborhoods, looking for a place where they might stay the night. On a side street, they had to stop for a group of children who were crowding the road with hockey sticks and nets, playing out the last minutes of daylight.

"Car!" shouted a girl Sal's age, and the goalie pulled his net aside to let the horses pass. Holly and Sal studied the other children. The players took no particular notice of them. Shaw Station was near the interstate, within reach of federal territory and the city; strangers passed through often enough that one family on horseback was unremarkable.

The place Brooke was looking for was still there: a motel joined onto a two-story house, where the side street met a commercial strip. Bare, ancient lilac trees grew at the edge of the sidewalk. Brooke recalled that the motel had been made over into apartments but that a room or two was kept free for travelers. Brooke hadn't known the owners. She had only heard they were decent—the kind of people that didn't allow chalk and didn't do business with the Hollands.

There were lights on in some of the units. Brooke knocked on the door of the main house. No one answered. She waited and knocked again, then a third time. Finally, a girl with a toddler on her hip opened the door. The girl wasn't familiar to Brooke, but that didn't mean anything. The girl would have been a toddler herself the last time Brooke was in Shaw Station.

"Do you still rent rooms?" Brooke asked.

"Sometimes," the girl said. She looked Brooke over, cast a

quick glance at Milo and the kids behind her. "It's kind of late. I can't show it to you now."

"We don't need to see it. We'll take it as is," Brooke said.

"Where you from?" the girl asked, looking harder at Milo.

"Buxton," Brooke said. "We can pay cash tomorrow."

"Uh-uh," the girl said, letting the squirming toddler down to run back inside. "I only take advance."

With a few more minutes of negotiating, Brooke agreed to leave one of the saddles as a deposit. The girl handed over a large brass key welded to a soup ladle and pointed them down the row of doors to the far end.

Inside, the room was clean enough, and the queen-size bed had been made up with fresh blankets since the last guests. Better still, the bath ran clear warm water. Milo showed Holly and Sal how to work the faucet and diverter—they shrieked and then laughed as water shot out of the showerhead.

Brooke stopped unpacking and listened.

They were laughing.

Things had happened, Brooke knew, that would stay with them forever. She had not been able to prevent it. But for now they were laughing.

After the water turned cold (more shrieking), Holly and Sal wrapped themselves in blankets and sat in front of the big picture window. The motel was on a hill, overlooking a wide spread of lights from town.

"What are we going to do now?" Holly asked.

Brooke sat down with them, gazing out over the town. "When places open up in the morning, we'll look for somewhere to cash that check." She hoped the exchange station would do it. The other option—the Shaw Station courthouse—she had no desire to see again. "Then we need to buy some food, and some warm things."

"Are we going home?" Sal asked around her thumb.

"Yes, Salamander," Brooke said. They would go home, together. Flood the bogs. Harvest what they could. Recover Star, if that was possible.

And then?

She remembered what Milo had said about giving everything up for her. She thought about Holly's loneliness on the farm.

"I have a brother," Brooke said, a shy flutter in her chest. "In the city. You guys have cousins."

"We do?" Holly craned around, eyes wide.

"I don't know how to reach them, though. I don't know, honestly, if Robin would want to hear from me."

"Of course he would," Milo said.

"I have—" Holly scrambled to her feet, rifling through her pile of things on the floor. "I have this." She held up Milo's old phone, like a trophy.

"You're still carrying that thing?" Brooke asked with astonishment.

"They've got places with reception here, right?"

Brooke exchanged a glance with Milo. It was true; Shaw Station had data hubs connected via satellite.

"Okay," Brooke said, taking the phone from Holly and meeting her daughter's dark, hopeful eyes. There was probably some way to find Robin on the Internet, though she couldn't guess where to begin. "I'll try."

When Sal's chin began dropping to her chest, Brooke and Milo ferried both girls onto the bed and tucked them in. They were asleep in seconds.

Brooke watched their sleeping faces. Sal's eyelids fluttered, and she flinched and whimpered in her sleep—the same high, muffled whine she'd made as a toddler, having her first nightmares.

Brooke felt Milo watching her and looked up to meet his gaze. Gold-flecked hazel eyes, brows arched like blackbirds' wings. The bones of his face, the shape of him, the warmth of him. She should have left him alone, walked away when she first felt her heart move, but she had always loved him, against caution.

"When were you on Highway 12?" Brooke asked, giving in to a sudden impulse.

"What?"

"Outside Buffalo Cross, on Highway 12, you said you'd been that way before."

"Oh, that. I was Holly's age."

"Where were you going?"

"The city, with my mum."

"You never told me you'd gone there."

"We didn't get through," he said. "You know how it was, right after the state fell. Things were shutting down. Mum had her birth certificate, so they had to let her in, but I was born out here and they wouldn't let me go with her."

"Why did she want to go?" Brooke had never known Milo's mother to talk much about her upbringing in the city. She'd been so much a part of the community in Buxton—volunteer, librarian, town councilor—it was hard to remember that she hadn't always been there.

"She wanted me to meet her family," Milo said. "She missed them. And I think she was scared."

"Scared?"

"You know. Being dark."

Brooke could hear the fatigue in his voice.

"I'm sorry for the stuff my mom said."

Milo raised his eyebrows. "I remember wondering if Mum was even planning to come back from that trip," he said. "Or if she was just fed up. She packed so much stuff. Maybe that's why they wouldn't let me through. Maybe she was trying to take me home."

Brooke imagined arriving in a Buxton where there was no Milo. She would have moved on in the spring as she'd planned.

"Thank you," she said. "Thank you for staying."

Milo smiled, and though he wasn't touching her, Brooke felt the quiet hum respond in her bones just the same.

Home.

They drew the dusty blind and climbed in on either side of the girls, shoving their heavy, unconscious forms to the center to make room. Brooke slept nearest the door, with the rifle next to the bed. Other than some teenagers shouting drunkenly in the night, nothing disturbed their rest.

THE EXCHANGE STATION WAS HOUSED IN A FORMER TRADE SCHOOL. FLUORES- cent tubes lit the lofty space that had once been the foyer, and the floor was waxed to a high polish. Brooke didn't remember the place being so rich. The flow of trade must have steadied in the years since she'd left. Oil, agriculture, drugs—the city needed to be fed, and the country needed money; it had always been so.

"I can't cash this without ID," the woman at the counter told her, pushing the check back at Brooke through a semicircular hole in her glass shield. Her fingernails were long and painted a thick wine color, with sequins stuck to them. "I don't know you."

"What's that got to do with it?"

"I don't know this is you." She tapped the name on the check with the tip of a talon: *click, click.* "Brooke Holland. I've got no way of knowing."

"Ask him," Brooke said, gesturing at another exchange officer seated farther down the counter. The woman was twenty-five, if that, but the man was older, thin and mousy, past sixty; Brooke thought she remembered his face.

The woman sighed and heaved herself up off her stool to confer with the other officer. He looked up from the check and peered at Brooke without approaching. Something flashed in his expression, too quick for Brooke to interpret.

"Could be," Brooke heard him say. "Looks like the mother."

"Well, they made it out to her, so if that's her I have to cash it," the woman said.

"It's got a serial number," the man said. "They'll pay it out either way."

The woman stumped back to the counter. "It's going to take a while," she said, making to slide her window shut.

"Wait," Brooke said, digging the old phone Holly had given her out of her pocket. "I need the Internet, too."

The woman sighed again and slid Brooke a plasticized card listing rates.

"I don't know how this works," Brooke said, returning to Milo and the girls with a sticky note bearing the wireless password in the woman's big, rounded letters.

"This thing is so old, I don't know if it'll even power up," Milo said, taking the phone and the sticky note from Brooke.

"It will," Holly said. "The new battery's good."

Milo held down a button on the side of the phone until the glass lit up blue. After a moment, the blue was replaced by an image of Brooke and the girls on their porch at home. Brooke had forgotten all about the photo. Milo had taken it when they were a few years into cranberry farming. Sal was a baby, drowsing in a bouncy chair. Brooke was steadying Holly where she sat on the porch railing, grinning to show the gap where she'd just lost her first tooth. That was the reason for the photo, Brooke remembered now. Milo had been capturing Holly's lost tooth to show his mother in town.

Milo poked a symbol in the corner and a keyboard appeared. He typed in the letters from the sticky note carefully, then waited.

A green wheel twirled in the middle of the screen, and finally a mess of colorful headlines and pictures appeared, ads that popped out of nowhere and traveled across the screen. Holly and Sal crowded over his shoulders, staring.

"What do you know?" Milo said. "That's incredible."

"It's working?"

"Yeah. Where do you want to go?"

Brooke named the e-mail platform, hoping it still existed; it was the only thing she remembered. Milo tapped the screen.

They waited. The screen changed. Milo handed her the phone.

The site looked different than Brooke remembered, but slowly, it came back to her, how to touch her finger in the box and get the keyboard to show. Holly and Sal reached out, unable to contain their curiosity.

"Give me some space," Brooke said. "You can see it after."

Brooke entered the password her teacher had made her memorize so long ago. It worked; a window opened. There were still those initial messages from when she and her siblings had first gotten their accounts (*Ha-ha, Callum says look up pornos*). But there were others, too, bolded. Unread. Brooke's breath quickened when she realized what they were.

He'd written intermittently in the years after she left.

Just in case, read one subject line.

Another: *Callum.*

Another: *Moving . . .*

The last one was from only a year ago, on her birthday: *Are you out there?*

He was working at a restaurant. He had a boyfriend named Rafe. Anita's kids were in school; they took after Anita, but mostly in good ways. He sent her an address in the city, and later another one, after they moved in with Rafe.

Robin said he knew Brooke would never see his messages,

but he wanted to believe she was alive. Delia's shot had grazed him that day in the alley; he was only lucky she hadn't stopped to check. When he recovered from the shock and saw Brooke lying there, motionless, he'd left to get help, but Edmund and Anita, returning to the spot, found her body gone. For years, Robin had given up the idea of leaving—their family was in mourning, and he felt responsible—but later, after it all fell apart anyway, he still had the money he'd saved, so he'd gone to the city with the kids. He hadn't been back to see Emily. It was too much, he said, too crazy. If Brooke was alive, he hoped she'd found something better.

Brooke read each of the messages twice, three times, laughing, wiping away tears when they blurred the words. When she looked up, the manicured officer was still at her counter. Holly and Sal were off exploring the far edges of the room with Milo. The phone battery was at 50 percent.

Brooke tapped on the arrow to reply.

For several minutes, she sat frozen, unable to think what to say to her brother. She had to tell him about Emily. That almost seemed easier than the rest of it.

In the end, she said nothing of how she'd gotten out of Shaw Station alive and left him behind. When they came face to face, she would try to explain. For now, she settled on a brief account— Buxton, the farm, Milo and the girls. She did not tell him what had happened to bring her home, nor how Emily had died. "It was quick," she told him. "She's buried in the garden."

She told him how happy she was to hear about his life, and that he was safe. She wasn't sure when she'd be able to check e-mail again, or how long until she could come find him, and meet Rafe and the children, but she would come, somehow, someday. She and Milo had the farm, still, and decisions to make. She told him she missed him, that his messages meant more than she could say.

She hesitated over how to end the letter. *I love you* felt too much like *goodbye*. So she just wrote her name.

WHEN THE EXCHANGE OFFICER HAD COUNTED THE BILLS OUT FOR BROOKE, AND Milo had pried the phone away from the girls, who had discovered (how?) a game of stacking marbles, they went in search of food and the other things they would need for their trip home.

They had outfitted themselves in new winter coats and boots and were standing in front of a grocery store window, listening to Holly point out ingredients she'd read about and never seen before, when a man approached and gestured Brooke aside. She recognized him as the mousy older man from the exchange station.

"You're Brooke Holland?"

"Yes," Brooke answered, instinctively cautious. Holly's explanation of umeboshi paste trailed off.

"What are you here for?" The man was nervous. His eyes darted around.

"Groceries," Brooke said.

"Are you staying in Shaw Station?"

"Why?" Brooke asked. She could feel Milo and the girls listening.

"Word's got around," the man said. "If anyone thinks you're selling—"

"I'm not selling anything. I told you, I'm buying groceries."

"You can't be coming in as an independent. If they think you're trying to get a line through the exchange station—"

"We're not staying. Don't worry."

"You'd be putting a lot of people at risk."

"I said, we're leaving."

"Then you'd better hurry." The man was moving away before he'd even stopped speaking.

THEY PACKED QUICKLY. MILO AND HOLLY WERE TENSE, SAL A NERVOUS WRECK. Brooke wanted to reassure them that it wasn't like before, that no one in Shaw Station wanted to bother with them, that they were simply getting out of the way of trouble. But she knew it wouldn't be so simple to dismiss their fears again.

When they were dressed and ready, Brooke retrieved the saddle and paid for the room. Their host seemed disappointed to see their money go until Brooke asked if there was a way to get off the property unseen; then the girl's face closed, she gave clipped directions to an alley behind the motel, and the door shut. Brooke heard a bolt slide.

Brooke led them through a tangle of back alleys, away from the center of town. Rather than go straight to Highway 12 and have their route observed, she took them down to the river. At dusk and dawn, people fished there, but at midday, the shore was deserted, hidden from view by sedge grass.

They followed the old footpath along the river, heading for the edge of town. The air was cold, and they wrapped their new coats more closely around them. In the distance, Brooke saw a green and white sign pointing the way up a rise of land to a picnic area and scenic lookout. There would be a view of the highway from the top.

Brooke hesitated. Below her, the river flowed past a boat landing, where it looked as if someone had lately been living; bits of a dismantled shelter were littered through the reeds. She knew this place. It was the same landing she and Robin had found that day, empty save for what Brooke had taken for a sandy-colored boulder.

Cawley's chin was not yet split, then. Brooke's shoulder not ripped. Robin not gone to the city in charge of orphaned children. They were still children themselves, that day, running through late summer grass, the sun on their skin. Soon, a siren would sound, calling them back to their parents, but not yet.

Brooke remembered standing out in the river, her feet on the burning rock. There'd been no sign of the snake until Cawley had shouted, pointing off to the right, and they had seen it swim out from the reeds into open water, head high, body a liquid line.

When the snake reached the middle of the river, the current had pulled it downstream, right past them. The three of them had watched amazed, as the snake fought to maintain its course. Then it was clear of the current and making once again for the far shore, only its head visible.

Finally, it was too small to trace and they lost sight of it.

ACKNOWLEDGMENTS

IN DRAFTING AND REVISING *THE CAPTIVE*, I WAS GREATLY ASSISTED BY THE thoughts and words of Howard Akler, Emily Anglin, Saul Davis, Susan Kernohan, Bob Kotyk, Mark Mann, Adina Muskat, Jocelyn Parr, Aidan Roman-Crossland, Hannah Spear, Julia Tausch, and Adam Wilkins. Thank you, friends.

Ray Bucknell shared valuable advice on horses, and James Robinson on guns. All errors that remain are my own. Historian Derek Murray's graduate work on the failed settlement narrative attached to my home community of Brudenell, Ontario, provided inspiration and helped clarify my thinking, as did Katherine J. Cramer's *The Politics of Resentment: Rural Consciousness in Wisconsin and the Rise of Scott Walker*.

Thank you to the Toronto Arts Council for supporting an early draft of this work.

Thank you to my agent, Martha Webb, for her clear sight, straight talk, and kind support, and for finding this book an excellent home.

Thank you to Jennifer Lambert, Sara Birmingham, and Zack Wagman, for their patience with a first-time author, for their excellent edits, and for treating this book with greater generosity and respect than I ever anticipated. Thank you as well to the excellent teams at HarperCollins Canada and Ecco who helped bring *The Captive* into the world, including heroic copy editor Sue Sumeraj.

Affection and appreciation to my outstanding colleagues at Frontier College, who do the vital work of raising literacy in Canada every day, and who sustained my efforts to be a working mom and a writer in the same lifetime.

Two writers of great heart have especially helped me over the years in ways big and small. Thank you to Sandra Gulland for giving me my first job and showing me this path even existed. And to dear friend Pasha Malla for directions, roadside repairs, and the occasional lift along the way. You will call it nothing, but it is not.

Deepest love and gratitude to my parents, my brother, and our motley family, to Etan's family, and, most of all, to our children.

Finally, I am forever thankful to Etan Muskat—story genius, feminist, true heart—who makes everything better. *Huspant*, you figured this book out with me, you adjusted our lives a hundred different ways so I could write it, and you kept the kids happy while I did. You inspire me, you make me laugh, and you give me strength. You're the best.